MATTERS OF THE HEART

CATHERINE MAIORISI

Bella
BOOKS

2016

Bella Books, Inc.
P.O. Box 10543
Tallahassee, FL 32302

Printed in the United States of America on acid-free paper.

First Bella Books Edition 2016

Editor: Shelly Rafferty
Cover Designer: Sandy Knowles

ISBN: 978-1-59493-493-3

About the Author

Catherine Maiorisi lives in New York City and often writes under the watchful eye of Edgar Allan Poe, in Edgar's Café near the apartment she shares with Sherry her partner, now wife, of thirty-eight years.

In the seventies and eighties while working in corporate technology then running her own technology consulting company, Catherine moaned to her artistic friends that she was the only lesbian in New York City who wasn't creative, the only one without the imagination or the talent to write poetry or novels, play the guitar, act or sing.

Since she found her imagination, writing has been like meditating for Catherine and it is what she most loves to do. But she also reads voraciously, loves to cook, especially Italian, and enjoys hanging out with her wife and friends.

When she wrote a short story to create the backstory for the love interest in her two unpublished NYPD Detective Chiara Corelli mysteries, Catherine had never read any romance and hadn't considered writing it. To her surprise, "The Sex Club" turned out to be a romance and was included in the *Best Lesbian Romance of 2014* edited by Radclyffe.

Another surprise was hearing the voices of two characters, Andrea and Darcy, chatting in her head every night, making it difficult to sleep. Reassured by her wife that she wasn't losing it, Catherine paid attention and those conversations led to her first romance novel, *Matters of the Heart*.

Catherine has also had two mystery short stories published in the *Murder New York Style* Anthologies, "Justice for All" in *Fresh Slices* and "Murder Italian Style" in *Family Matters*.

An active member of Sisters in Crime and Mystery Writers of America, Catherine is also a member of Romance Writers of America and Rainbow Romance Writers.

Acknowledgments

I'd like to thank my wife Sherry for never doubting when I said I was going to write a novel that I would; for treating me as a writer before I felt like one; for her tough love as my first reader; and for her ongoing support and encouragement.

Thanks also to my second readers and best friends Lee and Judy for their continued support, for patiently reading multiple versions of the same manuscript and still managing to offer constructive criticism.

Special thanks to Ann Roberts, Bella author of romances and the Ari Adams mysteries, for her generosity in reading *Matters of the Heart* and writing a wonderful critique and then taking the time to discuss the changes over the telephone. For me, one of the highlights of the Golden Crown Literary Society Conference in Portland was meeting Ann.

Last, but certainly not least, thank you readers. I assume if you're reading this, you've read *Matters of the Heart*. I hope you enjoyed reading it as much as I enjoyed writing it.

CHAPTER ONE

Dr. Andrea Trapani had plunged into disease-infested jungles filled with armed hostiles with less trepidation than she felt now about to enter the home of the cantankerous Ms. Darcy Silver. As she eyed the elegant mansion and its half-block walled garden, she wondered again why she'd thought this was a good idea.

But a commitment is a commitment. She squared her shoulders, picked up her suitcase and medical bag and passed through the wrought-iron gate. At the top of the curved stone staircase, she lifted the bronze eagle and knocked on the carved wooden door. Waited. Knocked again. About to knock a third time, she noticed the door was slightly ajar and stepped in, nearly tripping on a haphazard pile of suitcases and shopping bags just inside the huge foyer. Her nose twitched. The lovely fragrance of the colorful bouquet of fresh flowers on a small oak library table deeper inside the foyer was not at all what she expected. Could she be in the wrong house? She dug in the pocket of her jeans, retrieved the paper Julie Castillo had given her, and confirmed she was in the right place. According to Julie, they were expecting her. But where was everybody? Surely a house this big had servants.

Andrea placed her suitcase behind the library table to avoid it being taken by mistake, then peered into the large, sunny living room on the east side of the foyer. It was warm and comfortable-looking, rather than dusty, musty and forbidding as she'd imagined the house of the miserable Ms. Silver. In the formal dining room across the foyer, a magnificent chandelier glittered over a long rosewood table with, she counted, seating for thirty. She grinned, imagining the bitchy Ms. Silver sitting at the table scowling at her cowering minions, like in a Dickens novel.

As she moved back into the foyer, she became aware of voices from above. She grabbed her medical bag and followed the voices up four flights of steps and down the hall until she reached the door to a room where a woman in a hospital bed was engaged in a vicious shouting match with an angry blonde standing over her. Neither noticed Andrea just outside the bedroom. Feeling uncomfortable about interrupting, she waited for a lull.

"My bags are packed. I'm leaving, Darcy." The blonde leaned over the woman in the bed. "I didn't sign on for feeding you or washing you, and certainly not for giving you bedpans and serving on you twenty-four hours a day, but I tried. I can't do it. I can't tolerate your foul temper. I can't deal with your belittling me while I'm trying to help you. Most of all, I can't watch your self-destructive behavior. In the week or so you've been home from the hospital the aides you haven't fired have walked out because of your foul mouth and foul temper. Even the visiting nurse has refused to come back. That has to be some kind of world record." The blonde turned from the bed and began to pace, giving Andrea a glimpse of the red-faced, dark-haired Darcy Silver.

"What kind of woman walks out on a lover who can't do anything for herself?" Darcy Silver whined. "It's a terrible thing to be in pain. It's even worse to be in pain and helpless. But it's devastating to be in pain and helpless and abandoned by friends, by everyone you thought cared. You say you love me, Gerri, but if you did, you would stay and take care of me."

Gerri laughed. "Love you? How can I love you, Darcy? You live behind a glass wall and you've never once let me through. The sex was great but it was always all about you, you giving, you touching, you in control. You never let me touch you physically or emotionally. It's almost as if anyone who cares for you, who loves you, is worthless."

"You are worthless. Get your stuff and get out. I don't need you or anyone else."

"That's good since none of your precious" —Gerri made quote marks with her fingers— "'inner circle' of friends have shown up to see you, forget lift a finger to help."

"Get the hell out."

"You can't do a goddamn thing for yourself." Gerri glared at her. "I *should* leave you alone to starve to death or drown in your own piss and shit. That's what you'd do to me. But I'm a better person than you, so I've arranged for a live-in doctor to oversee your care and a nurse for the night shift. The doctor should be here shortly."

"Are you crazy? A live-in doctor? And a nurse? Did you discuss it with Candace?"

"I would have if she'd answered my urgent calls about you."

"Another ungrateful bitch. I refuse to have strangers."

"Too bad, baby doll. Even the exalted Darcy Silver doesn't always get what she wants. Anyway, I'm out of here as soon as the doctor shows up. Maybe she can sign you into some fancy institution where your money will buy tolerance for your nastiness."

"I'm not going to a nursing home."

"Up to you, darling. The agency I've been dealing with refuses to send anyone else so the nurse is from a new agency. I paid for the first twelve-hour shift out of the money you put in my account but the agency owner will be here tomorrow morning to get your oral approval since you can't sign. The doctor is not from an agency." Gerri leaned over the bed again.

CHAPTER TWO

Her veins were popping, her face was almost purple and she was breathing so heavily Andrea feared she'd stroke. As unpleasant as stepping into the middle of the screaming match would be, she needed to protect her soon-to-be patient. She knocked and entered. Her first full-faced look at Darcy Silver surprised her. Not only was Darcy much younger than she'd expected but even red-faced with rage, not a speck of makeup, and with her long dark hair splayed in clumps over a rust-stained pillow, the prominent cheekbones, the sensuous lips and the sparking sapphire eyes added up to striking.

At the knock, Darcy's eyes shot from Gerri to Andrea. She glared, eyes narrow, lips curled in a snarl. "Who the fuck are you? And why are you sneaking up on me?"

Andrea wasn't sure whether it was the foul language, or the vilest tone of voice anyone had ever hurled at her, but she froze, pinned by those blazing blue eyes. "Dr. Andrea Trapani. I was sent—"

"Get out. I don't need a doctor to wipe my ass."

"Good luck, Doctor." Gerri looked apologetic.

Darcy's head swiveled to Gerri. "Why are you still here?"

"Ta-ta, Darcy." Gerri breezed past Andrea, leaving a trail of flowery perfume in her wake. "Have a good life," she tossed over her shoulder.

They listened to her run down the steps, footsteps getting fainter with each flight of stairs until the only sound was Darcy's labored breathing. Andrea and Darcy regarded each other in awkward silence, then both jumped when the slamming of the front door echoed through the silent mansion. Gerri had left with a bang. "Well, Ms. Silver, do you want me to go?"

Insolent sapphire eyes raked her from head to toe with such intensity that Andrea felt she was being undressed and touched. Areas of her body that had been dormant for months quivered and, much to her chagrin, the flush infusing her body reached her face. It wasn't the first time she'd been scrutinized like that, but it was the first time a woman had done it, and the first time her body had responded.

"Do I look like I have a fucking choice?"

Darcy couldn't see her racing heart or the throbbing of her...body and she hoped the nastiness in the question meant that Darcy hadn't noticed her red face. She breathed deeply. Her best friend Julie Castillo, Darcy's cardiologist, had encouraged Andrea to take this job to get her mind off Nora and ease back into medicine. Though Julie had warned Andrea that Darcy was very, very difficult, she hadn't mentioned Darcy's age or beauty or her unpleasant, aggressive sexuality.

"I'll leave after you've made arrangements for twenty-four-seven coverage tomorrow, if that's what you want. But you need to calm down now and try to relax."

"I don't need you to tell me what I need to do. What you need to do is stop standing there like an idiot. If you're here to take care of me, how about you do your job and take care of me."

"I'd like to take your blood pressure, then settle in. Is there something you want now?"

"I'm thirsty. There should be cold water in the refrigerator behind me. And don't settle in too much, you may not be here tomorrow. I don't need another doctor. And I certainly don't need to pay a doctor to wash and feed me."

Andrea bit her tongue. Apparently, judging from the odor of sweat and urine, and the stained pillowcase, washing Darcy hadn't been a priority for her aides. And, apparently no one had told Darcy she definitely needed a doctor; then again, she probably hadn't listened. As she filled a glass with water from the pitcher in the refrigerator, she cursed herself for not wearing scrubs and a lab coat. Her scooped-neck top was going to give Darcy skin and cleavage to ogle.

She lifted Darcy's head and placed the straw between her lips. Darcy's perfect black eyebrows arched as her eyes widened but she didn't comment. When she finished, Andrea removed the straw. Darcy's sly smile telegraphed her enjoyment of her close-up of Andrea's breasts. Avoiding those impertinent eyes, she gently placed Darcy's head on the pillow and patted her lips dry. "I'm going to take your blood pressure now. I'm worried by the look of you."

"How sweet. Here five minutes and you're already worried about me."

Andrea ignored her. Darcy's eyes followed her as she retrieved the stethoscope and blood pressure cuff from her medical bag. She moved the light blanket aside to expose Darcy's right arm and was surprised to find Darcy naked, no hospital gown, no diaper. Her right arm was propped up by pillows, had a shoulder-to-wrist cast and was bent at the elbow in a V shape, awkward at best and not available for pressure. She covered the right arm and moved the blanket from the left arm. Its cast ran from just above her elbow to her wrist, with a couple of broken fingers as well, but the upper left arm was available for the blood pressure cuff.

"Neat huh? Just enough arm available for you to play doctor." Her voice was taunting and her eyes bounced from Andrea's face to her breasts and back. "I always loved that game."

God, what an offensive pig. Andrea had dealt with her share of pigs in the emergency room but they were always men. Andrea pumped then concentrated on listening. Just as she'd feared,

Darcy's pressure was in the danger zone. She'd let her relax for a while and take it again. If it didn't come down, she'd call Julie and have Darcy hospitalized. She undid the cuff.

"Not good? How high?" For the first time, Darcy spoke without sarcasm, anger, or nastiness.

Andrea met the inquisitive blue eyes. "Not good at all. Two-hundred-one over one-hundred-ten. We need to watch this, Ms. Silver, it's dangerously high."

"We do, huh?" The ridicule in her voice was blistering. "Okay, no jogging for me today."

"Jogging might be better than letting your anger get the best of you. Try to control that so we can get your pressure down and avoid a visit to the emergency room."

"No fucking way am I going back to the hospital, understand?" The anger and the red face were back.

Andrea touched her shoulder. "I understand, Ms. Silver—"

"Hey, sweetie, you're going to be wiping my ass so I think we can be on first name terms. Call me Darcy." She smirked. "Please."

"I understand, Darcy, but do you understand? You need to control your anger. If you don't, you could have a stroke or another heart attack. Either could leave you in much worse condition than you're in now." Green eyes held blue. "Do you hear me? You could die or be paralyzed or lose your ability to see, or hear, or speak or all of the above."

The blue eyes skittered over Andrea's shoulder. "I hear you." She sounded exhausted.

"Good. Did anyone give you your medication this morning?"

"I don't remember. I don't think so."

Andrea found the chart on the table behind Darcy's bed. She posted the blood pressure reading and her observation of Darcy's state, then scanned the previous entries. According to the chart, Darcy hadn't been given any medication since eight p.m. last night. As she closed the chart she noticed Gerri's contact number written on the cover and tapped it into her cell phone. "Hi, this is Dr. Trapani. Do you know if Darcy was given her medication this morning?" She listened, pocketed her phone, then made a note in the chart.

"So what did the bitch say?"

Darcy was calling the woman who went out of her way to arrange proper care for her a bitch. *Who's the real bitch here?* "Apparently, you threw the aide out at one a.m. this morning so Gerri sat with you all night, but didn't know what medication to give you." Andrea checked the chart again and gathered the pills. "These are your morning meds. I'll put them in your mouth one at a time followed by the straw so you can wash them down. Okay?"

"Nice of you to ask. Usually, they toss them in and walk away." Darcy opened her mouth.

When they'd finished, Andrea patted Darcy's lips dry. "Now, which bedroom can I use?"

Darcy's head popped up. "Why do you need a bedroom?"

"I was hired as a live-in so I can be available twenty-four-seven."

Darcy's eyes widened, her face reddened. "Who the—"

Andrea put both hands on Darcy's shoulders and stared into her eyes. "Take a deep breath, Darcy. I'll be leaving tomorrow morning, remember?"

Darcy held her eyes for a few seconds. "Any room on the second floor."

"No. I need to be near you." She could see a bedroom through the open door opposite Darcy's bed. "I'll take the bedroom next door."

"That's my bedroom." The eyes were shooting fire now. "If you're going to do whatever you want, why bother asking?"

Andrea pulled a chair close to the bed and sat so she and Darcy were on the same level. "Listen, Darcy, I know you're feeling helpless and out of control—"

"You don't know a goddamned thing about what I'm feeling."

"I'm here to take care of your physical well-being and to monitor your health. So I'll make the decisions I think are needed to best do those two things. I want to be close to you, even when I'm not technically on duty, therefore, I will sleep in the room next to yours." Andrea maintained eye contact. Her voice was gentle and firm, not confrontational. "Do you understand?"

Darcy glared at her. "Why should you care when you're off duty and not getting paid?"

Andrea held her eyes. "I'm a doctor. Your health is precarious and it doesn't get better just because I'm asleep."

Darcy blinked, then looked away. "Sorry."

Having won the first battle, Andrea stood. "I'll get my things from downstairs—"

"No."

Andrea frowned. "No?" This woman was the personification of the term *rich bitch*. If every little thing was going to require a battle, she would be happy to leave tomorrow morning.

"Use the intercom on the table there to call down to the kitchen. Ask Maria to have Gregg bring your things up."

"You have servants?"

"Not exactly. They're here between eight and six Monday through Friday. Gregg comes in early to make breakfast and to prep for the day's meals. Maria and Carlo come in a little later. Maria cooks, with Gregg assisting, and she oversees the people that come in to do the laundry and clean. Carlo serves and oversees the care of the grounds. Gregg does all the shopping and any heavy stuff needed. Maria will bring up my breakfast soon and she'll discuss the week's meals with us. If you need breakfast or coffee, let her know when you call down."

Us. Andrea turned toward the intercom to hide her smile. The awful woman was accepting her. Andrea did not like her at all. Her first instinct had been to tell her to shove her job, but there was no way she would leave her alone. Darcy was a control freak, no doubt about that. An out of control, control freak microseconds away from a stroke or a heart attack. Andrea had seen the violent temper and the uncontrollable rage frequently in the emergency room, and unless it was triggered by drinking or drugs, its cause was almost always fear.

She resolved to not let Darcy's needling and attacks rile her, to be patient, and to give her full attention to Darcy so she felt seen and cared for. Julie was so right about her being a challenge medically and temperamentally. The bigger challenge, though, might be dealing with Darcy's blatant sexuality and her own body's response to it.

CHAPTER THREE

She really was out of control. In the good doctor's place, she'd tell her where to go. Besides being nasty and abusive, she'd practically raped the poor woman with her eyes. She regretted it, but Gerri's leaving had panicked her and these days her eyes and her tongue were the only weapons she could wield when she felt threatened.

But while it was true she felt threatened, it was also true she'd found the doctor irresistible. A little taller than her own five-foot-nine, with a long lean body, full breasts, collar-length honey-red hair, gorgeous green eyes, ivory skin and sensuous lips, she was lovely. And she smelled sexy—a touch of sweat, a little citrus, some musk, some rosemary and tinges of woodsy.

A lot of good lusting and wanting would do her now stuck in this bed, helpless and in pain. Yet, she might not be as helpless as she felt. While the lovely doctor didn't seem distressed by her foul mouth and unbridled aggression, her flush indicated she'd responded to the sexual appreciation. Of course, it's possible she felt assaulted rather than flattered and it might have been an angry flush. But wouldn't it be nice if she were a lesbian?

But lust and sex aside, the doctor seemed to be kind, compassionate and caring. It might be nice to have Doctor Trapani taking care of her. A welcome relief from the brusque, all-business, slam-bam-don't-bother-me-ma'am treatment she'd been receiving so far from aides.

And what the doctor had said about having a heart attack or a stroke was scary. A massive heart attack had killed her dad without warning. She was unhappy and filled with anger and self-pity now but she didn't want to die or worse, lose her ability to speak or walk or any of the things Dr. Trapani had warned could result from her raging temper.

When had she become so angry? She didn't think of herself that way, but maybe she was remembering the younger, happier Darcy, the one who was in love and had a bright future where anything was possible. If she was honest, her life was a disappointment. The challenging, interesting, meaningful work to which she'd aspired had eluded her as had a lasting, loving relationship. Her failures embarrassed her and she hid the bitterness she felt behind an affable, fun-loving façade.

Since the accident, since none of her friends except Candace had even visited, forget offered to help, her rage had burned away the discipline and restraint that hid the real her. And where did this foul language come from? Of course she knew the words, had used them occasionally, but this savaging stream of hate and coarse curses surprised even her. It seemed when her rage exploded it flowed out of her like lava from a volcano.

She'd expected more from her friends, much more. And being abandoned by the inner circle she thought of as her family, being left in the care of a woman she'd been about to break up with when the accident occurred, had driven her to the edge. The beast had broken free. If her friends didn't care, why should paid nurses and aides give a damn about Darcy Silver, especially when she treated them like shit? Or doctors? If she wanted this lovely doctor to stay, she'd have to collar the beast.

She was hurt and lonely and scared, so she dumped all her anger and frustration on anyone who dared come close. She couldn't blame Gerri for leaving. It was surprising she'd lasted as long as she had. She hoped she hadn't become such a terrible person that if their roles were reversed she wouldn't have left without hiring someone to take care of Gerri. Enough self-pity. Despite being friendless, despite being a failure, Darcy wanted to live. She was disciplined. She could control herself. Her life depended on it.

CHAPTER FOUR

Gregg had not only brought up Andrea's suitcase, but he and Carlo had also changed the sheets on the bed, put clean towels in the bathroom and opened a window to freshen the room. She was all set. The room was huge, with large windows overlooking the garden, a king-sized bed, an easy chair with a hassock, a lovely chest of drawers with a large mirror over it, a desk and a walk-in closet. A wall unit facing the bed held a TV, a sound system, tons of books and many framed photographs. She was happy to see that in addition to the door connecting her room with Darcy's, another led out into the hall so she could come and go in privacy.

She'd only brought one small suitcase so she decided to unpack even though she'd probably be leaving in the morning. Standing in front of the dresser she noticed the mirror gave her a perfect view of Darcy's bed and she appeared to be sleeping. While touching her clothing might enrage Darcy, what she didn't know couldn't hurt her, so Andrea quickly combined several of Darcy's drawers to free up space for her underwear, shorts, running clothes, tank tops, T-shirts, scrubs and lab coats.

She entered the walk-in closet and was surprised to find it neat and organized, clothing clustered by type—pantsuits, jackets, slacks, jeans, shirts and gowns. Shelves held sweaters, shoes, boots and bags. Andrea sniffed, trying to identify the spicy, sexy fragrance in the closet, but couldn't. She shook her head. What the hell was she doing standing around getting turned on by the perfume of someone she found offensive?

She grabbed hangers, hung her jeans and shirts, put her sandals and running shoes on the floor, then closed the closet door. Despite herself, she checked the bottles of perfume on the dresser to find the name of the scent but some had handwritten labels and she didn't want to take the time to figure out which it was. She put her phone, her iPod, her laptop, her books, crossword puzzle books and travel clock on the bedside table, then shoved her suitcase under the bed.

Remembering the feeling of Darcy's eyes on her, she closed the door and changed into loose-fitting scrubs and a lab coat. Slipping into work shoes, she dropped her phone into her pocket, ran her fingers through her hair, and opened the door. A small, thin elderly woman was leaning over Darcy, talking intently in what sounded like Italian. Of course. With her dark hair and olive skin, it was likely that Darcy's mother was Italian. The woman tenderly tucked Darcy's hair behind her ears, held her face between her hands and kissed her several times. Perhaps her grandmother?

"Ah, Doctor. Sorry, I don't remember your name, but this is Maria."

Maria? Wasn't that the cook's name? She started to say, "Call me Andrea," but realized Darcy would probably respect her more if she had to call her doctor. She responded in Italian. "I'm Dr. Trapani. Nice to meet you, Maria. What menus have you discussed so far?"

Darcy scowled. "Speak English please, Maria, she understands us so we can't have any privacy."

Maria patted Darcy's face. "Be nice." She put her glasses on and read from her notes. "Dinners: linguine Alfredo, steak, fried pork chops, steak, veal chop; lunches: cheeseburger, pulled pork, *chicken parmigiana*, grilled ham and cheese—"

"No." The two women stared at Andrea. "Darcy needs a low fat, low salt diet."

"Who died and made you queen? I will eat what I want, when I want it. Got it, Doctor?"

Christ, the woman had perfected the art of the sarcastic shoot-down. Just the tone of voice could wither you on the spot. If you were vulnerable that is. And Andrea wasn't. In fact, she reacted exactly as she had the day the medicine man held a spear to her throat and insisted he would deal with the pregnant woman and babies. No way.

"Darcy." Maria's voice conveyed a warning.

Darcy Silver was a nasty bitch, but she was a patient, a patient who was in big trouble and either didn't know, didn't understand, or worse, didn't care. "Has anybody explained your condition?"

"You mean my heart? They said I passed out while driving because I have a clogged artery. They put a stent in to open the artery. It's fixed. Why shouldn't I eat what I want?"

Andrea was sure Julie would have discussed this with Darcy after putting in the stent, but maybe with the stress of the surgeries on her limbs, she hadn't taken it in. Or maybe, like many people, Darcy thought if she didn't feel pain, she was healthy. Or more likely, it wasn't what she wanted to hear so she ignored it. "That was the only *totally* blocked artery, but others are dangerously close to being blocked. What you eat is extremely important. I can't believe nobody discussed diet with you."

"Not that I remember."

Maria cleared her throat. "Gerri did say you need to be careful about what you eat. But you made her throw the papers away."

Darcy grimaced. "I thought Gerri was just being a pain in the ass."

Andrea steeled herself for an argument. "Remember what I said about making the decisions I feel are best for you."

Darcy lifted her head, her face red, and glared at Andrea. "Don't infantilize me, Dr. Trapani. It's my—"

"If you expect me to stay until tomorrow, you will allow me to order lunch and dinner for today and breakfast for tomorrow. When I'm gone it's up to you." It might mean an abrupt departure, but she had to draw a line or Darcy would walk all over her as she'd been doing with the aides and everyone else.

Darcy rolled her eyes. "I can't believe you're blackmailing me."

Andrea shrugged. "It's for your own good."

"Yeah, right." Darcy managed to convey a ton of nastiness in just those two words. Then she blew out a breath. "All right, Doctor, why don't you take Maria into the hall and tell her what we want while I nap. You can feed me breakfast when you're done." She closed her eyes.

Maria shook her head.

"See you later, *cara*." Maria kissed Darcy's forehead, then followed Andrea out. She smiled at Andrea. "Sorry Doctor, Darcy hasn't been herself since the accident. She's usually calm and happy and nice to be around." She glanced back into the room. "I'm worried about her." She turned to Andrea. "We can cook whatever you think is best. Tell me what you want?"

Andrea explained the basic diet she had in mind, then ordered lunch and dinner and breakfast. "Grilled chicken breast, steamed broccoli, half a cup of brown rice, and salad with a low fat dressing for lunch; for dinner broiled salmon, grilled vegetables, half a cup of quinoa, a salad and a peach or other fruit; and, for breakfast unsweetened, high-fiber cereal, one percent milk and a banana and berries, or poached eggs on a dry whole wheat English muffin and fresh fruit salad. And, Maria, no snacks."

Maria's eyes went to the woman in the bed. "Darcy likes cookies and muffins and chips. You tell her no snacks?"

"I'll tell her."

"Good luck to you." Maria smiled. "What about tomorrow?"

"If I'm here, we'll have grilled shrimp over a salad with a light dressing for lunch, and grilled pork tenderloin with steamed asparagus, half cup of quinoa, a salad and cup of strawberries for dinner. And, for breakfast the next morning, cold cereal or poached eggs, your choice. I'll have some menus and recipes for you tomorrow. Even if I'm not staying, maybe you can sneak in some healthy meals."

Maria grinned. "I think you be here tomorrow."

"Why do you say that?"

"Darcy is *una capa dost*, a hard-head. She never listens to nobody before."

CHAPTER FIVE

Darcy's eyes were closed when Andrea went back into the room. Such a striking woman. Such a vile temper. Too bad. Andrea sighed. She wouldn't be an easy patient, but dealing with Darcy had already pulled her out of herself and she was feeling more alive than she had for months. Julie had been right.

Darcy's eyes popped open and she immediately slipped into attack mode. "What are you staring at?"

"You. I was thinking that all that anger must be exhausting."

Darcy glared at her but didn't respond.

Andrea washed her hands, then moved the coffee and croissants Maria had brought for them to the bed tray. Some healthy breakfast. She raised the bed, wheeled the bed tray over and sat to feed Darcy. "How do you like your coffee, Darcy?"

"Lots of steamed milk, no sugar."

Andrea fixed Darcy's coffee, then put the straw in and held the cup so she could sip.

"Even through a straw, the first sip is wonderful."

Andrea attempted to cut Darcy's croissant with her knife and fork, but it was flaky and tough. Darcy snorted. "Use your fingers, Doctor."

Andrea hesitated, then tore off a piece of croissant with her fingers and fed it to Darcy. Much easier. She added milk to her own coffee and sipped. It was deep and rich and the steamed milk made it even better. Maria certainly knew how to brew a great cup. She smiled.

"Hey, stop daydreaming, I'm starving. Can I have more croissant or does your diet only allow one bite?"

Andrea broke off another piece and fed it to her. "Actually, my diet doesn't include croissants at all, so if I stay, it will be a while before you have another one." She took a bite of her own croissant. "Although I do see the attraction. This is delicious."

Andrea took her time with breakfast, alternating feeding Darcy pieces of the croissant and taking bites of her own with giving Darcy sips of coffee, then doing the same for herself. Neither spoke, but the silence was comfortable. Occasionally their eyes met, but even that was comfortable. When they were done, Andrea wiped Darcy's mouth and moved the tray away.

"I'd like to examine you now. Is that all right?"

"No." Calm Darcy had been replaced by angry Darcy. She closed her eyes, but a tear leaked out.

Andrea used a tissue to gently dry the tear. "Darcy?"

Darcy opened her eyes. "Do I have a choice?" Without the anger, her voice was low, husky. Sexy. Without the anger, her weariness was apparent. Without the anger, her fear and sadness were exposed.

Andrea felt bad for Darcy. She was totally dependent and the loss of control must be difficult. She pulled the chair close to the bed again and leaned in, keeping her voice gentle, her words direct. "You don't have a choice if you want to get well. But if that isn't your goal, you can choose to ignore your health and let the chips fall where they may. It's really up to you."

After a long moment of silence, Darcy spoke. "If I say yes, will you tell me about yourself?"

"Aha, tit for tat?" Andrea's voice was light, but she didn't know how much she cared to share with Darcy.

"Yes. After all, it's the closest I'm going to get to tit for a while."

Ah, the piggy was back, but the tone was light and teasing rather than insulting. "Do I detect a sense of humor?"

"I used to have one of those. So, what do you say?"

"Two questions, but not too personal since we've just met."

"Okay, examine away."

She pushed Darcy's hair aside to check the gash on her forehead. It was healing well, but it was still red and raw-looking. "Whoever stitched you in the emergency room did a good job. You probably won't have much of a scar."

"Can I see?"

Andrea looked around but there was no mirror. "Just a second." She went to the bedroom and retrieved the makeup mirror she'd seen there.

"I didn't know it was there." Darcy studied the gash. "Pretty bad, huh?"

Andrea nodded, then put the mirror down. With Darcy's eyes on her, she took her temperature and checked her respiration rate. Both were normal.

Darcy closed her eyes as Andrea moved the blanket aside and placed the stethoscope over her heart. Her heartbeat was sluggish but was probably normal for the state of her arteries. She shifted the stethoscope and listened to Darcy's lungs. "I'll try to be careful of your ribs, but I may hurt you." She rolled her to her side to get access to her back. Darcy grunted. Her lungs were clear and though she tried not to pay attention she couldn't help noticing Darcy's firm, full breasts and taut nipples. Damn. Now who's the piggy?

She checked for irritations on either side of the casts on Darcy's arms and the full casts on each of her legs, then listened to the pulses in her groin and both ankles. "Now I'm going to check for bedsores." She gently rolled Darcy to one side then the other, scanning her colorful bruised back, ribs and rear-end. Nice ass too. She smiled. In the ER there was always so much pressure she barely had time to register the sex of her patients and now here she was, ogling a helpless woman. Well, Darcy had done it to her so tit for tat. She checked Darcy's heels. No sores.

Darcy opened her eyes. "Why are you smiling?" She sounded grouchy rather than nasty.

"Was I?"

"You *was*. Don't act so innocent."

"I'm happy I didn't find any bedsores."

"Made your day, did it?"

"You could say that. I'd like to wash you now, if that's okay?"

She closed her eyes. "Can we do it later?"

She really needed a good washing but right now building trust was more important and she was intent on Darcy feeling more in control. "If you'd like." She picked up a bottle of skin lotion. "Your skin is dry, Darcy, at least let me put some lotion on it."

"Will it hurt?"

"I'll avoid your ribs. It should feel good. And, it will help prevent bed sores."

"Can you use my lotion, Darcy's Lotion #7, instead of that stuff? It should be in the bathroom."

Andrea went into the bathroom and scanned the bottles: Darcy's Body Wash #7, Darcy's Shampoo #7, Darcy's Cream Rinse #7 and Darcy's Lotion #7. She tested the lotion on her hand. Wow, thick and creamy. She sniffed her hand. A light version of the spicy, sexy fragrance that had turned her on in Darcy's closet.

Andrea held the bottle up for Darcy to see. "You can tell me to stop anytime."

It was hard to believe that none of the nurses or aides had done this. But Darcy's temper probably had made doing the simplest thing torture for patient and aide. Andrea put some cream on her hands and rubbed them together to warm them. She started with Darcy's neck, then down to the shoulders. "You have lovely skin; this should help it stay that way."

Darcy closed her eyes. She tensed as Andrea's hands neared the fractured ribs and shivered at the light rubbing of her belly, but slowly her tension eased. As she had when checking for bedsores, Andrea rolled Darcy first to one side then the other, applying the cream over her back and her buttocks. She finished up with Darcy's feet, massaging and rubbing the lotion in. Darcy lay with her eyes closed. "Thank you, Doctor. It's nice to be touched so gently. It's been a while."

Poor thing must be suffering sensory deprivation. "The last thing you need to be dealing with right now is bedsores, so I'd recommend doing that every day. Is this lotion made especially for you? The fragrance is...lovely." Actually, the fragrance was damned sexy.

"Yes, there's a perfume store in Brooklyn that creates fragrances for individuals. They got it right on the seventh try, thus number seven."

"Let's see if your pressure is down." She wrapped the blood pressure cuff around Darcy's upper left arm and pumped. "One hundred-seventy over seventy-eight. Better, but still not good. That's why your cardiologist wanted a physician with you at all times."

"My cardiologist? How did Dr. Castillo get involved?"

Not wanting to set Darcy off on another tirade against Gerri, Andrea considered the best way to answer. "As I understand it, your lov—, um, Gerri, was worried that you would hurt yourself and called her. Dr. Castillo recommended bringing in a professional for a few weeks to try to get your pressure under control."

"Well, I'll be damned. Gerri did that? More brains than I gave her credit for. And, more caring than I realized." Darcy stared at the ceiling. "She thought I wanted to hurt myself? What could I do, beat myself over the head with my cast?"

"Not that kind of hurt yourself. She felt you were out of control and might have a stroke, but she was overwhelmed and didn't know how to help you. In fact, she thought she was bringing out the anger and making it worse." *And, Dr. Castillo thought with your volatile temper and seriously impaired heart, you should have a doctor available.*

Andrea updated Darcy's chart, looked in the refrigerator to check what was there, then puttered around, straightening the messy room and arranging things to suit her, giving Darcy time to absorb what she'd told her. She dropped her pen and when she bent to retrieve it she was hit by the sour smell of urine from a clump of linens under the table, next to the refrigerator. She put on latex gloves and stuffed the sheets and pillowcases in the already full hamper in the hallway.

"Wow, now I'm overwhelmed. I guess I owe Gerri an apology. I've been a real bitch."

Those were the first words she'd heard from Darcy that showed some awareness of her impact on others. Maybe there was hope.

Darcy lay there chewing her lip. "So Dr. Castillo sent you, not the agency?"

"Yes. You'll be paying me directly, if that's okay?"

Darcy smirked. "And if it's not?"

"Then I guess you'll just have to pay me directly."

"Dr. Trapani, did you put something in the water you gave me earlier?"

"No. I'll always tell you when I'm medicating you. Why do you ask?"

"I feel calmer. Maybe rubbing me with lotion soothed the savage beast in me. Or, maybe it's you. Maybe I'm calm because you're calm."

Or maybe it's because you terrorized Gerri and the aides and nurses and they pulled back, leaving you feeling abandoned, which terrified you and made you lash out, terrorizing them. Andrea had hoped to soothe Darcy but didn't think it would happen so fast. "Calm is good, Darcy, whatever the reason."

"Before I ask my two questions, can I ask for two favors?"

Andrea was leery about saying yes, but they seemed to have moved to a good place and she didn't want to stir Darcy up. "Greedy little thing, aren't you? Ask away?"

"Yeah, I am greedy. Could you scratch my head; it's driving me crazy. And then could you raise the blinds so I can see out the window? I miss being outside and seeing the sky makes me feel a little better."

Andrea ran her fingers through the hair on Darcy's scalp. "Tell me when I've got the right pressure." She scratched.

"A little harder, down more. Use your nails and do the whole head. Aaah. Yes. Thanks, enough for now."

Darcy's already stained pillow was now covered with little brown flakes, Andrea's hands were pink and her nails had a red-brown coating under them. "I'm going to comb your hair then change your bed."

She washed her hands in the bathroom, then ran the comb she found on Darcy's dresser through Darcy's long black hair. Obviously her hair hadn't been washed in the several weeks since the accident and the tangles of sweat and dried blood made combing it slow going. By the time the comb moved easily through Darcy's hair, the pillowcase was covered with reddish brown flakes of blood and Andrea's hands were red again. It was better but still unacceptable as far as she was concerned. She put the comb aside and washed her hands again.

Darcy's eyes had been closed while she worked on her hair and Andrea wasn't sure she was awake until she spoke. "Thank you. That felt wonderful."

"When was the last time your hair was washed?" Andrea lifted Darcy's head, replaced the dirty pillow with a clean one, then deftly turned the dirty pillowcase inside out to contain the flakes of blood, and put a clean pillowcase on that pillow.

"Before the accident, I think. When I was in the hospital everything hurt and I couldn't stand to be touched so I wouldn't let anyone wash it." She flushed. "After I came home, one of the aides said I stank and wanted to wash it but she couldn't explain how she was going to do it and I was afraid she'd hurt me, so I refused. She said I smelled too nasty and quit at the end of her shift. No one else asked. It smells, doesn't it?"

"I got a lot of the dried blood out so it should be a little better if we keep on top of it." And, if she stayed, she would figure out a way to wash it.

When she'd replaced the sheets, Andrea raised all the blinds and opened a window to air the room. Darcy sighed. "It would be nice if we could have the sunlight in here all day. And the fresh air feels great." She sniffed. "It smells like spring. They must have cut the grass."

"Why don't we just leave the blinds up and the windows open? We're so high up, no one can see in."

"They said it was better for me to be in semidarkness. The aides, I mean."

"Bullshit." Andrea hadn't meant to be so vehement but it made her angry. "Sure they wanted it dim, so you would be more likely to sleep all day and not bother them. As long as I'm here, these blinds will stay up unless you ask for them to be lowered."

Darcy's eyebrows shot up. "Uh, thanks. I thought you medical types didn't criticize each other."

Hands on her hips, Andrea glared at Darcy. "Maybe some don't, but my priority is the patient and if a medical type does something wrong, it's wrong not to call them out for it. We deal in lives, after all." She took a deep breath. "Sorry. I didn't mean to condescend."

Darcy opened her mouth as if to respond, but closed it when Maria appeared with lunch. "It's nice and bright in here for a change. You call after you feed Darcy, Doctor, and Carlo will bring your lunch. Okay?"

"Sounds good." She moved the lunch to the bed tray. "Maria, we're out of clean sheets and pillowcases and I found some dirty sheets stuffed under the table. Is there someone who could bring up clean linens and collect laundry a couple of times a day?"

"Marta is supposed to check these things. I'll talk to her."

"Um, *Zia*…" Darcy looked uncomfortable. "Maybe I chased her out the other day."

Maria frowned at Darcy. "Maybe, *cara*?" She raised her eyebrows. "You feeling better?"

"*Si, Zia.*"

She patted Darcy's face. "So no more yelling?"

"I'll try, *Zia.*"

Maria studied Darcy. "Ah, it's your hair makes you look so nice. I see you later when I come to make dinner."

Zia? Maria is Darcy's aunt? Andrea began to feed Darcy.

Being fed could be infantilizing so to head off another Darcy attack, Andrea decided to make conversation. "You know, if you hang a bird feeder outside your window, you'd have something to look at. What do you think?"

Darcy swallowed the chicken she was chewing. "Sounds good. Ask Carlo to take care of it when he comes up with your tray." She watched Andrea spear another forkful of chicken breast. "Before you shove that in, can I ask one of my questions?"

Andrea's hand hovered near Darcy's mouth. "Fire away."

"Where are you from?"

She fed her the chicken.

Andrea considered whether this was appropriate information to share. "I grew up in Manhattan, the upper west side."

"Yes, but I hear a trace of an accent. Where are you really from?"

Andrea sat back. "You have good ears. I was born in Sicily but we moved here when I was ten years old. I learned English in Sicily but I became fluent at school here. I thought I'd lost my accent."

"It's very slight, just an occasional word."

"Yes, but it's amazing that—"

"What? That someone as egocentric as me would pay enough attention to hear it?"

"Well, yes." *Egocentric and selfish but paying attention to me. Not a good thing*.

Darcy laughed. "Ah, the good doctor is a truth teller."

Andrea leaned forward. "You know, you can't distract me from feeding you this not-a-cheeseburger lunch." She offered a forkful. Darcy opened her mouth, chewed and swallowed.

"It's delicious, so forget about me trying to distract you. I'm interested…in you. That's all." She flushed.

Andrea was pleased to see a blush but pretended to take the interest to mean interested in her background, rather than interested as in sexually. After all, she didn't even like this woman. But it was nice to know the outrageous Darcy Silver could be embarrassed too. She'd left not a shred of doubt that Andrea's body interested her but had controlled herself while the lotion was applied. Andrea, on the other hand, had enjoyed touching Darcy's lovely body way too much. Maybe it was time for her to get back in the dating game. She'd call Julie and Karin soon and agree to go out with the friend they wanted her to meet.

Darcy swallowed the last of her chicken. She smiled. "So, how old are you, Dr. Trapani?"

Andrea got up and called down to Maria. She was starving and looking forward to a quiet half hour while she ate. "Forty-one. And you?"

"Hmm, I don't remember granting you any questions. But since you ordered me such a tasty lunch, I'll answer this one. But remember we do tit" —her eyes flashed to Andrea's breasts even though they were invisible beneath her lab coat— "for tat. I'll be forty in December."

Andrea's body responded to Darcy's blatant flirting with a blush. She didn't know what to say but she was saved by the arrival of a slender, virile man with a full head of white hair, an old-world manner and a jaunty air. He reminded Andrea of her relatives in Sicily.

"Doctor, this is Carlo, Maria's husband."

He smiled at Andrea. "Where do you like the tray, *Dottore*?"

Before Andrea could say *put it in the bedroom*, Darcy spoke. "On the bed tray, *Zio*, the doctor will talk to me while she eats lunch."

They were doing so well; Andrea didn't want to upset the fragile stability. If she stayed beyond today, she'd draw some boundaries—separate meals and no flirting. "Carlo, would it be possible to hang a bird feeder outside this window?"

He turned to Darcy. "*Vuoi questo, bella?*"

"Yes, I want it, *Zio*. You know I like birds."

He kissed two of his fingers and touched them to Darcy's lips. "*Va bene*." He nodded at Andrea, removed Darcy's empty dishes, put Andrea's lunch on the tray and left.

Darcy watched Andrea take her first bite. "I'm sorry. I'm sure you could use a break from me, but, as we've established, I'm greedy and egocentric and you're the first, uh, interesting company I've had. I promise I'll take a nap later so you can have some time for yourself."

Andrea was moved by the request to sit with her and the understanding that she needed some time to herself. She nodded and swallowed. "Tell me. How do you amuse yourself?"

Darcy had a mischievous gleam in her eye and Andrea rushed to cut off whatever sexual innuendo was coming. "Other than terrorizing people, I mean." She smiled to take the sting out of her words.

Darcy chewed her lower lip.

Andrea noted her lips were chapped and made a mental note to put some lotion on them.

"Well, other than making people squirm, I spend lots of time staring at the ceiling. Sometimes I watch TV but mostly it doesn't interest me." Her voice became distant, sad. "I guess I mostly space out."

And probably stoke your rage at being abandoned, Andrea thought. "What would you like to do? Given your current condition, that is?" Got to herd this woman in the right direction. She took another bite.

"Wow, nobody's asked what I'd like. I'd love to sit in my garden but we know that's not going to happen. I'd love to read a book, but I can't hold one. I'd love to listen to music, I'd love to go to my house on Fire Island." Darcy's voice drifted off. Looking like she wanted to cry, she shifted her eyes over Andrea's shoulder, toward the window.

"What kind of books do you like?"

Her eyes swung back to Andrea. "I read, used to read, a lot of different things. I like well-written romances and mysteries with lesbian characters." She held Andrea's eyes as if waiting for confirmation.

Andrea returned her look but didn't provide the information she was seeking. Darcy was already too sexual for her comfort.

"But I also like literary novels, mysteries, thrillers, as long as they're well-written and have interesting characters and plots. Mostly I read non-fiction, political books, history, particularly English, American and Italian, biographies and psychology."

"Eclectic, huh? What about music?"

"Eclectic in music as well. Classical, opera, blues, country, rock, depending on my mood. Nothing too raucous."

"Do you have an iPod?"

"I did, but it was in the car when it burned."

"How about after I eat, I give you my iPod? We can put together a playlist, I'll put the earbuds in, and you can listen. Maybe it will help you relax."

Darcy's smile said *yes, yes, yes*.

"And, what do you like to do my good doctor?"

"I enjoy hiking and running. I'm pretty eclectic in books and music too, except I throw in some medical books to stay up in the field."

"Is your field cardiology?"

"I'm an emergency room doctor."

The color drained from Darcy's olive skin. "Am I so bad that I need someone like you with me twenty-four-seven?"

Without thinking, Andrea gently brushed the hair off Darcy's forehead. "No, no. Don't worry. I just happened to be available." She could see the question forming in Darcy's mind so she stood. "I'll get my iPod." She bolted next door to her bedroom. She left the door open but went into the bathroom, closed that door, and leaned against it. *What was I thinking touching Darcy so tenderly?* Shit. Darcy would probably use the gesture as fuel for her sexual harassment.

After she caught her breath, Andrea washed her face and hands, then picked up her iPod and returned. Darcy either hadn't noticed or didn't find it noteworthy, so she relaxed and they spent some time discussing music. It seemed they liked many of the same things.

Darcy grinned. "Definitely Ravel's *Boléro*. It makes me feel sexy."

Here we go again. All conversations with Darcy led to sex. "We should probably skip it then."

"Afraid I'll become a raging beast?" Darcy's tone was mocking.

Damn she hadn't meant to say that aloud. And, probably for the millionth time in her life, she wished she wasn't so fair-skinned that every little blush flashed like the warning light at an intersection. "Would you be offended if I said yes?"

Darcy shook with laughter, a deep belly laugh. "Not at all. As you've seen, I can be a raging beast. And, I'm sorry to say, you've also experienced me using my eyes and my words to be a sexual beast. But, I promise to control myself."

"Was that an apology?"

Darcy reddened. "For the tone and the delivery, not the sentiment." She tensed.

Andrea narrowed her eyes. True the tone was insulting and the sentiment could be viewed as a compliment. Darcy seemed to get it. "Accepted." She turned back to the iPod. "What else?"

They cycled through the options. "Great, I love Adele. And, all the oldies like Stevie Nicks, Joan Baez, Judy Collins, Janis Joplin, Tracy Chapman, Nancy LaMott, Cowboy Junkies, Emmylou Harris. Can we get some opera and—"

"Hey, this isn't your last chance to make a playlist. Why don't you listen for a while?"

"Sorry, I told you I was greedy. It feels like ages since I've heard music so I want it all now. But it would be nice to listen for a while."

Andrea plugged her in and turned the iPod on. The smile on Darcy's face as she listened touched Andrea's heart. Then, with one eye on Darcy, she continued cleaning and setting the room up to her liking. When Darcy's face went slack, Andrea crept into her own room. She left the door between them open and sat in the easy chair by the window. From there she could watch Darcy in the mirror over the dresser. She sighed. The day had been stressful, but she was feeling more optimistic now. She thought about where they were versus where they'd started and realized that she'd enjoyed talking to Darcy while she ate. Poor woman was starved for company and conversation. Then she had an epiphany. Darcy would feel less isolated if they ate meals together and that would help her relax. Such a simple thing. She picked up the intercom and Gregg answered. "Gregg, please tell Maria I would like my meals served at the same time as Darcy's so we can eat together." That done, she picked up *Love by the Numbers*, the romance she'd started the night before.

"Dr. Trapani." Darcy called from the other room.

Andrea looked up, shocked that nearly an hour had passed.

"Coming, Darcy." She put her book down and went into Darcy's room. "Have a nice nap?" One of the earbuds was lying on the pillow. "Do you want to listen to more music?"

"Not now, but thank you so much. I feel like I slept for hours."

Andrea removed the other earbud and put the iPod on the table near the bed. "Actually, it was only about an hour."

The catheter drainage bag was nearly full and Darcy probably needed a bedpan by now. She'd been surprised that Darcy wasn't wearing a diaper but diapers were difficult for most patients and she thought it would be particularly difficult for someone like Darcy. Well, bedpan or diaper, they'd have to face it eventually. She braced herself. "Darcy, I noticed you're not wearing a diaper. Isn't it difficult for you to sit on the bedpan with the leg casts?"

Darcy flushed. "It's uncomfortable but I won't wear a diaper." Her voice was hard.

Andrea could see she'd tensed for an argument. It was probably better not to make an issue of it. If there was a problem, she'd come back to it another day. If there was another day. "Fine. I'm going to empty your drainage bag. Should I put you on the bedpan first?"

Darcy looked miserable.

Damn. Darcy was embarrassed. Andrea wondered if she'd she done something to elicit that reaction. No, she'd had her stray thoughts about Darcy's body but she was sure her behavior had been professional. Darcy would probably go on the defensive and attack but she'd just have to gird her loins since there was no way to avoid this discussion. She retrieved the bedpan but she wanted Darcy to feel in control so she pulled the chair over again, putting them on the same level. "I'm a doctor, Darcy. I know how the body works and believe me I've seen a lot of excrement in the emergency room. Plus, let me remind you that we all do it."

Darcy refused to meet Andrea's eyes. "Yeah, but it's embarrassing. I don't want to ask you to do that, to see me like that."

No attack. Score one for me. "We don't have too many choices here, Darcy. And, you know, in the greater scheme of things, it's not the worst thing for either of us, so let's not make it a big deal. Okay?"

Darcy was silent. Then she nodded slowly. "Thank you, Dr. Trapani, for being patient with me." She smiled. "I guess if you're willing, I shouldn't complain."

Andrea cleaned and reconnected the urine bag, then quickly and efficiently took care of Darcy and the bedpan. It went smoothly. She was pleased they'd gotten through it without either of them stressing, another small battle won.

Darcy asked to listen to music again. She also asked Andrea to stay in the room with her. Given Darcy's tendency to sexualize everything, Andrea decided it was best to not announce her sexuality by bringing her book in, so she sat nearby doing a crossword puzzle.

At six, Carlo delivered their dinners and told Andrea to leave the dirty dishes on the cart in the hall and he'd pick them up in the morning. He also gave her keys to the house so she could lock up after the nurse arrived at eight o'clock. Before he left he kissed Darcy on the cheek.

Darcy's eyes widened when she realized Andrea intended to eat with her. She smiled sweetly. "Thank you, Doctor. I appreciate," her voice broke, "the company." Her eyes filled. "Everyone else shoveled it in and disappeared. I've been lonely."

"I thought it would be more interesting for both of us." She placed a fork full of salmon in Darcy's mouth. "Do you remember that a nurse will be here from eight tonight to eight tomorrow morning?" She took a bite of salmon. No question, Maria was a wonderful cook.

Darcy chewed slowly, seeming to enjoy the fish. "I remember. You'll be in the bedroom, right?"

"Yes. I might go out for a run after I get the nurse oriented, but then I'll be right there in the bedroom if you need me."

"A run sounds wonderful. I used to run. Around the reservoir in Central Park when I was in the city and on the beach at my Fire Island house."

"You'll be walking again in a couple of months."

"It's hard to imagine. I feel like I've been trapped in this room for years. A couple of months seems like forever. Do you think I'll be able to run again?"

"I assume your legs will be fine and with time you'd be able to run but I'm not sure about your heart. By the time you feel like running Dr. Castillo should be able to tell you. Have you ever run along the Hudson River where the marina is?"

"I haven't been there in years." She shrugged. "Maybe someday, if I can, I'll go there. I've heard they've made it really beautiful."

"It is beautiful." Andrea waved the fork. Darcy opened her mouth, chewed and swallowed. "Um, this not-linguine-Alfredo dinner isn't half bad." She opened her mouth for more.

When the last spoonful of fresh fruit salad had been eaten, Darcy sighed. "Are you sure this diet is good for me?"

"Did you enjoy the meal?"

"I did. I've been afraid I was going to gain a lot of weight because I'm barely moving. Do you think your diet might help keep the weight off?"

"It should but don't worry about the calories now, your body needs more than usual while it's healing."

"If you don't feel like running tonight, you might enjoy sitting in the garden. Have you seen it? It's private and it's safe. You get to it through the kitchen."

"I think I'll run tonight, but I'll keep it in mind." Andrea carried their dishes to the cart. "Okay, Darcy, time to check vitals again. She smiled at the blood pressure reading. "One hundred fifty over seventy-five. Not perfect but much better."

Darcy didn't respond.

Now what? "Something wrong?"

Darcy cleared her throat. She gazed at the windows. "I was just trying to figure out how to get you to not leave tomorrow."

So Maria was right. Andrea wasn't surprised she'd enjoyed the challenge of taming the beast but she was surprised she'd enjoyed Darcy's company and surprised to realize she wanted to stay. She had no illusions, Darcy's underlying issues, fear of being alone and feelings of abandonment, were not gone, but once she got past her terror and rage, Darcy was an interesting woman.

"Let's see now." She tapped her finger on her lips. "Hmm. You could try asking me to stay."

Darcy turned to Andrea, her face hopeful. "Dr. Trapani, would you stay and take care of me? Please?"

"I'd be delighted, Darcy." And she meant it. She knew it would be up and down but she felt alive, a hundred times better than the depressed lethargy she'd been stuck in for the last few months.

Darcy smiled. "Thank you. I feel…safe with you. It's…I like it. I like you." Her eyes filled. "Hey, can I ask what this night nurse is going to do to me?"

"Why don't you think of it as doing *for* you rather than to you? Mostly she'll take your vitals a few times, watch over you while you sleep and be available if you need water or a bedpan or anything else overnight. I'll be right here if there's a problem. And since I didn't get a chance to wash you today, I'm going to ask her to do that before you go to sleep."

CHAPTER SIX

After changing into her wicking V-neck tee and ankle-length running tights rather than her usual shorts and tank top, Andrea stretched, then went to Darcy's room to tell her she was leaving. Dressing discreetly didn't prevent Darcy's candid appraisal. Those lovely blue eyes danced over every inch of her body, leaving no doubt Darcy liked what she saw. Once again Andrea's body responded to the frank assessment with a burst of heat. Before today that had never happened from just a look. Or was it before Darcy? As she ran down the four flights of steps, Andrea realized that she enjoyed Darcy's company but found her temper and piggy ways offensive. Obviously her sexual response to Darcy was just a chemical reaction, the result of Darcy's pheromones attracting her due to her self-imposed abstinence in the last four months. Actually, it had been a very long time since she'd had anything but casual, almost mechanical, sex, so her physical reaction to someone as sexual as Darcy flirting with her was understandable. Wasn't it?

Right now Darcy was helpless and dependent, and, it was clear, she was anxious and feeling abandoned and deprived. Andrea guessed flirting made her feel alive, more like her old self. In a way, she needed it to help her through these next few months until she regained her independence. But, chemicals and her body's response aside, Andrea had no desire to become involved with Darcy so she would have to be the adult in the room and keep things professional.

When she was at home on the west side, she almost always ran in Riverside Park along the Hudson River but she did occasionally run around the reservoir in Central Park, so she was comfortable running there tonight. As usual she let her mind roam free and tonight her thoughts kept coming back to Darcy, how to help her, how even with her potty mouth and sarcastic attacks she was sexy and beautiful, how seductive she was, how her flirting seemed to touch places in Andrea that didn't usually get touched. Chemicals, she reminded herself.

Andrea stretched on the front steps, steps that were new and strange when she'd arrived less than fourteen hours ago. It had been a long and stressful day and although the run hadn't cleared her mind as it usually did, it had worked out all the tension she was feeling from her first day at work in four months. Now she'd shower, read a little and sleep.

Darcy was asleep. The earbuds were in place and she looked peaceful, a huge difference from this morning. Andrea waved the nurse, Francine, out to the hallway. "How has she been?"

"Good." She handed Andrea the chart she'd brought out. "Her pressure was about the same as when you took it earlier."

Andrea looked at the chart and handed it back.

"She didn't need much from me other than water and the iPod. But she insisted you said you would wash her in the morning. I didn't want to argue and get her pressure up so I let it go but I'm happy to stay and do it in the morning after you discuss it with her. Other than that, she's been very pleasant and easy to be with. She said she was tired and I should just relax and read my book."

Andrea shook her head. "I told her I was going to ask you to wash her."

Francine looked alarmed. "I swear—"

Andrea held up a hand to stop her. "Don't worry, I believe you. I guess Devious Darcy wants me to wash her."

Francine's shock came through in her voice. "But you're a doctor. Really, I can do it before I leave in the morning."

Andrea laughed. "It's okay, Francine. It won't be the first time I've washed a patient and probably not the last. I worked in Africa with Doctors Without Borders. We were always short-staffed so we did whatever was necessary to treat the patient."

Francine gazed at her. "If you're sure."

"I'm sure. Wake me if you need help getting her on and off the bedpan, or if she wants me, or her pressure goes high again."

"We've already managed the bedpan once, so I don't foresee a problem."

"As I said earlier, keep an eye on the catheter bag and her pressure." She thought for a second. "She really needs to rest, so let her sleep till about three before waking her."

"Gotcha."

"Now, unless you have questions or need something, I'm going to take a shower and go to bed."

"See you in the morning."

Very pleasant indeed. What a difference twelve hours could make. Although she'd worried about leaving Darcy with another new person, once Francine arrived Andrea had relaxed. She'd worked with enough nurses in her time to recognize that Francine, a plump earth-mother type with curly chestnut hair, soft brown eyes and a warm, caring, no-nonsense professional manner, was one of the good ones. Apparently, Darcy had responded well to her. Progress. Andrea found herself humming in the shower.

As she dried off and put on her pajamas, she examined the family pictures displayed on the bookshelves. Assuming the couple in the photos was Darcy's parents, she had her father's height and blue eyes but otherwise looked like her mother. The early pictures showed Darcy as an infant then a baby. Around three or four another little girl appeared between Darcy and her dad. The very small and very blond girl didn't resemble Darcy or her parents. In all the photos after that, the two girls were together, often with the blonde between Darcy and her dad, right up through what appeared to be college graduation. If they were the same age, probably not a sister. Adopted? Maria and Carlo's daughter? She'd have to ask Darcy. Other photographs looked to be from college. One that caught Andrea's eye showed Darcy in the arms of a very tall, very blond young woman, the two of them looking at each other with such love it was touching. Obviously a past lover. She wondered what had happened.

She climbed into bed and powered up her laptop. Darcy had mentioned several books she was interested in reading, so Andrea downloaded the two available as audio books, a mystery and a political analysis, to her iPod. Then she switched to Gmail and typed the email update she'd promised.

Dear Julie,

You were right. Darcy is in danger. She's very volatile and her pressure was 201/110 when I arrived. In fact, I considered calling you or making a trip to the ER but I realized you'd probably say wait and see if it comes down. And it did.

As you warned, she is difficult. But when she's not in a screaming rage she can be engaging and interesting. Not to mention, charming. She's also a big flirt and much to my surprise, I find my body responding. It's nice to know I'm not as dead as I thought. In fact, I already feel more alive than I have in months.

Love…Andrea

She hit Send, powered down and was asleep in minutes.

CHAPTER SEVEN

Andrea woke with a start, and with years of emergency room and field medical experience with Doctors Without Borders, she was fully conscious immediately. She relaxed when she recognized the sun-filled room in Darcy's house and remembered she was in Darcy's bed. She glanced at the clock. Seven fifteen, much later than her usual six a.m. She rolled out of bed, washed her face and brushed her teeth, pulled on clean scrubs and a lab coat and slipped into her shoes. Eight minutes later, she ran the brush through her hair, then walked into Darcy's room to review the night with Francine.

Darcy was pale, her eyes were closed. "Good morning, ladies, how did it go?"

Francine was standing at the table behind Darcy, writing in the chart. She looked worried. Darcy didn't respond. Andrea raised her eyebrows at Francine.

Francine shrugged, then pointed to the chart.

Puzzled, Andrea dropped her voice. "Oh, I didn't realize Darcy was still sleeping. Let's review the chart before you leave,

Francine." She walked behind the bed and reached for the chart. "Read this part first, Dr. Trapani," Francine said, handing her a handwritten note.

> Dear Dr. Trapani,
> For the most part, the shift was quiet. Darcy slept except for when I woke her to check vitals, but she awakened about five this morning and was very agitated. She asked 'What time is it?' every three to four minutes until just before you came in. And her eyes were glued to your bedroom door the entire time. At six, I asked if she wanted me to wake you. She got a little nasty and said, 'I'm fine, I don't need her." It was clear to me that you were exactly what she needed/wanted but I felt it was important to respect her wishes. I hope I did the right thing.
> I just took her blood pressure and it was 180/80 much higher than overnight as you'll see when you check the chart.
> Francine

"Hmm, pressure is up again. I'll have to see what I can do about that today." Andrea spoke loud enough for Darcy to hear. "Thanks, Francine. We'll see you tonight."

Realizing Francine was upset, Andrea walked to the hallway with her and spoke softly. "Don't worry, Francine. Respecting Darcy's wishes was the right thing to do." She looked into Darcy's room to check on her. "Not to change the subject, but I'm planning on washing her hair tomorrow morning and I'd like your help."

"Sure. I can stay later."

"No need. I'll come in earlier, about seven. An hour should be enough time."

After Francine started down the stairs, Andrea took a minute to brace herself. She didn't know why Darcy was upset but she was sure an attack was in her immediate future. *Oh, well, here we go again.*

Darcy's eyes were still closed, her jaw was tense, her mouth white and her breathing uneven. Whatever it was had frightened her. Andrea touched Darcy's shoulder. "Good morning, sleeping beauty."

Darcy squeezed her eyes tighter.

"Remember me? Dr. Trapani?"

"Doctor who?" Darcy's voice was harsh.

Andrea stiffened. She'd expected it, but it still didn't feel good to be on the receiving end of that tone of voice. She kept her own voice gentle. "Not Dr. Who. Dr. Trapani, your very own live-in."

"Mine? You must be mistaken. I don't have a…anyone."

That Darcy was angry was clear but Andrea's heart broke at the pain and abandonment she heard underneath the harshness and the anger. She sighed. *Square one it is.* She pulled the chair over and placed her hand on Darcy shoulder, trying to connect. "Can we talk?"

"Talk about what?" Darcy spat the words out.

"There's the weather or the problems in the Middle East, but talking about what you're feeling will do more for your blood pressure." She gently squeezed Darcy's shoulder. "Why are you so angry?"

Darcy's face softened. Her heart went out to Darcy. She was temperamental and difficult but being so helpless would make anybody crazy.

"I dreamed you'd left me. It felt so real." Her voice was a whisper.

"You asked me to stay and I said yes. I would never leave without telling you first. Why didn't you ask Francine to wake me?"

"I was afraid to find out that you really were gone, that I'd driven you away like everybody else."

"And why did everybody else leave?"

Darcy hesitated. "Um, because I'm a nasty, punishing bitch."

"There you go. Stop being a bitch."

Darcy opened her eyes. "If that's what it takes to keep you here."

"That's what it takes because it's not good for you to work yourself up like this, your pressure is dangerously high again. Promise you'll ask Francine to wake me any time you need me, as often as you need, to feel safe." She plucked a tissue from the box and dried Darcy's drippy nose.

Darcy sniffed. "I promise."

"Francine was worried about you. She could see you were upset but she didn't know why. She was caught between you telling her not to wake me and her instinct that you needed me."

"I didn't mean to worry her."

"I want you to have as much autonomy as possible, but I'm going to tell her to trust her instincts in the future. Okay?"

Darcy nodded.

"So, how about we start the day over?"

Darcy smiled. "Good morning, Dr. Trapani."

"Ah, good morning, Darcy. Sleep well?"

"Better than I have in a while, except I had a nightmare."

"Do you want to talk about it?"

Darcy looked puzzled. "Um, we already did."

Andrea smiled. "So we did. And that's good because not talking about it makes it feel real." She patted Darcy's hand. "I hear the breakfast trays. I'll brush your teeth, then after we eat I'll wash you and we can talk business." She looked up as the cart rolled in. "Ah, morning, Maria."

Maria moved the dishes to the bed tray.

Andrea glanced at Darcy. "I'll be staying, so you can proceed with the menu we discussed yesterday. And, if you give me a second I'll get the menus I promised you."

As Andrea went into the bedroom, she heard Maria speak to Darcy. "Is good she stay, I think, *cara*." She kissed Darcy's cheek.

"I think so too, *zia*."

"Here you go." She handed Maria the menus and recipes. "By the way, what do we do about meals on the weekends?"

"No worry. Gregg cooks."

Gregg? Really? He looks about fifteen? "Perfect. As long as he follows the diet."

Maria left and Andrea turned to Darcy. "Okay, let's get some food in you."

"Coffee first."

Andrea raised the bed. "We're on the same wavelength there." She fixed Darcy's coffee and held the straw to her lips. Then, she picked up the spoon to feed Darcy her cereal.

"No. You have some coffee first, then I'll eat." Darcy watched Andrea fix her own coffee and drink some.

"Do you like your fruit in your cereal or separate?"

"Bananas in, berries on the side."

Andrea dumped the bananas into the cereal and spooned some into Darcy's mouth. She grinned. "Remember, no croissants today so you'd better eat everything."

"You look awfully happy about depriving me of one of the few pleasures in my life these days. I hope you're not a sadist."

Andrea fed her some berries. "We'll just have to see, won't we?"

"I'm sorry I gave you and Francine such a hard time."

Andrea spooned cereal into Darcy's open mouth. "I understand, and I'm sure Francine does as well, that you're very vulnerable right now. Being dependent is a bitch. It's infantilizing and I imagine it's very scary for someone who likely has never needed anyone on such a basic level, at least not since childhood." She patted Darcy's cheek. "It's probably not the last time you'll feel that anxiety. You can't will the feelings away but it would be good to work on verbalizing them rather than trying to hide them and getting so worked up that your pressure goes sky-high."

"And, speaking of being dependent, my nose is running again. Could you—"

"Of course." Andrea reached for a tissue and held it to Darcy's nose. "Want to blow or should I just wipe."

"Wipe."

She tossed the tissue.

"Thanks, my nose always runs when I get emotional. Hey, let me rest a minute while you eat some breakfast."

When they'd both eaten, Andrea moved the dishes to the cart, then sat to talk. "Your chart says they put the catheter in three days ago because you refused to wear a diaper. I know using the bedpan is difficult but you risk infection by keeping the catheter in too long. I'd like to remove it before I wash you this morning. Is that all right?"

"The night before they put the catheter in, I asked for the bedpan several times and the aide apparently didn't hear me so I had an accident. The aide also didn't hear my request to clean me and change the sheets and I lay there in my urine for almost four hours. The truth is I wasn't very nice to her and she was getting back in the way she could. I fired her the next morning and before I knew it, the nurse came and put the catheter in, and not gently, I might add. Incidents like that happened all the time which is partly why I was in the state I was in when you came."

"I'm sorry. That was cruel and unprofessional, at the least."

"I guess I deserved it. But what happens if I have another accident?"

"Oh, Darcy, nobody deserves to lie in urine. I promise to wash you and change the sheets immediately. And, if any nurse we bring in does anything less than that, I want you to scream for me and I'll get rid of them on the spot. And make sure they have a bad reference."

"Okay, take it out." She chewed her lip as she watched Andrea get ready to bathe her. "Doctor, I'm feeling anxious about you washing me."

Really? Is everything going to be an issue with this woman? "Why did you tell Francine I would wash you?"

Darcy cleared her throat. Her eyes shifted to the windows. "Because, um, I didn't know her." She flushed. "And I wanted you to do it."

Andrea resorted to her ER face to prevent her amusement from showing. While it was true they had spent the day together, it wasn't like she'd been caring for Darcy for weeks. "And now?" Andrea kept her back to Darcy. "Would you rather wait until Francine comes in tonight?"

"No, I want you to do it."

She faced Darcy. "Why does it make you anxious?" That's it, play dumb Andrea.

"It's so intimate."

"It is intimate, Darcy, but no more than the other things I've been doing for you. Does the idea of Francine washing you make you anxious?"

"No."

"Then, why don't we wait—"

"No, I want you to do it." Darcy looked down.

Andrea studied Darcy. "I'm confused."

"Me too."

She put a finger under Darcy's chin and lifted it so they were looking into each other's eyes. "I'm your doctor, not a sexual partner. I wash you to make sure you're clean and comfortable, not to turn you on. I'll wash you this morning if you wish, but if I sense that you make it into something sexual, I'm going to insist that Francine, or whichever nurse is on, washes you in the evening. Do you understand?"

"Yes." Her voice was small.

Andrea felt for her. Darcy was confusing being touched with sexual contact. Well, it was up to her to set the ground rules to keep this from getting too charged for both of them. "I'm not rejecting you, Darcy. You have a long way to go to get back on your feet. If you want me with you on this journey, we have to be clear about our relationship or things could get sticky and I'll end up having to leave. I don't want to do that. I want to be with you all the way, but—"

"I get it. And, I'll try to control myself. No. I will control myself."

"Good, so am I washing you or do you want to wait for Francine?"

"You."

Damn. As she'd told Francine, working in the field with Doctors Without Borders she had often washed bloody or dirty patients, before operating or delivering a baby, and hadn't given washing Darcy a second thought. But clearly Darcy had. And now Andrea was anxious. She reached for a pair of latex gloves. She wanted Darcy to enjoy being bathed but she didn't want to turn her on, so she was self-conscious about her touch, striving for gentle and caring, but not too caring.

CHAPTER EIGHT

An hour later, she was washed, her hair brushed and the linens changed. She'd managed to stop fantasizing about Andrea and just focus on the pleasure of being touched. Even if it was a professional touch and not the caresses she longed for. She smiled at herself. It had only taken one day for the lovely doctor to become the girl of her dreams. She knew the truth was that she was vulnerable and needy and lonely so she'd focused on the one person she perceived as caring. But Andrea Trapani was pretty and sexy and she seemed intelligent and a lovely person to boot. Maybe too good for nasty old Darcy, but she reserved the right to fantasize about her whenever she wanted and to pursue her when she was back on her feet and able to pursue.

"What's so funny? You're lying there with a big smile on your face and a faraway look. Was it that good for you?"

"You can't have it both ways, my dear doctor. No sexual innuendos allowed."

Andrea flushed. "Just teasing, but you're right, I need to behave too."

Darcy grinned. Dr. Trapani looked uncomfortable. Had she caught the doctor flirting with her?

Andrea waved the stethoscope. "Vital signs, then business." When she finished, she said, "Your pressure is coming down but it's still too high. So try to relax. Other than that you're good."

The intercom buzzed and Andrea turned to hit the button. It was Maria. "Darcy, Candace wants to tell you she is coming at eleven to sign the papers for the agency lady and the doctor."

"Okay, Maria." Darcy waited until Andrea switched the intercom off. "About fucking time she showed up." The rage was back. She scowled at Andrea. "Did you call Candace?"

"I have no idea who Candace is." She put a hand on Darcy's chest. "Calm down."

"She's my attorney." Darcy bit her bottom lip. "And supposedly my sist...friend. Gerri must have called her to come and take care of the contracts." Her eyes filled. "I really do owe Gerri an apology and a thank you for making sure I was taken care of." She blinked. "God, I hate being teary all the time." She stared out the window for a minute. "So what's this business you want to talk about? Are you going to demand a higher rate because I'm such a difficult patient?"

Andrea smiled. "No, nothing like that. I'd like to get you some things I think would make you more comfortable, but they're expensive and I'm not sure about how to pay for them."

"Like what?"

Carlo came in to retrieve the cart with the breakfast dishes, stopped to kiss Darcy's forehead, sniffed. "You smell nice this morning."

Darcy sniffed. "I do, don't I. Thanks to the good doctor I'm starting to feel human again."

He smiled at Andrea, then turned to wheel the cart out. Watching him, Andrea asked the question that had been bothering her. "Carlo," she asked in Italian, "do you and Maria carry trays up and down all those stairs?"

He laughed. "No, Doctor. *Usiamo l'accensore*," he said in Italian as he walked out.

Stunned, she spun to face Darcy. "You have an elevator?"

"Did you think they floated me up four floors? I had it put in when my mother was sick. It opens near the kitchen."

"Then it's near the door to the garden?"

"Exactly. We built a ramp so she could go into the garden. She loved to sit there and read." Darcy sounded so wistful, it tugged at Andrea's heart. And gave her an idea.

"Back to business. I'd have to clear it with your surgeon but I was thinking I could order a chair for you, a recliner, but one that can bring you to an almost standing position. With the help of Carlo or Gregg I could move you in and out of bed without putting weight on your legs. They run several thousand dollars. What do you think?"

"I wouldn't have to be in bed all the time?"

"That's right. You could sit up in the chair or lie back if that's what you wanted. We'd have to buy some loose clothing so you wouldn't be nude when we move you."

"Are you trying to deprive Carlo and Gregg of the sight of my broken body or protect yourself from temptation?"

Andrea chose to ignore the last part of that remark. "Carlo, Gregg and any other visitors you have. I think it would be a good idea if you invited a friend or two to visit you, to help break up the days. Maria told me you have lots of friends but none have visited. Why is that?"

Darcy shrugged and turned her head toward the window. "I don't know why. I guess they aren't the friends I thought they were." There it was again, underlying the words, the feeling of being abandoned.

"Maybe we could call some of them?"

"I won't beg." Her anger was sharp and cold. Not something Andrea enjoyed being on the receiving end of. Darcy turned to Andrea, frowning.

"What's the matter?"

"My forehead is itchy."

Andrea scratched lightly.

"Let's give Candace the information and she'll order it and pay for it." Darcy yawned.

"Do you want to take a nap before they come?"

"Yes, if you promise to wake me when Candace gets here."

"Of course."

"And speaking of being naked, is there something I could wear on top? I don't think anything of mine would go over the casts."

"Hmm, they sent all the hospital gowns back when you refused to wear them. How would you feel about wearing one of my scrub tops? It's not glamorous and it might be a little big but we can cut the sleeve if it won't go over the cast. I have blue, green and turquoise. The blue would look lovely on you."

Darcy narrowed her eyes. "My dear sweet doctor, are you offering to give me the shirt off your back?"

Andrea noted the upgrade to dear sweet. "Well, not quite that dramatic but I am offering my shirt."

"I would love it. And, I'll replace it if we cut it. Can we try it now?"

Andrea retrieved the top, slit the sleeve so it fit over the cast and slipped it over Darcy's head. Darcy was ecstatic. She sniffed. "It smells like you. I'm not giving it back." Her eyes were sparkling. "I feel like a new woman. Thank you, thank you, thank you."

"You're very welcome. Now close your eyes and see if you can get a little rest."

Darcy woke when Maria buzzed the intercom to say Candace was on the way up. Andrea raised the bed, then noticed again that Darcy's lips were chapped. She leaned in to apply cream to Darcy's lips, their faces close. At the sound of a low whistle, Andrea whirled. "Hey, Darce, I didn't expect to find you making out, but I should have known."

Andrea flushed. "We weren't—"

The woman laughed and extended her manicured hand. "Dr. Trapani, I presume." She was impeccably made up, her light brown hair was streaked with gold and she wore it in a sophisticated cut that fell to her chin and highlighted her lovely dark eyes and good-humored face. Her tailored soft green pantsuit hugged her body and her four-inch heels put her at about five-six. Small and compact, she was still an imposing figure.

"Go fuck yourself, Candace, that's your name isn't it? It's been so long since I've seen you, I forget." Darcy scowled. "And, for your information, I should be so lucky as to be kissed by my good sweet doctor. Doctor Trapani, this impertinent bitch is my attorney and used-to-be best friend, Candace Matthews of Silver, Levitz and Forbes."

"Ms. Matthews." Still not recovered from the accusation, she shook the hand Candace extended. Up close, Andrea could smell Candace's light but intoxicating perfume.

"Call me Candace, please."

Andrea let go of Candace's hand but Candace held on and did a slow scan of Andrea's body. Christ, Candace was as piggy as Darcy. Happily, her body didn't respond at all to Candace's assault but it annoyed Andrea. She cleared her throat and stared at her trapped hand until Candace grinned and released it. Her amused brown eyes studied Andrea. "Maria told me Darcy is listening to you, Doctor, so as her attorney and friend, I felt it was imperative to determine what drugs you're giving her. But now that I see you in person, I understand."

Before Andrea could respond, Maria appeared with Mrs. Gordon, the owner of the agency. After introductions, Darcy spoke. "I gave Francine a bit of a hard time this morning but I like her. How does she feel about taking care of me?"

"To be frank, I don't understand what your friend Gerri was worried about when she called. She said you could be very difficult and had a hard time keeping nurses and aides. Francine didn't mention any problem. In fact, she said you were very pleasant."

The other four women in the room avoided each other's eyes. Candace jumped into the silence. "Well, Darcy, if you'd like to continue with Francine and whoever is her backup, I'll sign the contract."

"I do want to continue, please sign and let's get on with the rest of our business."

Candace read the contract, then signed and handed it to Mrs. Gordon. "Send the bills to the address on the contract and call me at the number listed if you have any payment problems."

Maria escorted Mrs. Gordon out and the other three waited until they heard the elevator doors close before bursting into laughter. Andrea walked to the refrigerator to get ice and water for Darcy.

"I'll ask again, Dr. Trapani, just what drugs are you giving Darcy?"

"No drugs except medications prescribed by her other doctors, I swear."

"Are you sure? I've investigated you thoroughly so I know all about your past."

Andrea stiffened and felt her blood drain. She wasn't ready to discuss Nora or her reason for leaving the hospital with anyone. And, given Darcy's inclination to sexualize it would be a lot easier if she didn't know she was a lesbian. She turned to face Candace. Luckily, Andrea was standing behind Darcy so she couldn't see her face.

But Candace saw it. And scarcely missed a beat. "And, I found nothing improper, so I guess I'll just have to chalk Darcy's good mood up to your excellent care." She took some papers out of her briefcase and handed them to Andrea. "Your contract, Doctor. I hope payment on the first and the fifteenth is acceptable. I've signed it but you should look it over before signing it."

"While we're waiting for Dr. Trapani, Candace, I've told her to call you when she wants to order equipment or supplies and I want you to order what she says and handle the payment. We'll start with a special recliner and some clothes that fit over my casts."

Candace wrinkled her nose. "She can order without your approval?"

"No, Darcy." Andrea looked up from the contract. "I suggest we discuss the things I think will help you, then we call Candace and order the ones you want."

Darcy looked at Candace. "Does that work for you?"

"If it works for you, it works for me. Just don't let the pretty doctor throw fairy juice in your eyes."

Andrea glared at Candace. It was hard to know if she was being playful or sending a message. When Darcy and Candace burst out laughing, she smiled. Candace was good for Darcy. It was nice to see her relaxed and enjoying herself. She turned away from Candace and found Darcy staring at her, her gaze warm and sweet rather than sexual. Andrea smiled then broke the connection when she noticed Candace looking from her to Darcy. Flustered, she signed the contract and handed it to Candace. "Please mail the checks here."

Candace glanced at the contract, placed it in her briefcase, then pulled out another sheaf of papers. "I've received a substantial offer for the two buildings on York Avenue."

"Does it include the provisions I specified for the current tenants?"

Candace leaned over Darcy. "No, but they exceeded the asking price and you should accept it."

The blood rushed to Darcy's face. "Is that a recommendation or an order?"

Candace straightened at the heated tone. "Just a—"

"I think I've been clear. Each and every tenant is to be relocated to an apartment of the same size at the same rent in a comparable building and those who want to move back when the new building is ready receive the same size apartment at the same rent and remain tenants as long as they live or they decide to leave. What don't you understand Candace?" She was shouting.

Christ, the woman could go from zero to a hundred in a matter of seconds. Andrea elbowed Candace aside to bring herself into Darcy's line of vision. "Calm down, Darcy."

Darcy lifted her head trying to see behind Andrea. "I'm waiting, Candace. You know the money is not my priority."

Damn. Candace didn't seem to have any idea how fragile Darcy was. "Stop. Can't this wait?"

Candace looked from Darcy to Andrea, then stuffed the papers in her briefcase. "I'll go back to them and discuss the requirements. If they're not amenable, I'll turn down the offer, but you may have to build the building yourself."

"If I have to build it, I will. Are we clear?"

"Sorry, honey, I didn't mean to upset you." Candace leaned in to kiss Darcy's forehead. "Forgive me, please?"

"As long as we're clear." Darcy took a deep breath, smiled and turned to Andrea. "I'm okay. Could I have some water?"

She held the straw for Darcy. "If you're done arguing, I'll give you two some time alone. I'll be in the bedroom. Let me know when you're leaving, Candace."

Candace took Andrea's hand. "You'll have to excuse us; we always act like thirteen-year-olds when we're together." She handed Andrea a business card. "Email the information about the chair and the clothing."

Andrea went into the bedroom and stood by the window. She could hear the murmur of their voices mixed with laughter, the ease of old friends. She thought about the look she and Darcy had exchanged, and wondered why it had felt so intimate even though it wasn't sexual. Darcy was a paradox. She could be sweet and thoughtful when she was relaxed and vulnerable, but vicious and hateful when she felt threatened. Andrea was appalled by Darcy's blatant sexuality and she wasn't sure she even liked her. Yet Darcy was able to touch her, without touching her at all. It was strange.

She shook her head and turned to call Darcy's surgeon and get his approval for the recliner (and a surprise wheelchair) she had in mind…That done, she sat in the chair with her eyes closed, wondering.

CHAPTER NINE

Candace pulled the chair over to the bed. "Come clean. What's the deal with the sexy doctor?"

Darcy grinned. "What do you mean?"

Candace tapped her manicured nails on Darcy's arm cast. "Come on, don't hold back on me. Were you kissing when I came in?"

"I wish. She was putting lotion on my lips."

"Whatever she's doing, though, is working. You seem much more grounded than when you threw me out of here last week. Are you feeling better, honey?"

"She makes me feel safe. And, yes, I'm feeling better. But I freaked this morning because I thought she'd left."

Candace frowned. "She just started. Why would she leave?"

Darcy blushed. "You know what I've been like. I was nasty to her. I said I didn't need a doctor to take care of me but Gerri was gone so we agreed she would leave this morning after I got an aide to take care of me. But she's wonderful, Candace. By the end of her shift I knew I'd die if she left, so I asked her to stay. But then I had a nightmare about her leaving me. I got scared."

"I doubt she's going to run away."

"She said she would stay until I'm independent, but if I tried to make it a sexual thing, it would complicate her ability to care for me and she would have to leave."

"So—"

"So, I'm going to concentrate on healing." Darcy grinned. "But as soon as I'm back to my life you can be sure as shit that I'm going after her."

"Whoa, you really are smitten."

"You bet your sweet patootie." Darcy tried to blow the hair out of her eyes.

Candace extended her hand. "Can I help you with that without getting my head bitten off?"

"Yes."

Candace brushed the hair off Darcy's face.

"Thanks." Darcy smiled. "I guess I owe you an apology for—"

"Forget it, Darce. Besides, I owe you an apology for not doing what I promised but it's hard seeing you so broken and helpless."

"I feel abandoned by you, Candace, and by the whole inner circle. Nobody's come or called."

"I'm truly sorry I've failed you." Candace looked down. "I guess everybody is busy."

Darcy nodded. "And I owe Gerri an apology. I thought she was abandoning me but she made sure I was well taken care of before she left. I think I should send her flowers and replace the money she laid out for the nurse. Do you know where she's living?"

"Do you want Gerri back in your life?"

"Not as a lover, no. Remember, I had decided to break up with her before the accident."

"I'm glad *you* remember. My advice would be to wait a month or so to send the flowers and the money, so she doesn't misread the gesture as an invitation to return. For some reason, the girl does care for you."

"Candy, would you shop for me? But first ask Lucia if she has some things that would fit over my casts. She knows my size and what I like."

"At my hourly rate you want me to shop?"

"I was thinking of it as something one friend does for the other, not as a billable service." She yawned.

"Okay, because we're friends I'll bring you some things tomorrow. But you're tired. I should go."

"Could you sit with me until I fall asleep?"

"Sure sweetie. Can I hold your hand?"

"If you can find it under the covers."

* * *

Andrea was sitting by the window reading when Candace knocked lightly on the door. She waved her in, but left the door half open so she could see and hear Darcy.

"She's sleeping," Candace whispered. "I thought she'd just doze but it looks like she'll be out for a while so I'm going to leave."

"I think she really enjoyed seeing you. But her heart is very weak and it's not good for her to get so upset."

"Sorry, she can be thick-headed. It's a great offer but I don't have the authority to accept or refuse a deal so I had to discuss it with her even though I knew it would make her mad."

It seemed to Andrea that Candace was playing innocent. Bringing an offer that she knew didn't meet the terms that were important to Darcy was provocative. Maybe Darcy had the power and that was how Candace got back at her. Hopefully, Candace now understood the situation. "Darcy obviously enjoys your company, so please come frequently but try to avoid discussing things that put her over the edge."

"She kicked me out last week, said she didn't need me standing around gawking. I was planning to come back today, even if Gerri hadn't taken the bull by the horns, so to speak."

"She was in a bad way when I got here yesterday. I was sure she was about to stroke."

"You're doing something right." Candace glanced toward the sleeping Darcy. "Listen, Doctor, I'm sorry I made that crack about your background. I did look into you, of course. Without a friend or relative in the house, I had to be sure you were who you seemed to be. I called Dr. Castillo to confirm she needed a doctor, then I spoke to a couple of people at the hospital. I'm sorry about what happened and what you've suffered."

"Did you—"

"No. I saw by your face that you didn't want me to say anything."

"I prefer to keep my personal life private, but I think Darcy has picked up that I'm a lesbian. At least she's been shamelessly flirting with me."

"That's my girl."

"She's very vulnerable and needy, and, though she might disagree, she needs a caregiver more than she needs a sexual partner right now. I'd like to keep our relationship professional."

"She gets that." Candace turned to leave, then turned back. "Oh, she asked if I would shop for her rather than have you take the time to do it online. Is there anything special I need to look for?"

"Either sleeveless or sleeves wide enough to go over her arm casts. And legs wide enough to go over the leg casts. Don't get anything tight and look for soft fabrics."

Candace studied Andrea for a minute, then seeming satisfied, nodded. "I'll be back tomorrow with some things."

While Darcy slept, Andrea powered up her laptop and went into Gmail.

Dear Candace,

It was nice meeting you today. It was wonderful to see Darcy laughing and joking with you. She needs that and she needs her friends, so I encourage you to visit as often as possible and encourage her other friends to do the same.

I've attached the information about the recliner we discussed. Also, Darcy won't wear a hospital gown so I'd like to get her some scrub tops to sleep in. See the link below to order.

I haven't discussed this with her but I'd like to surprise Darcy with this wheelchair (see attached), so we could sit outside in the garden or go to Central Park. I know this will lift her spirits.

Dr. Andrea Trapani

CHAPTER TEN

The next morning Andrea was out of bed and dressed by six. She'd figured out a way to wash Darcy's hair and the night before she'd purchased the plastic bags, tubs and pails she needed at the CVS drugstore on Lexington Avenue.

When she entered the bedroom at six thirty, Darcy was chatting with Francine and she immediately noticed the containers in Andrea's hands. "Are you going to chop me up and put me in storage?"

"That's a good idea for another day." Andrea put the containers down. "But today, Francine and I are going to wash your hair."

"Really?"

Andrea placed the supplies on the floor and huddled with Francine. Darcy tracked them as they separated and began to prepare.

Francine lined the floor with large green plastic garbage bags. Andrea carried in a pail of warm water from the bathroom, then slipped some pillows into plastic bags. Together they lifted

Darcy onto the pillows so her body was higher than the bed. Francine held Darcy's head to support it while Andrea placed a plastic tub under it.

"Are you comfortable, Darcy?"

"I guess." Her eyes skittered around the room.

"I promise we won't hurt you, and if you can relax, I think it'll feel good. Close your eyes."

Darcy took a deep breath, then closed her eyes.

Andrea soaked Darcy's hair, warmed some shampoo in her hands and massaged it in. Doctor and nurse grinned at the moans of pleasure coming from their patient. There was still some blood in her hair and the shampoo turned pink and barely foamed. "We're going to rinse now, then shampoo again. Are you comfortable, Darcy?"

"Yes, please don't stop."

Andrea rinsed, then applied more shampoo. This time it foamed as she worked it through Darcy's hair and onto her scalp. When she was satisfied that Darcy's hair was clean, she rinsed until the water ran clear, then rubbed conditioner in, eliciting more moans. She went to the bathroom and filled the pail with warm water again. After she rinsed the conditioner away and wrapped a towel around Darcy's head. Francine quickly dismantled the makeshift sink, and they removed the pillows so Darcy was flat on the bed.

Darcy lay with her eyes closed, a smile on her face. "Was it as good for you as it was for me, Doctor? Francine?"

Damn, Darcy was always ready with the sexual innuendo, but still, Andrea was thrilled that Darcy seemed so pleased. She smiled and shook her head.

Francine giggled. "You are too much, Darcy."

"*Moi*, too much?" Darcy said, her eyes still closed.

They dumped the water from the pail and the tub in the bathtub, then while Francine washed them out, Andrea removed the plastic bags from the extra pillows and picked the bags off the floor.

Andrea slapped palms in a high-five with Francine when she came back. "Thanks, I can take it from here."

Darcy opened her eyes. "I love you, Francine. Thanks."

"I love you too, Darcy. See you tonight, ladies."

When they were alone, Darcy smiled. "But I love you most of all, my sweet doctor."

Andrea pulled the towel over Darcy's face and began to rub her hair dry. Darcy's shampoo and conditioner both had that sexy, spicy fragrance that she found so tantalizing and it was difficult to stay professional even without Darcy murmuring endearments and staring into her eyes. It was annoying. No, it was damned irritating. And it was getting to her. Darcy moaned but kept her eyes closed as Andrea moved on to combing her damp hair. Maybe it was time Andrea started dating again. She'd definitely call Julie about the woman she'd been wanting to fix her up with.

She bathed Darcy and rubbed lotion over her body, changed the sheets, then dressed her in one of her scrub tops. She finished just as Maria arrived with breakfast.

She glanced at Darcy. "Good you washed her hair, Doctor. She was stinky."

Darcy's eyes popped open. "I wasn't that bad."

"Oh, yes, *cara*, your hair was *sporco*, dirty. Now is nice." She patted Darcy's head and left.

"Did it smell so bad, Doctor?"

"There was blood from the accident. And, you do sweat a lot, so, maybe a little?"

"I'm embarrassed."

"It wasn't something you could do anything about, Darcy. Besides, I assure you I've dealt with patients who smelled a lot worse than you did."

"But Darcy Silver doesn't smell."

"Well, Ms. Silver, you smell good now and as long as I'm with you, you will never smell bad for any reason. How about we eat some breakfast?"

"I knew it felt dirty and was a little funky but I didn't know anybody else could smell it."

"Calm down, Darcy. Most people wouldn't notice it. But Maria always leans in to kiss you and I scratched your head and got close to wash you and comb your hair. I assure you most people probably had no idea. So calm down or I'll shove this breakfast in to keep you quiet."

"Are you about to abuse me, Doctor? I mean shove my breakfast—"

Andrea spooned some cereal into Darcy mouth. "Hush. You're going to raise your pressure."

Darcy chewed slowly, then swallowed. "What I meant to say was thanks for figuring out how to wash my hair so I feel clean and smell like myself again."

Andrea smiled at the abrupt turnabout. "My pleasure."

"Where did you get the pails and buckets and plastic bags?"

"I went shopping last night."

Darcy opened her mouth for some coffee but kept her eyes on Andrea, watching her drink her coffee and take a spoonful of her own cereal. "Don't forget to send the receipts to Candace." She opened her mouth for some berries.

"My treat. It wasn't that much."

"You shouldn't be spending your money on me."

"It was worth it." She snorted. "Now I don't have to smell that awful smell."

Darcy opened her mouth. Closed it. Stared. Then burst out laughing. "You are a terrible person. If I wasn't such a calm, easygoing woman, you'd be in big trouble."

They laughed together, then finished breakfast.

Darcy was listening to the political book Andrea had downloaded to the iPod. Andrea sat nearby reading a mystery. "Doctor, I've had it with this book for now. The partisan analysis of the current political situation is making me angry so I think I'll stop before I figure out a way to toss your iPod against the wall."

Andrea removed the earbuds and put the iPod on the table next to the bed. "What kind of work do you do, Darcy? Are you in politics?"

Darcy flushed. "No, I'm not in politics. I do a little of this and a little of that."

"So being laid up for a couple of months is no problem?"

Darcy looked away and didn't respond. Andrea didn't want to push what seemed to be an uncomfortable subject. She certainly understood Darcy not wanting to talk about why she wasn't working. She picked up her book.

Darcy cleared her throat. "I actually don't have a job. I went to Harvard Law after college and worked for a few years for Brandon, Corwin and Diamond, one of the biggies, but I hated it. I hated the pompous asshole partners, I hated the unsavory attitude toward the law and I hated the dog-eat-dog competition to make partner so you could be the one in charge of abusing the lawyers working on abusing the law. After that, I spent some time as an Assistant DA and another year or two in the Public Defender's Office. I found all of it beyond depressing. It's rarely about justice. None of it was what I expected the law to be like." She grinned. "I bet I'm the last person you'd have thought was idealistic."

Andrea thought about it. "I don't know you well enough to have an opinion about that."

"Anyway, while I was at the Public Defender's Office I got a masters in political science from Columbia. After that I got a Ph.D. in Modern European History, also from Columbia. I wanted to teach but it was a bad time to be looking for a college-level job and it didn't happen. Since then, I volunteer at a women's shelter and as a big sister, and I worked in Obama's first campaign, things like that, but nothing I get paid for."

Her smile was full of regret. And something else Andrea couldn't interpret. Shame?

"You must think I'm a dilettante, flitting from one thing to another."

Andrea thought for a minute. "No, I don't imagine that you're a dilettante. But I do wonder why someone as intelligent as I think you are hasn't found her niche. I mean a law degree opens doors to many different careers. Surely you had some dream, some idea of what you wanted to do when you went to law school."

Darcy bit her bottom lip. "It wasn't my dream, it was my dad's dream that I be a lawyer like him, that someday he could add another Silver to the name of his firm. I did it to please him. But ultimately I disappointed him. He didn't understand why I couldn't find my place in the law like Candace. He thought I wasn't serious enough. It never occurred to him that it wasn't what I wanted."

Chasing someone else's dream rather than your own would make anyone bitter. "It must have been torture being in law school when you hated the law."

"Quite the opposite. I love learning new things. I graduated at the top of my class at Harvard and passed the bar with no trouble. But I found the practical application of the law tedious and disappointing."

"What would you have done instead of law?"

"I always wanted to teach college history or political science and if I'd gone for my Ph.D. right after I graduated Smith, it's likely I would have been able to follow that dream. But by the time I got around to it, teaching positions were few and far between. I did have an offer from a small religious school in Indiana but I didn't think I'd do well in a religious environment, so I turned it down." She shrugged. "So for all my bluster, doctor dear, I'm a failure."

And underneath all the sexual bluster and rage and nastiness, Darcy was vulnerable and unsure. Andrea was touched by Darcy's willingness to share her feelings. "I don't think you're a failure, Darcy. I would say you just haven't found your place. Maybe teaching isn't the only way to use your degrees."

"I'm almost forty. Don't you think I should have found my place by now?"

"It's never too late. Some people are late bloomers. And you did spend a lot of years chasing your father's dream. Maybe when you're back on your feet, you can chase your own dream for a while."

She smiled. "Thank you for the vote of confidence."

CHAPTER ELEVEN

Two days later, late in the afternoon, the recliner arrived. Darcy's face lit up when they carried it in. After the men had stripped off the plastic wrapper and left, Darcy turned to Andrea. "Can I inaugurate it tonight?"

Andrea looked at her watch. "Gregg will be up in about a half hour to help me move you into the chair, so which of the outfits Candace got you do you want to wear for dinner?"

"The red one."

"Good choice." Andrea retrieved the clothing from Darcy's closet, threw the covers off and removed the scrub top Darcy was wearing. She slipped the scooped neck red top over the left arm cast and then over the right and buttoned it. The scattered red stones glittered in the afternoon sunlight. She eased the red pants over the casts one leg at a time, shifted Darcy left and pulled the pants up over her hip and then shifted her right and did the same.

Darcy lifted her head trying to see how she looked. Andrea brought her the hand mirror from the bedroom. "You look beautiful, Darcy. Everything Candace bought for you is perfect. And speaking of Candace, you do remember she's joining us for dinner tonight?"

"How could I forget? She called Maria three times today about the wine. I think she's more excited than me."

"Would you like her to feed you, just for variety?"

"Are you saying you'd like a break from feeding me?"

"No. I'm asking if you would like your friend to feed you."

"Absolutely not. I know Candace. She won't be able to resist making choo-choo and airplane sounds with every forkful. You know my rhythm and you're able to do it without making me feel two years old."

It only took a few minutes for Gregg and Andrea to move Darcy into the chair but instead of dashing out as he usually did, he stared at Darcy. "You look nice, Darcy." He blushed. "Um, I'd better go help Maria with dinner." He ran for the door.

"Thanks, Gregg," Darcy called after him. She grinned. "Well, at least someone around here finds me attractive."

It was lovely to see Darcy's joy at being dressed and out of bed and admired. She couldn't seem to stop talking about how different everything looked from this angle, how different she felt, when was Candace coming and how long until dinner.

"Doctor, could you come here, I want to show you something."

Andrea walked over. "What?"

"Come closer. Lean over, it's there on my shoulder."

Andrea leaned in to see what she was talking about and Darcy kissed her cheek. "Thank you for this."

"Geez, did I catch you two kissing again?" Candace stood in the doorway grinning.

Andrea straightened. "No—"

"If you must know, I kissed her cheek to thank her for this chair. Don't you dare say another word about it."

Candace stuck her tongue out. "Wow, you look gorgeous in that outfit, Darce. Be nice to me, I come bearing gifts." She held up the bottle of wine she was carrying. "Maria was assembling the trays when I came up." Candace looked around. "Ah. I see the bed tray I ordered arrived. I figured if I was going to have dinner with you from time to time, it should be as civilized as possible, given the circumstances."

The sound of the dinner cart rolling down the hall got their attention. Maria was beaming as she brought the cart into the room. "I made fish stew for you tonight. I know you love it, Candace. And Darcy, you learning to love fish since the doctor come, so enjoy." She kissed Darcy and Candace on their cheeks. "You know where to leave the dishes, Doctor. Goodnight."

Maria loves Darcy, Andrea thought, and the fact that Darcy was happy and starting to see friends made Maria happy. And Maria was connected to Candace, as well. Andrea felt a twinge of jealousy. She was sure it was feeling excluded from their close-knit circle, not that Darcy and Candace seemed to be more than friends.

Candace poured the wine. Andrea thought about cautioning her to give Darcy just a half glass but reconsidered. At worst she would get tipsy. But Darcy surprised her.

"Only half a glass, Candy, I haven't been drinking for a while and," she shot a mischievous look at Andrea, "I wouldn't want to throw up all over the good doctor."

"Good thinking, Darcy. After all, you don't know what I might do to get back at you."

Andrea's mouth watered as she arranged the bed trays. First, the stew, a fragrant tomato-based broth filled with shrimp, scallops, clams and chunks of fish that reminded her of Sicily as did the couscous, then the mixed green salad glistening with an olive oil dressing and a sprinkling of cranberries and pecans and, finally, bowls of melon and berries for dessert.

She put a straw into Darcy's wineglass, tucked a napkin into the neck of her blouse and sat next to Candace, facing Darcy. As she speared a shrimp, Candace raised her glass.

"To a speedy recovery."

Andrea put the shrimp back, raised Darcy's wineglass to her lips. With her other hand she sipped her own wine. "I'll drink to that."

Darcy was watching Candace, probably looking for a sign of disdain at her sipping her wine through a straw. Andrea didn't dare look at Candace but judging from Darcy's face, Candace hadn't reacted.

"Nice wine, Candace." Andrea fed Darcy a shrimp, then ate a shrimp from her own stew. She turned to Candace. "I've been forcing Darcy to eat healthy but Maria makes everything taste so delicious she hasn't noticed."

"Ah, that explains the healthy glow. Maria must be thrilled that you're finally eating more than steak, eh Darcy?"

"Yes."

Andrea alternated giving Darcy stew with eating her own. At one point, she held Darcy's fork in one hand and her wineglass in the other. She met Darcy's eyes, held the fork up, then the wine. Darcy tilted her head at the wine, accepted the straw and sipped, without breaking eye contact. Andrea's stomach flipped. What was it about this often obnoxious woman? She cast a sideways glance at Candace who seemed focused on her stew.

Andrea dipped her bread in the spicy broth, then did the same with Darcy's bread. Feeding her with her fingers felt intimate and as their eyes met again she felt a warm surge through her body. Darcy licked her lips and smiled into her eyes but let her fingers go without a fight. Why did everything feel so sexual? It had to be Darcy because she'd never responded to anyone like this.

"You know, Candace, I am enjoying the fish and the healthy food. Who knew it could be so tasty. A little more wine, Doctor."

Andrea put the straw in Darcy's mouth. Something had shifted. Whether it was Candace being relaxed about her being fed, or Andrea's attempt to be unobtrusive, or maybe the wine, or just possibly that connected moment, Darcy relaxed and began to relate. As she did when they were alone, she asked Andrea for what she wanted. And, she began to talk. They talked politics and books and laughed a lot.

Candace helped Andrea stack the dishes and offered to take the cart down to the kitchen and put the dishes in the dishwasher, something Andrea had gotten into the habit of doing after Francine arrived. When she left a little after seven thirty, Candace kissed both Andrea and Darcy on the cheek.

"Thank you for having me. This was the most delightful dinner I've had since your accident, Darce. Everybody is so boring these days. Please invite me again."

"I enjoyed it too. I felt normal again. Aside from being fed, that is."

"Don't knock it, Darce. How often have you had a beautiful woman gently stuff tasty morsels into your mouth, give you wine and pat your lips dry? It's not worth getting all broken up for, but hey, I say enjoy it while you can."

So she had been watching.

* * *

"Is it okay if I take your clothing off now, then when Francine arrives we can just slide you into bed? I'll cover you with a blanket."

"You can undress me any time, sweet doctor." Darcy's husky voice sent a shiver through Andrea's traitorous body.

"Oh, oh, no more wine for you." She felt Darcy's eyes on her as she unbuttoned the red top. Her ribs were still tender so she wasn't wearing a bra and her nipples were erect. Andrea averted her eyes as she slipped the top off.

"Did you enjoy yourself, Doctor?"

"I did." Darcy grunted as Andrea shifted her pants down over her hips and pulled them off. Andrea turned to put the clothing on a hanger. "But, you know Darcy, all this flirting and sexual innuendo makes me uncomfortable. Do you think you could turn it down a little?"

Darcy flushed. "Sorry. The last thing I want is to make you uncomfortable. I tend to be outrageous sometimes, though it's usually a teasing game I play with close friends, when I used to have close friends. I'm not denying I find you attractive but I think flirting and teasing helps me feel like my old self. I'll try not to make you uncomfortable but it's sort of automatic, not something I can easily control."

Andrea turned around. "I'd appreciate it if you would try." She sat next to Darcy. "Did you enjoy yourself?"

"I did. Did you notice that Candace drank the entire bottle of wine except for my half glass and your glass?"

"Is that a problem?"

"It could be. She was drunk so often our junior year in college that our sorority sisters did an intervention and gave her an ultimatum: give up alcohol or leave the sorority."

"Which did she do?"

"Gave it up with the help of the group of friends we called the inner circle. We made sure one of us was with her at all times."

"What a loving thing to do. Did you meet in college?"

"We've been best friends since nursery school. When we were three and a half her parents asked my parents if they could leave her for a month while they went to India, then they didn't come back for thirteen years. So we grew up together. She even called my parents mom and dad. We went all through school together and were roommates freshman year in college. We both came out that year and bedded a lot of women. Candace was interested but I realized you could love someone, be best friends forever and not want to have sex with them. We talked about it and agreed it was better for us to not get involved sexually."

Andrea tucked a blanket around Darcy. "And now?"

Darcy considered. "That hasn't changed for me. But sometimes I feel…I don't know, sometimes I feel Candace would like a go at being a couple."

Just what Andrea thought. "And, are you willing to give it a try?"

"No. I love her like a sister and I have no desire to change our relationship." Darcy opened her mouth but seemed to change her mind and quickly looked away. It didn't matter. Andrea had seen what she was feeling in those expressive blue eyes. Please don't say it, she pleaded silently.

Francine walked in. "Hey, look at this spiffy new chair. How's it been sitting up?"

"Great. And we just had a fabulous dinner with my friend Candace."

"She was leaving as I arrived. She seemed to enjoy it too."

"Are you ready to get back into bed, Darcy? If not, I can help Francine move you later."

"No, I'm ready. This way Francine can do her nightly duties, you can do whatever and I can go to sleep. All the socializing and the wine knocked me out."

"Ooh, you let her have wine?"

"Yes. And she showed remarkable restraint for a woman who's being denied all the pleasures of life. She only had half a glass."

"Good thing for you, Ms. Smarty-Pants Doctor, because who knows what I would do if I got drunk."

"Come on, Francine, help me throw this woman into bed before she gets too aggressive."

CHAPTER TWELVE

"About time we had a sunny day," Darcy grumbled. "It's bad enough to be stuck in the house but three gloomy days in a row are too much."

"It's sunny today. Shouldn't you have been grumpy yesterday and the other days when it was gloomy?" Andrea fixed Darcy's coffee. "Maybe a little caffeine will help."

"The world *does* look a little brighter after a sip of coffee."

"I bet it'll feel even brighter after you eat your eggs."

"You feed me cold cereal on the wet, gloomy days and eggs on the sunny day. That seems ass backwards to me."

"Don't get surly. It's not good for your pressure." Andrea forked more eggs into Darcy's mouth.

Darcy chewed and swallowed. "Am I surly?"

"It's going to be warm today. Would you like to go outside?"

Darcy groaned. "You know I'm dying to go out. Are you going to throw me on your back and carry me to the elevator? Or maybe you'll roll my bed to the elevator. Or have you hired a crane to lift me out the window?"

"None of the above. I promise no manhandling."

"I *could* do with some woman handling." She wiggled her eyebrows.

Andrea sighed. As promised, Darcy had cut down on the sexual comments in the last couple of weeks but they still slipped out more often than she liked. "Finish your breakfast and let me get you dressed, then who knows what could happen."

"Did you hire an ambulance to take me downstairs?"

"You're not eating. Come on." She held the fork to Darcy's lips and smiled at the quizzical look on her face. "Humor me. *Mangia*. Eat."

"Ah, my love…erly doctor whispers sweet nothings in Italian. How can I resist?"

After breakfast, Darcy's eyes tracked Andrea as she moved around the room.

"What would you like to wear today?"

"Am I going to the doctor's office?"

"No, just to the garden."

"Just to the garden? I've been dying to go to the garden and you damn well know it. How about the pale gray outfit?"

Smiling at Darcy's excitement, Andrea pulled out the pale gray top and pants, according to Candace another outfit designed by their friend Lucia. The pants were plain but the scoop neck top was embroidered in an exquisite multi-colored pattern. Lucia's designs were beautiful, Candace knew which would look spectacular on Darcy and Darcy seemed to have unlimited money. A nice combination. "Good choice. You look lovely in this outfit." She slid the pants on.

"When I wear Lucia's clothing I feel like a woman instead of the Pillsbury Doughboy."

Andrea slipped Darcy's arms in and buttoned the top. She stepped back, assessed her work and smiled. No question she looked like a woman. But, in her opinion, Darcy always looked like a woman, beautiful, sensual and sexy, casts or no casts, dressed or undressed.

"You look pleased with yourself."

"I am. I do nice work; don't you think?" Andrea buzzed the kitchen and spoke into the intercom. "Come on up, Gregg."

While they waited, Andrea pulled together the things they would need: her stethoscope, an extra blanket, a mystery for her, a romance she could read to Darcy, the iPod, tissues and a bottle of water.

"You're not going tell me, are you?"

"Uh-uh. You'll just have to wait."

"This suspense can't be good for my blood pressure. I might have to report you to Dr. Castillo for abuse." Darcy surveyed the room. "Are you and Gregg going to carry my bed downstairs?"

Andrea loved seeing the excitement and anticipation on Darcy's face. Her eyes were sparkling, her cheeks glowing and her smile endearing. God, she was beautiful. She was excited too, giving Darcy this gift. She was thankful Candace had gone along with her little surprise and had invited her to join them for lunch in the garden.

Andrea heard Gregg coming along the hall and peeked out. Carlo was with Gregg and he grabbed the handles of the wheelchair and started toward her. As they entered, she stood aside "Tada."

"A wheelchair? I thought—"

"I cleared it with Dr. Stern. This wheelchair is fitted to give you the support you need, just like the recliner."

"In that case, can we go now?"

Andrea moved the wheelchair near the bed and put the brakes on. She leaned over, put Darcy's right arm on her shoulder and swung her legs so she was sitting on the edge of the bed. "Okay Gregg, put your hand behind her back and under her thigh, er, cast." Carlo watched as she and Gregg lifted Darcy into the chair. "Enjoy," Gregg said, as he left

Andrea arranged pillows behind her and under her arms and legs, then covered her with a blanket. She stepped back and smiled. "Comfortable?"

"You bet. Let's go."

Carlo grinned at Darcy's excitement. "You want me to push, *Dottore*?"

"No, thank you, Carlo, I've got her."

The three of them walked to the elevator. Carlo pressed the button for the kitchen level and they started down. The only sound besides the creaking of the elevator was the sound of Darcy's rasping breath. Andrea put a hand on Darcy's shoulder and leaned over to whisper in her ear. "Easy. Take a deep breath. Good. Now take another one. That's it."

Darcy turned her head. "Doctor?"

"Yes?" She leaned over to listen.

Darcy spoke softly, her mouth close to Andrea's ear. "You breathing in my ear is not calming me, but it does divert my thoughts to things other than finally being outside."

Andrea tapped her on the head. "Control yourself, woman." She straightened and took a deep breath. *And you breathing in my ear takes my body to places it shouldn't go.*

The elevator stopped and the door slid open. Maria was waiting, a huge smile on her face. "Enjoy the sunshine." She hugged Darcy. "I bring nice lunch later."

Carlo opened the outer door. Andrea rolled Darcy down the ramp, into the bright sunshine and over to the bench she'd scouted out the night before. She parked the wheelchair and settled herself. When she looked at Darcy she was alarmed to see her doing a slow imitation of the girl from the exorcist, her head moving side-to-side then up and down. "What's wrong?" She touched Darcy's shoulder. "Are you in pain?"

Darcy laughed. "Far from it. I'm happy and trying to suck it all in at once. How can I ever thank you, Andrea?"

Hearing Darcy say her name sent chills down Andrea's spine, but she couldn't allow it. On the other hand, she didn't want to put a damper on the day, so she'd let it go and correct her only if she did it again. "Relax and enjoy yourself. You can listen to music or an audio book, or I can read to you. I have *Love by the Numbers*, the Karin Kallmaker romance." Andrea flashed the cover of the book.

"Did you send the bill to Candace?"

"It's a gift."

"Thank you." Darcy's smile was sweet. "I just want to sit for a while."

Pretending to read a medical journal, Andrea surreptitiously watched Darcy breathe in the fragrance of the newly blooming lilacs and the freshness of the spring air. Her pleasure at being outside was palpable.

Darcy closed her eyes and turned her face to the sun. After a while, she looked up at the trees and cocked her head at a rowdy pair of birds going at it. "We take so much for granted in life. You never think how lucky you are; you never think about what you'd miss. At least I never did."

Andrea lowered the journal and listened.

"I hope my life will go back to normal in a couple of months, my injuries and limitations will be gone. How do people whose 'normal' is so circumscribed exist?"

Andrea enjoyed this side of Darcy: the sweet, honest, introspective woman open about her feelings and fears. She put her journal aside and adjusted Darcy's blanket. "They have to accept where they are and move on from there or they're doomed to unhappiness."

"Maybe the accident was a wake-up call for me. A reminder to be more mindful of my surroundings, of other people and myself. I'm luckier than most and I should be doing something good with my life. Like you." She looked embarrassed. "I don't know what I'm talking about."

"Don't denigrate yourself, Darcy. It sounds as if you've been thinking about what's important to you. That's a lot better than sailing along not making choices." She waited for Darcy to continue, but she was silent. "I think you've learned a lot about yourself."

Darcy snorted. "I've certainly learned what a bitch I am and how talented I am at abusing and belittling people."

"Maybe you've seen a part of yourself you don't like, but seeing is the first step in changing. You've also learned how important the outdoors is to you, how it's all right to let yourself be taken care of, that you don't always have to be in control or perfect."

"You think I'm not perfect?"

Andrea batted Darcy's arm with her magazine. "No, I don't think you're perfect but in the few weeks I've been here, I've seen you're capable of changing. And, you know, a lot of people aren't." Andrea studied Darcy. "How are you doing, are you warm enough, tired?"

"No, I'm happy sitting in my garden speaking to my… doctor."

"Tell me about how you got here? About the accident?"

"There's not much to tell. Carlo and Maria were moving back to Italy and I planned to go with them to help them settle, so I was driving home from Fire Island on a Monday afternoon. I'd had a spectacular argument with Gerri right before I left and I was in a screaming rage." She flushed. "You've seen one. Anyway, I was speeding and some guy with two kids in car seats cut me off, not once but twice. The fact that he would risk his kids' lives like that added fuel to the already raging fire. I was so out of control I was banging my fists on the steering wheel. The next thing I remember is waking up in the hospital wrapped like a mummy."

"Wow."

"Wow, for sure. They told me the car flipped several times, rolled down an embankment, then burst into flames. If a stranger, a fireman, hadn't jumped out of his car and run down to pull me out I would have been burned alive. Apparently, I blacked out because of the blocked artery." She shrugged. "I guess it was good I didn't die. And I'm thankful no one else was hurt."

Andrea felt sad for the poor little rich girl who guessed it was good she didn't die. "Oh, Darcy, if you don't learn to control your anger, it will kill you."

"I didn't get that until you came. You talked about my blood pressure being too high, how Gerri was afraid she was killing me and how Dr. Castillo was worried enough to send you. And, I felt you cared about whether I lived or died. Silly, huh?"

"Not silly at all. I do care. A lot. I hope I can help you learn to control your anger and eat healthily. I want to help you live."

"Yoo-hoo, ladies." Candace came into the garden. "Lunch is coming soon." She kissed Darcy on the cheek. "This looks like a very serious conversation."

"It is. We're talking about the birds and the bees and the flowers. And life." Darcy smirked. "Do you have anything you want to add, Candace?"

"Only that you're looking dashing in that outfit I bought for you. And you actually have a little color in your cheeks. Is it the sunlight or the conversation?"

"A little of both. You showed up just in time to hear the gory details. We do tit for tat, you know."

"Tit?" Candace raised her eyebrows. "Really?"

"God you have a dirty mind. Anyway, I was just about to ask Dr. Trapani how it was that she was available to ride in on her white steed to save this damsel in distress, but I see Maria coming with lunch, so it will have to wait until we've eaten."

Candace glanced at Andrea. "Oh, pish, I'm sure it's a really boring story. Why don't we talk about something interesting? For instance, have you read that romance I see lying on the bench next to the good doctor?"

Andrea sent silent thanks to Candace for sidetracking Darcy's questions. "Candace, please wheel Darcy to the table while I help Maria."

"Oh, no, I'm sure Candace doesn't know the right way to push a wheelchair. I'm afraid she'll dump me on the ground."

"And, well I might, darling, if you're not nice to me. Don't you know you should never bite the hand on the controls? Oops, are there brakes?"

"She's going to kill me. Save me, Doctor."

Andrea stood with her hands on her hips. "You two are impossible. Come on, no more wrestling in the sandbox. Lunch is served."

Darcy's eyes widened when she arrived at the grape arbor to find Maria and Carlo sitting down to eat with them. "Did you?" she whispered.

Andrea nodded.

"Thank you. Remind me later that I owe you a kiss."

"What was that about kissing?" Candace frowned at them.

"I don't know how Andrea did it, but I'm really happy that you, *Zia*, and you, *Zio*, are joining us for lunch."

"We want to celebrate with you, *cara*." Maria spoke in Italian. "Let's drink a toast to Dr. Trapani for making everything better for you." They all raised their water glasses and drank.

"And let's drink to friendship and family." Candace made the toast in Italian, surprising Andrea.

A teary-eyed Darcy looked from one to the other of them sitting at the table. "Even if it's barely green yet, it's like old times, eating under the grape arbor. All we need is Mom and Dad to make it complete." She turned to Andrea. "My dad had the grapes planted and the arbor built for my mom and Maria and Carlo to remind them of the good times in Italy. We used to eat here all the time in the summer."

That comment brought forth stories about fun times they'd had at this table.

Andrea turned to Maria and Carlo. "Where will you settle when you go back to Italy?"

"We come from outside Florence." Carlo took Maria's hand. "When Darcy can travel, we'll all go back and stay in the villa there and see how we feel."

"You should consider Sicily," Andrea said. "The winters are mild and the island is beautiful."

They discussed the issue for a while, then when they'd finished eating, Maria and Carlo excused themselves so Maria could take a nap and Carlo could tend to some things.

Candace, Darcy and Andrea spent the next half hour over coffee, laughing and talking. Candace entertained them for a while with stories about the many lovers she'd had and lost, including the one she'd just dumped because she was too serious. After that, Darcy seemed to drift away from the conversation. Taking that as a sign that Darcy was tired, Candace said she had to get back to the office. She hugged Andrea and kissed Darcy lightly on the lips, saying she would see them tomorrow sometime.

After Candace left and Gregg had cleared the table, Andrea wheeled Darcy around the garden so she could see all the flowerbeds. Following Darcy's lead, Andrea didn't speak but when they got back to their bench, Darcy seemed depressed.

"Hey, what happened? You look down in the dumps."

Darcy smiled weakly. "Sorry. I just realized, over lunch, that whenever I'm not involved with someone, Candace dumps her current girlfriend so she's single too."

"And that makes you feel bad?"

"Yes. What I sensed is true. Candace is waiting for me so she makes sure she's available when I am. I really care for her and I want her to be happy, but I can't be the one."

CHAPTER THIRTEEN

They were in the orthopedic surgeon's waiting room for Darcy's four-week checkup. "Don't get your hopes up, Darcy."

"You said they were going to remove the casts, right? This is the beginning of the end."

Andrea squatted in front of Darcy's wheelchair. "Look me in the eye, Darcy."

"What?" Darcy was annoyed.

"You have this wonderful talent for hearing what you want to hear. What I said was, they will X-ray your arms and legs to see if they're healing properly but it's too early to remove the casts."

"Don't yell at me."

"I'm trying to make sure you understand. The point of this visit is to confirm that your limbs are healing as they should, not to release you for physical therapy."

"But maybe I'll be healing so well, they'll take the casts off."

Andrea rested her hands on Darcy's shoulders. "If you were sixteen, sweetie, you might have a chance. But you're forty. It's highly unlikely that you won't need more healing time."

"I'm not forty yet and I don't understand why you're trying to bring me down."

"Because I don't want you to go off the deep end."

That got Darcy's attention. "*Moi*, go off the deep end?" She glared at Andrea. "Did you just call me sweetie?"

"No." *Oops*, thought Andrea, *I'll have to watch those slips. She doesn't miss a thing.*

"You did."

Andrea stood. "I'm your doctor. Why would I call you sweetie?"

"Because you can't help yourself, you care for me."

"Ms. Silver, we're ready for you." The technician led them back to a room. "Dr. Trapani and I will put you on the table so I can take X-rays. It will take a little while to develop the pictures, then Dr. Stern will come in and talk to you. Okay?"

"Well, if it was up to me, you would remove the casts and Dr. Trapani and I would leave."

The technician laughed. "Everyone feels that way." They lifted Darcy to the table. "But I guess with both arms and legs in casts, you probably feel it more than most." She arranged Darcy's arms. "Please step behind the shield, Dr. Trapani." The machine hummed, then the technician came back and arranged Darcy's legs. The machine hummed again and Andrea and the technician returned. "Are you comfortable on the table?"

Darcy nodded.

"Dr. Stern will be in as soon as I develop the pictures." She left them alone.

"How quickly can we get a physical therapist?"

"Darcy." Andrea knew she sounded annoyed, but Darcy was setting herself up for a fall. And she couldn't stand to watch her suffer. "Don't, please."

Darcy looked hurt. It was the first time Andrea had been anything but patient with her. They avoided eye contact as they waited for the surgeon in silence.

Dr. Stern breezed in. "The X-rays look terrific, Ms. Silver. I did a terrific job, if I must say so myself. I'll see you again in two weeks." He pivoted toward the door.

"You're leaving the casts on?" Darcy struggled to stay in control.

He turned, frowning. "Let me remind you that it took multiple surgeries and a number of plates and many screws to put your limbs back together. You're lucky they're healing so well." Seeing the distress on Darcy's face, he moved closer and spoke in a gentler voice. "You were pretty badly damaged and your bones need the time to mend. Removing the casts too soon would be a mistake. When you come back in two weeks, we should be able to remove the arm casts and you can start therapy. We'll check the legs then, but my guess is they'll need at least another four weeks."

Darcy gasped.

The ride home was excruciating. Despite Andrea's warning, Darcy had allowed herself to believe the casts would be coming off and she was sinking fast. Andrea yearned to hold and comfort her. But of course, she couldn't. When they got back to the house, Darcy didn't want to sit in the garden; she wanted to go to bed.

Carlo helped Andrea shift Darcy into the bed. She lay there with her eyes closed. He looked at Andrea, a question on his face. She walked him to the elevator and told him in Italian what had happened. He went down looking depressed. Back in the room, Andrea pulled the chair close to the bed and sat listening to Darcy's ragged breathing. "I'm so sorry, Darcy."

"Well, that sure makes me feel better." Nasty Darcy was back.

"I know you're hurting. I'm sure four weeks feels like an eternity, but if you don't heal properly, you'll suffer for the rest of your life."

"You don't know a damned thing." She turned her head away.

"Darcy, please don't isolate yourself like this."

"What do you care, *sweetie*?"

Andrea could kick herself for letting that pop out. "I care. Can't you tell?" And, she realized, she really did. In fact, she had a sudden urge to climb into bed with Darcy, to kiss her and soothe her and make her forget about her casts. She rubbed her eyes, trying to clear the image, then focused on Darcy. Was that a shoulder shrug under the blanket?

Andrea struggled to calm her racing heart and slow her breathing. Where had those feelings come from? And what was she going to do about them? Darcy's soft voice pulled her back to the room.

"I know you tried to warn me and so did the technician, but I wanted to believe I would be done with all this. And, you called me sweetie, but then you denied it and made me feel crazy. Everything got all mixed up, having to live like this for another four weeks, and feeling you'll never love me made me feel hopeless."

"I'm sorry. I denied calling you sweetie because I'm trying to keep our relationship uncomplicated. And I do care."

"But?"

"Listen to yourself, Darcy. I'm the person you're dependent on for everything. It's natural you would fixate on me, to think that you love me. Psychotherapists call it transference. Right now, I have all the power because you need me. Doing anything, making any commitments, when you're so vulnerable, is a recipe for disaster. I'm trying to protect you."

"I don't want to be protected, I want to be loved."

"You're fragile, you need to be protected and taken care of more than you need love that might prove transitory. Do you understand?"

"No. And, I can't talk about this anymore. I know what I feel for you. I know what I want from you. It's bad enough I have to ask you to blow my goddamn nose because it's running and to dry my face because I'm crying and to do all the other things you do for me. Don't make me beg for your love, Andrea, it's too demeaning."

The hurt in Darcy's voice felt like a gut-punch but she couldn't give Darcy what she wanted. Andrea helped Darcy blow her nose. "Can we put this aside for now? It's not good for your pressure. After dinner I'll read to you a while if you like, or you can listen to music."

"Will you stay with me until I fall asleep tonight?"

Andrea was hoping to run across the park to Central Park West where Julie and Karin lived. Maybe they could help her figure out how to handle Darcy's feelings. And hers. "If it's important, I'll call Francine and ask her to come in later."

"It's important."

Andrea stepped into her bedroom to call Francine. She said she'd come in about ten because Darcy was usually asleep by then. She also called Julie who agreed to meet her in front of the house about ten thirty. They would sit in the garden and talk.

Darcy calmed down. They were quiet while eating dinner, each off in their own thoughts for the most part, then Darcy opted to be read to. About nine, Darcy's eyes started to close. "Andrea, would you get in bed with me until I fall asleep?"

"What?" She couldn't hide her shock. "Absolutely not."

"I don't mean under the covers or anything, just lie next to me so I can feel a warm body. I promise not to make a habit of asking but I feel so alone."

Andrea rubbed her forehead. Unless she was upset, Darcy was straightforward, so if she said she wouldn't make a habit of it, she wouldn't. She was really needy tonight. In fact, she'd asked Andrea to sit close to the bed while she was reading and then had maneuvered her hand out from under the blanket and rested her fingers on Andrea's arm. Andrea's mind warred with her body. Her mind triumphed. "I'm your doctor, Darcy. I couldn't do something so unprofessional."

"Sorry." Darcy turned her head away. "I didn't mean to put you in a compromising position. I just need…"

Andrea cupped Darcy's cheek. "Hey, it's all right, you don't have to apologize. At her touch, Darcy began to sob. "I'm so fucking pathetic. I make myself sick."

Andrea felt like crying herself. She turned Darcy's face toward her. "Please open your eyes and look at me, Darcy." It took a minute but Darcy complied. "I hear you. I really do. And I feel your loneliness. I want to make you feel better but it wouldn't help either of us if I did something that made me so uncomfortable that I felt I had to leave. Please understand this is not a rejection but an affirmation of my desire to see you through this."

Darcy nodded. "I get it, but I still feel lonely."

"If I sit here with you until you fall asleep, you won't be alone."

"Could you at least touch me so I feel that you're here?"

Andrea lowered the lights, pulled the chair closer, and reached across Darcy to rest her hand on Darcy's shoulder. Darcy turned her face away.

"Are you all right?"

"Touching helps but I miss being held."

"It's the best I can do, Darcy." As she leaned in trying to see whether Darcy was crying, Darcy turned to face her again. They were so close, Andrea thought, it would take the tiniest movement for their lips to come together but it was taking a gigantic effort to resist. "Hey, you're all wound up, close your eyes, try to relax. I'll stay with you until you fall asleep."

Darcy closed her eyes but didn't turn her head away. "Thanks. Your breathing and the warmth of your breath are comforting. The weight of your arm on my shoulder too."

Andrea watched Darcy's face in the dim light, feeling the warmth of Darcy's breath on her face, the rise and fall of Darcy's chest, the ragged beat of Darcy's heart and the yearning in her own body for more.

CHAPTER FOURTEEN

It took Andrea a couple of seconds to realize where she was when Francine woke her. She was mortified to find her head on her arm on the bed sort of half draped over Darcy and stiff because of her awkward position. Francine helped her ease herself off Darcy and followed her into the bedroom to talk.

"So is there something I should know?" Francine asked, grinning.

Andrea flushed. "Yes, she's extremely needy tonight. Despite what I told her, she expected Dr. Stern to remove her casts today. When that didn't happen, she went off the deep end which was complicated by my slipping and calling her sweetie then denying it when she called me on it."

"Oh my. You know she's in love with you, don't you?"

"I know she thinks she's in love with me. She's so labile; her feelings fluctuate from happy to angry to sad to happy again in the blink of an eye. I don't trust she really knows what she feels."

Francine hesitated, then spoke. "It's none of my business, but it seems to me you have feelings for her."

"Of course I have feelings for her. She's my patient. I empathize with her situation. I want to help her get well."

"No, Dr. Trapani, that's how I feel. You may fire me for saying this, but it's pretty clear to me that you're in love with her."

Andrea collapsed in the chair and put her head in her hands. "In love? I don't think so. But I am attracted to her." Was Francine right? Was she in love with Darcy? Or was it her own loneliness and the day-to-day proximity to someone who valued and desired her? She'd insisted that Darcy was vulnerable and needy and couldn't possibly know her real feelings. Wasn't she in the same boat, vulnerable, needy, lonely and wanting to be loved? If she was in love with Darcy, she wasn't ready to admit it yet. She hadn't even let herself know the extent of her attraction until she had found herself so close to Darcy tonight.

"Is it such a bad thing to love a patient?"

"I think it's unprofessional. She's so raw and stressed that...oh, I have to go. I'm meeting my friend Julie, Darcy's cardiologist, in the garden to discuss this. Call me immediately if she wakes up and you think she wants me, or needs me. And Francine, don't worry about me firing you. I appreciate your honesty."

* * *

Julie was leaning against the banister in front of the house, holding a bottle of wine in one hand and two long-stemmed glasses in the other. She opened her arms and Andrea walked in for a hug and a kiss on the cheek. They'd been a couple in medical school but with internships and residencies at opposite ends of the country, Julie had broken things off with her, saying being good friends was a safer bet. And, best friends they remained. Except Andrea had never stopped loving her. Until now.

Andrea led Julie into the house and out the garden door to her favorite bench. Julie handed her a glass and filled it, then did the same for herself. She sat next to Andrea. "You sounded like you might need that. What's up?"

"Darcy thinks she's in love with me." Andrea sipped her wine. "And I'm attracted to her."

"And this is freaking you out because?"

Andrea swiveled so she could see Julie's face. "Because it's unprofessional? Because she's on an emotional seesaw and I don't trust what she thinks she feels?" She sipped her wine. "And because it's happened so fast. I've only known her a little more than three weeks and I don't trust either of us."

Julie studied her. "You're attracted, but not in love?"

She wasn't ready to admit that, not even to Julie. "I'm confused, Julie. I have feelings for her but I can't put a name to them yet."

Julie swirled her wine. "It seems to me Darcy's emotional state is irrelevant to you loving her. As for unprofessional, doctors are just people and you wouldn't be the first doctor to fall in love with a patient. But putting all that aside, falling in love takes what it takes. Some people fall in love at first sight, others after years of friendship. It's not something we mere mortals can control." Julie sipped her wine. "I guess in terms of an actual relationship you'd want her to be more stable. But Andrea, it's been a long time since you've let yourself love." She studied Andrea over her wineglass. "I've often thought you were still in love with me."

Andrea gasped. She thought she'd hidden her feelings all these years. "You knew?"

Julie put her wineglass on the ground and wrapped her arms around Andrea. "I hoped you would find someone but it seemed as if you locked your heart away and made do with women like Nora. Nice, but not someone you could love."

Andrea breathed in Julie's familiar fragrance, a combination of her shampoo, her cologne, and the sanitizing products used in the operating room. "Oh, Julie, I'm so sorry."

"For what? I'm the one who should be sorry. I never thought ending our relationship would cause you so many years of pain." She held Andrea away so she could see her face. "But if there's anything I've learned, it's that we don't have a lot of control over our hearts, the physical or emotional ones. Come on, smile. I'm ecstatic you're at least letting yourself feel attracted to Darcy."

Andrea's smile was shaky. "I still love you but it feels different. I've hardly given you a thought recently."

"Should I be insulted?"

"No." Andrea took Julie's hand. "Tell me what to do, oh wise one."

Julie looked into Andrea's eyes. "Trust your heart. Unless you let yourself love her, you're sentencing yourself to the same limbo you've been in for years."

Andrea squeezed her hand. "You make it sound easy."

Julie studied her friend. "You need to think about why you're complicating it."

Was she overthinking? Could she trust Darcy's feelings? Or, hers for that matter? She bit her lip. "I'm worried about Darcy's heart—"

"So you said."

Andrea punched Julie's shoulder. "Not her emotional heart, well, that too, but her physical heart. I'd like you to examine her, but traveling is stressful. Would you consider a home visit?"

Julie took her phone out of her pocket and checked her calendar. "I'm booked solid all week and that's without any emergencies. If I skip lunch tomorrow, I could do noon."

"Why don't you join us for lunch?"

"Lunch sounds great. And, it'll give me time to examine and assess Darcy's physical and emotional hearts."

CHAPTER FIFTEEN

The sound of Andrea's door closing about six thirty woke Darcy. She hoped she hadn't scared Andrea away with her meltdown and her ranting about loving her. She was sure she was in love with Andrea, that it wasn't just her situation talking. No question she was needy but not since she and Tori had been a couple in college had she felt so close to someone, so happy just to sit quietly in the same room. Yes, her attraction to Andrea was sexual, but it was so much more than that.

She'd acted like a big sniveling baby yesterday, not very attractive. And, worse, she'd presumed that Andrea was in love with her when she wasn't even sure she was a lesbian. After all, people called each other sweetie all the time. It didn't mean they were in love. And Andrea in particular was so kind and giving and affectionate that she probably called all her patients sweetie. Darcy flushed, embarrassed she'd asked Andrea to sleep with her. It would probably have been uncomfortable with both of them on this narrow hospital bed, but it sure felt nice to have that arm draped over her, to not feel so alone.

She would drive Andrea away if she continued to act like a spoiled brat. And though as she'd said to Candace she would pursue Andrea once she was back on her feet, right now she couldn't think of anyone she'd rather have taking care of her. So if she hadn't already driven Andrea away, she would apologize this morning and tell her it was the stress of yesterday that made her so outrageous. And, for the rest of the time trapped in this bed, she would do her best to be respectful toward her. Well, she wouldn't be able to stop flirting, but she would try to avoid putting her on the spot, demanding she declare her love. But later there would be no stopping her. She was confident she would get the girl. After all, Andrea wouldn't be the first supposedly straight woman to fall in love with Darcy Silver.

"Good morning, Miss Sunshine." Francine stood at the end of the bed smiling. "Sleep okay?"

"Yes. Thanks. Did you see Dr. Trapani when you came in last night?"

"Of course, she was right here."

"I kind of gave her a hard time. Was she all right?"

"I heard about the casts. Bummer. But Dr. Trapani was fine. Emergency room doctors can take a lot of abuse. Don't worry about her."

"Have you seen her this morning?"

"No, but I heard her moving around. I think she went out for a run."

Darcy's eyes kept darting toward Andrea's door.

Francine stepped in front of Darcy, breaking her connection with the door. "Don't worry, hon, she's not going anywhere. She'll be in after she showers and dresses."

"How can you be so sure?"

Francine grinned. "Trust me."

Darcy wondered about that grin. Was it just to reassure her or did Francine know something she didn't know?

Francine stood between Darcy and the door again, this time waving the bedpan. "You slept through the night, you must be in dire need."

"Now that you mention it."

Francine cleaned Darcy and the bedpan, checked her temperature, respiration rate and blood pressure, then updated the chart.

Darcy lay staring at the door, thinking about her new strategy for dealing with Andrea. She was going to be cool. When she heard Andrea moving around in her room, Darcy glanced at Francine and caught her watching. Francine raised her eyebrows.

Darcy felt her whole body heat up. Francine was no fool, she knew. "Francine?"

"What do you need, hon?"

"I...could you, um, could you not say anything about. . . um, this, to the doctor, to Andrea?"

Francine smiled. "Now you know I have to talk to the doctor about your vitals and all things medical. Is there something else?"

"No." Darcy grinned. "Nothing else."

The door opened and Darcy and Francine both turned. Andrea looked from one to the other. "Whoa, what are you two cooking up?"

"I didn't hear her say good morning, did you, Francine?"

"Can't say I did." Francine turned to hide her smile.

* * *

Ah, so we're going to be playful this morning, thought Andrea, *that's better than last night.* And it solved her dilemma about how to deal with last night. "Oh, sorry, I meant to say good morning."

"Much better, my good doctor, a much better start to the day than accusing us of plotting against you."

"Doctor Trapani," Francine said, "if we could go over Darcy's chart, I'll leave you two to, um, to whatever."

Andrea looked at the chart. Darcy's pressure was high again. Then she scanned the note Francine had written:

She slept until she heard your door open and close when you went out this morning, then she seemed anxious.

I told her you'd gone for a run and would be back and she settled a little. She didn't relax until she heard you come in again. Her eyes were glued to the door, waiting for you.

Francine left and Andrea gathered what she needed to wash Darcy. "I'm worried about your heart so I've asked Dr. Castillo to come and listen for herself. The only time she has free is her lunch break, so I invited her to eat with us. I hope that's all right with you."

"Did you tell Maria?"

"I left her a note but I'll call down later to be sure." Andrea brushed Darcy's teeth, then washed and dried her face.

Darcy took a deep breath. "Dr. Trapani, I owe you an apology for my infantile behavior yesterday. I had no right to take my frustration and disappointment out on you or try to manipulate you into my bed. And while flirting is in my nature and I can't promise I won't do it, I want you to know I understand that calling me sweetie or any other term of endearment doesn't mean you love me. I mean, you're probably straight, and the last thing I want is to make you uncomfortable. I also understand that given our circumstances, it's not unusual for the patient to be grateful and confuse the care you give with love."

Stunned, Andrea stopped washing her. On the one hand, Darcy was letting her off the hook and she didn't have to say anything about her feelings. On the other hand, she felt devastated because Darcy was saying the only reason she cared was their circumstances. "I see."

"You're very important to me, Doctor, and I want you to stay with me for however long it takes me to get back on my feet. I'll try not to harass you. Please don't run away from me."

"Thank you for clearing that up. I meant what I said, I'll be here as long as you need and want me."

Andrea was super conscious of Darcy watching her. Her emergency room face, which didn't let the patient see how bad things might be, came in handy. Only this time it was the doctor who was hurting.

When she finished washing and dressing Darcy, they ate the breakfast Maria delivered and chatted about what they would do this afternoon. "Would you like to go for a walk in Central Park?" Andrea dabbed at the egg yolk on Darcy's chin.

Darcy shook her head. "I'd prefer the garden. I don't feel comfortable having strangers ogle me in the wheelchair."

"Ogle?"

"You know what I mean. I look grotesque splayed out with these casts."

"No one will stare. Besides, you'll look beautiful, as usual."

Darcy was silent as Andrea removed the napkin she'd tucked into her collar. "You think I look beautiful like this?" Her voice was low.

Andrea had spoken without thinking but given yesterday's *sweetie* incident, the truth was her only option. "Yes, I do. The casts and being in a wheelchair don't diminish your natural beauty." She forced herself to look at Darcy. "So what's your pleasure now?"

"Thank you, Doctor." Darcy smiled sweetly. "I'd like the iPod, please."

With the earbuds in, Darcy closed her eyes.

Andrea stared, admiring Darcy's long eyelashes and perfect eyebrows, her full lips. She was gorgeous. Maddening, but gorgeous. With her eyes on Darcy, she processed what she'd said about last night. On the one hand, Francine's note indicated that Darcy had been afraid she'd left. And last night Francine was definite that Darcy was in love with her. So maybe she'd scared herself by being so open last night or maybe she was afraid she'd scared Andrea and driven her away. If that was true, if Darcy loved her and was covering it to ensure that she stayed, then maybe it was a good thing. She'd see what Julie had to say later. Feeling better, she picked up her book and sat near Darcy, reading, until Julie arrived.

Darcy had dozed off listening to music, so Andrea leaned over her, removed the earbuds and lightly touched her cheek. "Darcy."

She opened her eyes. When she saw Andrea she smiled sweetly and her face seemed to fill with love.

All Andrea's doubts fled.

"Hi Darcy."

Darcy's eyes swung to Julie Castillo who was standing at the foot of the bed. "Dr. Castillo. Sorry, I was asleep. Nice to see you."

Julie laughed. "I'm sure you'd rather be doing anything else, but Dr. Trapani is worried about your heart."

Darcy's eyes slid back to Andrea.

"So I thought I'd come and listen myself, if that's okay with you."

Darcy focused again on Dr. Castillo. "Thank you for the house call. It's hard getting around these days. You're having lunch with us too?"

"Yes. And Carlo, I think his name is, said he would bring it up in fifteen minutes. So how about I get to work so we have some time to relax while we eat."

Andrea removed the blanket to allow Julie to take Darcy's pressure.

Julie looked at Darcy. "One seventy-five over eighty. Is this because you're excited by my visit?"

"I'm afraid not," Andrea said. "It's been in that range for a couple of days." She lifted the scrub top so Julie could listen to Darcy's heart and the pulses in her stomach, her groin and her ankles. Then, Andrea and Julie raised Darcy so Julie could listen to her lungs.

Julie put her stethoscope and pressure cuff away and sat next to Darcy. "I think I'll add a diuretic to your medications, Darcy. You'll pee more, but it should bring the pressure down. But I am worried about what I'm hearing in your heart. Do you remember what I told you after we put the stent in?"

"No, but Dr. Trapani told me that you thought I'd eventually need bypass surgery."

"Right. Eventually may be sooner than we expected. I'd like to get you in the hospital to do an angiogram—"

"I can't deal with heart surgery now."

"You already had an angiogram when we put in the stent. It's not surgery in the sense you mean, Darcy. We'll give you a mild sedative, put a catheter in through your groin, then introduce dye, which flows through your arteries and shows the blockages. Unless there are complications, you'll come home the same day."

"And if there are complications?"

"Depending on what we find, we could put in another stent, or decide it can wait a while, or recommend immediate surgery." Julie stood. "To be honest, Darcy, I would prefer to wait and do the bypass when the casts are gone and you're walking. But we may not have the luxury of waiting."

Darcy's eyes settled on Andrea.

"Don't worry, sweetie, I'll be with you all the way."

"I'd like to be in the wheelchair for lunch, so I can feel like a big girl." Darcy's joke broke the tension. Julie and Andrea lifted her into the wheelchair just as Carlo arrived with lunch. He set the dishes out on the bed trays and left.

"So, Dr. Castillo, do you do the cutting?"

"I do. Of course, you can have any surgeon you choose."

"Can Dr. Trapani be in the operating room with me?"

"If she wants. What do you say, Andrea?"

"I said I'd be there all the way and that includes the OR." She held up a shrimp and Darcy opened her mouth.

The three women chatted about vacations, beach vs. mountains, sunbathing vs. hiking, until Dr. Castillo received a reminder text from her assistant. "Sorry to cut this lovely lunch short, but duty calls."

"Come back any time, Doctor. I enjoyed spending time with you."

"Likewise. You two decide on the timing for the angio and call my office to schedule it." She stood. "Please walk me to the stairs, Andrea."

"You can take the elevator," Darcy said.

"Thank you, but walking down the four flights of steps will be my only exercise this week."

When they reached the stairs, Julie hugged Andrea. "I would say you two are a match made in heaven and she's definitely head over heels in love with you but trying to hide it."

"I think she scared both of us last night and now she's decided if she wants me to stay she has to pretend she's not in love. She thinks I'm straight, but I can live with that. I'll feel better if we continue without any romantic commitments as long as we can."

"Well, neither of you is very good at hiding your feelings. At least it was obvious to me."

"That's because you are the most wonderful, perceptive and loving friend a woman could ask for."

"I'd better go while I'm still held in such high esteem." Julie kissed Andrea's cheek and dashed down the steps.

CHAPTER SIXTEEN

Something had shifted for them. Darcy relaxed and didn't push. Andrea relaxed and didn't worry about setting limits. They settled into a comfortable routine of just being together. Every once in a while, their eyes met and the connection would flare between them, neither spoken nor denied, no commitments made, no promises given.

They spent most days in the garden, eating lunch and dinner there unless Darcy was tired. Outside or in, Darcy listened to music or audio books, Andrea either read to Darcy or read her own books but still kept her lesbian books in the bedroom. They both loved to do crossword puzzles, so Andrea got a subscription to the *New York Times* crossword puzzle and they often worked on one together.

It didn't take Candace long to notice. She'd been out of town for a week on business and came by for lunch her first day back. She chattered away as usual, going on about the people she'd met and the places she'd been, but her eyes darted between them as Andrea fed Darcy. "Still in baby mode, I see?"

Andrea's hand paused midair, fearing Darcy would be hurt and lash out. But Darcy took the food off the fork, chewed and swallowed. She smiled at Candace. "And don't you wish it were you?" She didn't say whether she meant as the feeder or the fed.

"What's going on with you two? Something is different. You didn't get engaged or married while I was away, did you?"

They all laughed.

"Nothing so dramatic, Candace. Dr. Castillo came to check me out and said my heart is pretty bad, so I'm trying to go with the flow, as they say, rather than go crazy and burst it."

Candace shook her head. "Uh-uh, Darcy, I know you. I can't put my finger on it but there's something. I'll have to think about it." She finished her lunch. Then, pleading a desk piled high after a week away, she left them alone.

A little while later, Maria came out. She sat, clasped her hands on the table and leaned forward. "Candace was upset when she left, *cara*, she thinks something happened while she was away and you don't tell her. I say Dr. Trapani takes good care of you and you feel happy again. It's been a long time, no? But she insists there is a secret."

"No secret, Maria. You're right. Dr. Trapani takes good care of me. I feel safe with her. And yes, she makes me happy."

"That's what I told her, but you know how she gets when she's jealous."

"You think she's jealous, *zia*?"

"Yes, always when you have something she doesn't. No matter how we love her." She kissed Darcy's forehead, patted Andrea's arm and rolled the cart with the dirty dishes back to the kitchen.

Darcy stared after her. "Interesting."

"Maria and Carlo seem to really care about you. How long have they been with you?"

"All my life, but longer with my parents."

"Really? Why don't they live in, you certainly have the room?"

"It's a long story."

Andrea's eyes sparkled. "It's about time you entertained me."

Darcy nodded, then took a few minutes to collect her thoughts. "My father was a pilot in the air force during World War II and he was shot down over Italy. Maria and Carlo were fifteen-year-olds in the Italian Resistance when they found him bleeding and barely alive after his plane crashed. They hid him and nursed him back to health. There was no way for him to get back to the American troops so when he was able, he joined them and the three of them fought side by side until the Americans invaded Italy. It was during this time he met my mother who was also a teenager and part of the Resistance. But she didn't live in the mountains and fight the way Maria and Carlo did. She was a member of the aristocracy and continued to live in her villa and carry on with her life, but she gathered information and smuggled food, medical supplies and messages to the fighters. The four of them became friends."

She cleared her throat. "Water, please." She sipped, then continued.

"My dad was older than the three of them, but after the war my mom, Francesca, married my dad, who, it turned out, was also from a wealthy family. Dad insisted they bring Maria and Carlo to live in New York but my mom fought him. You see, Maria and Carlo were uneducated peasants, scratching a living out of the small piece of land they had, while my parents were both educated and, let's not forget, wealthy. However, being a good guy and feeling eternally grateful for all they had done for him, he brought them over anyway. Neither spoke English well and they had difficulty finding jobs so Dad decided Maria would cook and Carlo would drive him and work around the yard. Mom put her foot down. She didn't want these nearly illiterate peasants living in her house as if they were relatives. Dad had just completed a high-rise apartment building around the corner and he gave them an apartment. He told them it came furnished but I think Maria eventually figured out that he paid for everything.

"He sounds like a great guy."

"He was. And mom wasn't as bad as she sounds, but when she grew up peasants didn't socialize with the upper classes. Of course, things were different during the war and in America.

Mom gave in to Dad, but insisted on hiring one of Italy's top chefs to train Maria to cook more than pasta and teach the two of them the proper way to serve. She eventually relaxed and learned to love them. And they were devoted to her, which is why the three of us were able to care for her at home when she was sick."

"Did they teach you to speak Italian?"

"Actually, being peasants, Maria and Carlo only spoke a dialect, not Italian. When I turned three, Dad brought in an Italian teacher and the three of us, and later Candace, learned to read, write and speak Italian together. Mom, Maria and Carlo always spoke Italian when Candace and I were around, but Dad spoke to us in English, so we grew up bilingual."

"Why didn't Maria and Carlo move in and take care of you? I'm sure they would have in a second."

"They wanted to. But they're in their eighties and I didn't want to stress them, so we compromised. They would cook and run the house with support staff but stay in their apartment. And Gerri would continue to live here and oversee the agency people she brought in to care for me."

"Maria and Carlo don't have children?"

"No. Something about the war and the bad nutrition. In fact, everyone was surprised when my mom got pregnant with me in her mid-forties. I'm just as much their child as I was my parents'."

"And, it's your villa they'll live in?"

"Yes, my mom's family's place which we've always kept up. They're not sure they'll feel comfortable there but my parents left them quite a bit of money so they can buy an apartment if they'd rather. I plan to visit often."

"It's a nice story."

"It is. I wish my mom and dad were still in it."

"So besides this house, you own various apartment buildings, a villa in Italy and a house on Fire Island?"

Darcy snickered. "Did I forget to tell you that besides being beautiful, intelligent and sexy, I'm very, very wealthy and a great catch for some woman?"

"Umm, I'll keep that in mind."

CHAPTER SEVENTEEN

As Carlo set lunch on the table in the garden, Andrea wheeled Darcy over. He smiled. "Candace is coming for dinner tonight and she brings a special guest for you."

"Did she say who?"

"No, just she is special guest."

Andrea fed Darcy some salad. "Do you have any idea who she might surprise you with?"

Darcy chewed slowly and swallowed before answering. "She knows how much I love Tori so she's the most likely surprise. Or maybe Lucia, since she got my clothes from her. But I'd be happy to see any of the others from the inner circle, even though none of them has bothered to visit."

Andrea extended a bite of chicken. Darcy hesitated. "I just hope it's not someone I would be embarrassed to have see me being fed." She opened her mouth for the chicken.

"Would Candace do that to you?"

She swallowed. "Maria did say she was jealous." Darcy tipped her head toward the iced tea. "And she's been strange lately, don't you think? I look up and she's staring at you or at me. She thinks we're hiding something from her and she gets pissy when she feels excluded." She sipped from the straw in the glass Andrea held for her.

"She senses you're more at peace and doesn't know what to make of it." *And she senses our relationship has shifted in some profound way, and it confuses her, fuels what Maria indicated was her usual jealousy of Darcy.*

Darcy shrugged. "I guess we'll see later. More iced tea, please."

After lunch, they sat in the garden reading until Darcy started yawning, then Andrea wheeled her upstairs for a nap so she would be refreshed for Candace and the mystery guest. Andrea noted in the chart that Darcy tired easily and was napping more, sleeping more overnight. Her heart was slowing her down and underneath the tan she'd acquired sitting in the garden, she was often pale.

Andrea took advantage of the time to do some research on physical therapists. The appointment with the ortho surgeon was in just three days and she wanted to be ready to bring someone in immediately. She called people she knew at the hospital to get recommendations. Three people recommended someone she knew so she called and arranged for her to be on standby the day of Darcy's appointment. It was important that Darcy start therapy right away so she could feel that she was making progress. Once Darcy's cast was off she would be able to feed herself. Good for Darcy, a loss for her.

When she woke, Darcy wanted to dress for dinner so she'd look nice for her mystery guest. The blue of the outfit she selected was lighter than her eyes but, as always, she looked stunning. Andrea brushed Darcy's hair, musing about the guest. It might be nice to meet Lucia, the talented clothing designer, although if Tori was the tall blonde in the picture in the bedroom, it would be much more interesting to meet her. When Darcy's hair was glossy, Andrea dabbed some of her spicy, sexy perfume behind her ears and applied the lipstick she requested. Then, Andrea buzzed Gregg to come up and help move Darcy to the wheelchair.

But it was Carlo who came. When he saw Darcy propped up in bed, he grinned. "*Che bella.* How beautiful."

Darcy reflected back his grin. "Thank you, sir."

The three of them rode down in the elevator. Carlo went back to the kitchen; doctor and patient settled in the garden to wait for the guests. Andrea hoped they would be on time, since three hours seemed to be the longest Darcy could go without a nap.

"Continue reading, please. I'm anxious to know how it ends."

At Andrea's skeptical look, Darcy laughed. "Yeah, yeah, I know the girl always gets the girl, but I like to see how the writer works it out."

Andrea picked up the romance they were reading. "Have you ever thought about writing?"

"Hasn't everyone? Actually, I took some writing courses in college and my professor said I had promise, but I didn't have what it takes. Writing a novel seems easy when you read a well-written one, but it takes fortitude and persistence and butt-in-the-chair hard work. I wasn't serious enough about it to ever write more than a chapter or two, so I gave it up."

"You like history and politics; have you tried nonfiction?"

She laughed. "That too. I started a book on the Italian resistance, but I didn't think it was good enough, so I put it in the drawer with my novels."

"Maybe my dad could take a look—"

"Where's Darcy?" Candace's voice boomed from the kitchen.

"Oh, oh. This can't be good." Darcy glanced at the door to the house. "Candace isn't usually so loud."

Candace burst through the door. "Ta-da. Look who I brought." She opened her arms and swiveled so they could see the woman behind her. Gerri.

Darcy stiffened. Andrea put a hand on her shoulder. "Stay calm."

Candace stumbled toward them. Gerri followed slowly, as if not sure of her welcome.

"Ya said you wanted to send her flowers to thank her, so I sent them and the check for what you owed her for Francine, with a note inviting her to dinner. I figured now that the doctor has cured your temper you and Gerri should reconnect." She plopped down on the bench.

Gerri looked mortified.

As Gerri approached, Andrea smiled and lifted a hand in greeting. "Hi Gerri, I'm Dr. Trapani. We sort of met in passing."

"Hi Gerri, nice to see you again." Darcy's voice was gentle. "Please sit, I tire if I have to look up too long. I did want to tell you how sorry I am for treating you so badly and how much I appreciate your kindness in spite of it." She looked at Andrea. "Dr. Trapani tells me if you hadn't intervened I probably would have blown my mind or my heart. I owe you for that. Thank you for coming."

Carlo arrived with the food and, with his usual flair, set the plates on the table, then poured the wine. He waved them over. "Please, sit." He helped Candace and Gerri with their chairs, placed napkins on everyone's laps, tipped his head to Darcy, then walked away.

Darcy smiled at Gerri. "How is art school?"

Gerri looked grateful. "It's good, Darcy. Thank you for continuing to pay the tuition. I was sure you'd stop it when I left."

"A promise is a promise. Besides, you're a gifted artist and I'd love to see you make a success of your art. Let me know when you think you're ready to show your work and I'll introduce you to some women who can help you."

A month ago, Andrea would have bet these two women would have ripped each other's throats out. But now she felt the connection and caring that must have brought them together in the first place. And, Darcy's generosity and desire to support Gerri's talent was touching.

Darcy indicated she was ready to eat and Andrea fed her salmon followed by rice pilaf.

"See, I told you she needed you, Gerri." Candace waved her fork at Darcy. "Look, she still can't even feed herself."

Darcy chose to ignore Candace. "Where are you living, Gerri?"

"I moved in with my friend Annie. And because you're paying my tuition, I'm able to get by with a part-time job. I have a painting for you. Maybe I'll drop it off one of these days." Gerri smiled. "I know I was kind of nasty too and I apologize."

"No need, Gerri. Dr. Trapani didn't see half of it but she can testify to how abusive I was to you. And you were right. I would have dumped you. I can only hope that I would have done it in as positive a way as you did. Anyway, let's put it behind us and move on."

Andrea fed her some more salmon.

Candace poured herself more wine. "Did you see, Gerri? Did you see she's still helpless? She needs you. And if you come back, we won't need Dr. Trapani."

Gerri looked down at her plate.

Darcy stiffened.

So that was it. Blinded by her jealousy, Candace thought only about getting rid of her perceived competition and chose to ignore Andrea's warnings about the precariousness of Darcy's health. Andrea fought the desire to scream at Candace, to ask her if she couldn't see how much she was hurting the woman she supposedly loved. But this was Darcy's fight.

Gerri stood. "Thank you for everything, Darcy, but I think I'd better leave."

"I'd like us to have dinner sometime. In a couple of weeks all these casts should be gone and I'll give you a call. I'm sorry this—"

"No, Darcy, I'm sorry. I knew it couldn't be true, but Candace convinced me you wanted me back." She walked out with her back straight and her head high.

"What's the mat—"

Darcy turned her attention to Candace. "Who do you think you are screwing with people's heads? Don't you ever do anything like this again and don't you ever, ever show up here drunk again."

Candace started to cry. "I was just trying to help."

"I don't want to see you until you're sober and you've figured out what was wrong about what you did here today. You owe me, Dr. Trapani and Gerri, especially Gerri, an apology. Now, get the fuck out."

Darcy was shaking, her face was fuchsia and her veins were popping. The very last thing she needed.

Candace was having trouble getting out of her chair so Andrea went to help her. "Stay away from me, bitch." Candace pushed herself up and staggered to the garden door. Maria and Carlo, who must have heard the ruckus from the kitchen, stood silently watching. Carlo put his arm around Candace and helped her up the three steps into the house. Maria looked at Andrea and pointed at herself. Andrea shook her head. Darcy needed time to process this. Maria turned and went into the house.

Andrea knelt next to Darcy and put her hands on her shoulders, the closest she could get with the casts in the way. "Take a deep breath, sweetie, come on, a really deep one. Now do it again. You've every right to be angry but it's not good for your heart." Andrea held on to Darcy until she stopped shaking and her breathing slowed, then she leaned back to look at Darcy's face. The pain she saw there brought on an overwhelming urge to comfort her. She looked away. She was attracted to Darcy, but was this love? No, it was probably compassion. Julie always teased that she was too compassionate to be a doctor. She had to admit though, as she spent time with Darcy, she became more loveable, less awful.

Darcy offered a small smile. "Throwing yourself on your knees in front of me is a lovely gesture, but you ain't as young as you used to be, my sweet doctor. Besides, it would be nice if you could save it for when we have sex."

"You are incorrigible. And, how did we get from my comforting you to having sex?" Andrea leaned on the wheelchair and dragged herself up. She bent over stretching her legs and her back.

"We'll always get to sex, my lovely doctor, always, and don't you forget it. You're lucky I didn't kiss you when you were holding me."

"Yuk, what a disgusting thought." She pushed the hair out of Darcy's eyes, then took a tissue out of her pocket and dried Darcy's face. "Please don't push me away with jokes, Darcy. I'm sure this is painful for you. Want to talk about it, while we eat our cold dinners?"

"I'm not hungry."

"Doesn't matter. You have to eat. Don't make me force feed you." Darcy's pressure was probably up in the stratosphere and Andrea was hoping that the intimacy of eating together would relax her. "First a sip of wine." They ate in silence for a while. "So, do you want to talk about it?"

Darcy shrugged and looked away. "I guess it would be better." After a long pause, Darcy spoke. "I feel betrayed." Her anger was underscored by sadness. "I haven't seen Candace drunk since college. And telling Gerri I want her back is beyond the pale. She's the one who advised me to wait a few months before contacting Gerri so she wouldn't get the wrong idea and think I wanted her back." She shook her head. "I don't get it."

"Would you like a little more wine?"

"Sure. Are you trying to get me drunk so we can get back to the sex part?"

"It seems I don't have to get you drunk for that, but I do for you to relax."

"As an outsider, what's your take on it, my dear doctor?"

Andrea took a minute to think about what she wanted to say. Candace's friendship was important to Darcy and she didn't want to get in the middle of that. But, maybe she was already in the middle. "Since your meltdown the night you found out the casts weren't coming off, you've been different. Something shifted for you, in you, and in our relationship. I think Candace senses that and imagines you're hiding something from her. Remember when she asked whether we'd gotten married or engaged while she was away?"

Darcy nodded.

"My interpretation might be off the wall, but I think she believes she's losing you to me and that scares the hell out of her. Maybe Candace sees Gerri as a placeholder until you're ready to commit to her. Is that crazy?"

"It is a little weird, but Candace is definitely capable of that kind of convoluted thinking."

"You need to talk to her, help her work through it."

"Are you kidding?"

"No, Darcy, I'm not. Candace is important to you and you should do whatever is necessary to keep her in your life. It is possible for women to be friends even if one is in love with the other."

Darcy studied Andrea, but Andrea had slipped that bland emergency room face on. "I have friends who have done it."

CHAPTER EIGHTEEN

Candace called five times the next day and five times the day after that. On the third day, with Andrea's encouragement, Darcy relented and agreed to see her. They were waiting in the garden, when Darcy decided she'd rather meet Candace in her room with Andrea out of sight but nearby in her bedroom. Andrea settled Darcy near the windows and when they heard the elevator open and close, she went into her bedroom, leaving the two old friends alone. She sat in the chair by the window with her book in her hands, but she was poised to dash in to protect Darcy if she heard raised voices. She closed her eyes and listened to the murmur of voices but was unable to hear the words.

* * *

Candace slunk in like a cat who didn't want to be noticed. Her eyes skittered around the room and landed on Darcy.

She did a quick double-check to see whether they were truly alone. "Hi Darcy." Her smile was bright but strained. Her voice pitched low.

"Hi yourself." Darcy's concern for Candace had replaced her anger. She hoped Candace was sober. "Sit." She thrust her chin in the direction of the chair she'd had Andrea place directly in front of her. "We need to talk."

"I guess I owe you an apology."

"I'm not the only one."

"I've already called Gerri and smoothed things over. And I apologized to Maria and Carlo at their apartment last night. I'm mortified that I was drunk in front of them." Her foot tapped the floor. "Where is the doctor?"

"Dr. Trapani is in the next room; you can see her before you leave. Does smooth over mean apologize or does it mean dance around what you did?"

Candace flushed. "I apologized. I practically had to prostrate myself before she would even let me speak."

"Glad to hear it. Now, how about you tell your oldest and dearest friend what the hell is going on with you."

Candace looked over Darcy's shoulder, out the window. "I'm not sure."

She shook her head. "I don't believe that for a minute. This is me you're talking to, Candace. You knew exactly what you were doing but had to get wildly drunk to do it."

Candace's lips quivered. Darcy had loved Candace for almost her entire life and it pained her to see her so unhappy. But she refused to comfort her as she always had in the past. Candace needed to take responsibility for her feelings and her actions. Darcy needed to help Candace understand it was time to move on. To understand that she could never love Candace in the way she desired, that if it wasn't Andrea, it would be someone else, never her.

Candace lifted her shoulders, arms out, palms up, in a gesture of helplessness.

Darcy was losing patience. "Come on, Candace, how bad can it be? Spit it out."

Candace looked down at her hands, then out the window. "I'm afraid I'm losing you. You seem so far away. At least when Gerri was here I was the one you talked to about her, about how you felt, about your frustration. Now you and Andrea seem like a closed unit. I guess I thought if Gerri came back, things would go back to the way they were."

"You know, Candace, Andrea and I spend just about every waking hour and some hours when I'm asleep together. She does everything for me, every single thing. And she never infantilizes me or makes me feel unseen or less than her. She's focused on making my life the best it can be in these circumstances and helping me get well as fast as I can. As I recall, when I asked you to come here and help me so I wouldn't have to be dependent on Gerri, you ran the other way. Of course, Andrea is paid to do these things, but I would have paid you to be with me and help out if that's what you wanted."

Candace opened her mouth to speak but Darcy shook her head. "I'm not done yet. So yes the doctor and I *are* kind of a unit, but it's certainly not exclusive. Actually, you exclude yourself. You make fun of me because I'm unable to feed myself. I wonder what you would do if you saw her put me on the bedpan. You're the one putting up the walls. You want things to go back to the way they were before the accident? Well, I sure wish they could, but you know what, I'm not the person I was then and things will never be the same."

"Are you in love with her?"

"Yes, though she says it's because I'm vulnerable and dependent on her. Time will tell." She looked Candace in the eye. "You're important to me, Candace. I want you in my life, but the love I feel for you is different. I love you like a sister."

Candace looked down at her hands. "What I did was awful. Can you forgive me?"

"I don't want to lose you, so, yes, I do forgive you. But I can't forgive drunken and hurtful behavior so make sure it doesn't happen again."

"I promise I'll try." She kissed Darcy on the cheek. "You look tired."

Darcy nodded.

"Is it all right if I come back, you know, for lunch or just to hang out with you?"

Darcy smiled. "I'm always happy to see you. Sober."

Candace smoothed her skirt. "Should I knock on the door and apologize before I go?"

"Sure. She doesn't bite." *Although I wish she would. Wow, I am so horny I disgust even myself.*

The tentative knock brought Andrea to the door in a shot. She looked past Candace to Darcy in her wheelchair and relaxed when she saw the smile on her face. "Hello Candace."

"Hi Dr. Trapani, um, I'm afraid I owe you an apology." She laughed and shrugged. "Maybe two. I'm sorry I subjected you to my drunken behavior and I'm sorry I called you a bitch when you tried to help me stand."

Andrea stepped back into the bedroom and motioned Candace to follow. "You know, Candace," Andrea said softly, "I'm just the hired help so calling me a bitch doesn't hurt me at all, but I do find your drunken behavior offensive. I can forgive you for both those things. But what I can't forgive, though I'm sure she forgave you, is the pain and stress you caused Darcy. Let me remind you that I'm here because she's extremely vulnerable physically."

Candace paled. She looked down. "It was stupid, I was stupid. The last thing I want to do is hurt Darcy. I appreciate your honesty."

Andrea put a finger on Candace's chin and lifted her face to look in her eyes. "I, of all people, know we all have our not so wonderful moments." She stepped away from Candace. "I hope the next time we see you it will be more enjoyable for all of us."

CHAPTER NINETEEN

They were sitting in the garden when the two-way radio that Carlo had given her, vibrated. It was Maria. "Tori is here to visit Darcy. Okay she comes now?"

Andrea shot a questioning look at Darcy.

Darcy's face lit up. "Hallelujah, one of my friends is amongst the living. Yes. Yes. Yes."

The happiness on Darcy's face tugged at Andrea's heart. How could Tori and Darcy's so-called inner circle abandon her when she so clearly needed their love and support? "Send her out, Maria." She put a hand on Darcy's shoulder. "Easy."

Andrea watched the tall blonde with the looks and strut of a runway model amble toward them, carrying a basket of flowers.

Seeing Darcy splayed in the wheelchair, the woman's face crumbled. She dropped the basket and got to her knees to embrace Darcy. "Oh, honey, I didn't know. I just heard about the accident but I didn't get any details. I'm so sorry."

"Just heard? It's been at least six weeks." Darcy looked puzzled. "Candace didn't call you?"

"No." Tori stood, then retrieved a tissue and dabbed at her eyes. "Alex's sister Irena ran into Maria and Carlo late last night. She thought they'd already left for Italy, but Maria explained about your accident delaying them. Alex called me right away. I feel so bad." She caressed Darcy's cheek. "You must have thought we abandoned you."

"I did." Darcy turned her head to kiss Tori's hand. "But I'm ridiculously happy you're here now."

"Those flowers are for you." Tori studied Darcy. "Are you in pain? How is it possible that you look happy?"

"Tori, this is Dr. Trapani, my live-in caretaker. Doctor, this is Tori, an old friend and" —Darcy hesitated— "I haven't seen her in a while."

Andrea could sense the connection whether Darcy spelled it out or not. And she recognized Tori as the young woman embracing Darcy in the picture in her bedroom. An old lover. Well neither of them was a virgin, that was for sure. *Where did these thoughts come from?*

"Nice to meet you, Tori."

"And I'm very glad to meet you, Doctor." She took Andrea's hand and held it while she did an overall assessment.

"Tori," Darcy said in the indulgent tone one would use with a child, "that's the hand that feeds me. Give it back to the doctor."

Tori released Andrea's hand. "Sorry, Doctor, I'm an unrepentant flirt, something I learned at Darcy's knee."

The tenderness on Darcy's face was moving. "God, I've missed you, Tori. Please stay for lunch?" Clearly, she loved Tori.

"I'd love to catch up with you and get to know the lovely," —she smiled at Andrea— "Dr. Trapani, is it?"

Andrea grinned, amused by Tori's flirting. So blatant, just like Darcy. As she keyed the radio, she wondered why Tori's flirting didn't bother her and why she felt so comfortable with Tori despite her obvious connection to Darcy. When Gregg responded to the radio, Andrea told him Tori would be staying for lunch.

"Okay, we'll be ready in about a half hour," blasted from the radio.

Andrea poured Tori a glass of lemonade.

Darcy cleared her throat. "So, Candace didn't tell you or anyone else about the accident?"

"No. And we didn't worry about not hearing from you because you were supposed to be in Italy with Maria and Carlo helping them get settled. But we hadn't seen you in so long Maya joked the other night that maybe Candace had finally spirited you away to a private island to get married and live happily ever after. All by yourselves."

"Is it that evident? About how Candace feels about me, I mean."

"Sure. Though she tries to cover it up."

"Why didn't I know? How long has this been going on?"

"In my opinion? Since you and I were together in college. She's always hidden it well but in the last year it's been obvious to the group. She comes alive when you're around. And, we've all noticed her efforts to separate you out from the pack."

Andrea could see that Darcy was starting to feel bad. "So how did you two come to be friends?"

"Just let me say one last thing about not knowing and then I will regale you with the lurid, sexy story of how Darcy, a big, beautiful junior, seduced me, an innocent freshman, and convinced me to allow her into my panties. And anywhere else she chose to go." She wiggled her eyebrows.

Darcy laughed. "Ah, the good old days."

Andrea smirked. "Darcy seducing an innocent? That can't be."

"I must really be rusty, my dear doctor, if you haven't noticed my powers of seduction."

Tori smiled at the banter but then her face darkened. "Alex said you were in casts but I never imagined both arms and legs. It's nice to see you in good spirits. I'd probably have slit my wrists by now."

"I probably would have, too, but the casts are in the way. And, since Dr. Trapani came into the picture, life has been easier. And better."

"Maria did mention that to Irena. Anyway, my dear, I wanted to tell you that Alex and I have been on the phone to put the word out about your accident. I hope that's okay, because I would guess you'll be having a ton of visitors."

"Thanks, Tori. I've wondered why you all abandoned me." Darcy blinked but the tears escaped. She turned to Andrea, who gently dried them with a tissue.

Tori observed their interaction with a warm smile but didn't comment. "So let me tell you how Darcy seduced me." Tori launched into the story. "So there I was an eighteen-year-old skinny, flat as a board, six-foot-two-inch beanpole freshman sitting in the student union engaged in a heated conversation about racism with the few friends I'd made in my first few weeks of college. At some point, I noticed a couple of them staring over my shoulder. I turned to see what they were looking at and there at the next table was the gorgeous, wonderful, popular Darcy Silver with her chin in her hand, listening. She smiled. I checked behind me to see if one of her friends had come in. When I turned back, she pointed at me. I felt my face flame, though Darcy later claimed fuchsia was more like it. I didn't know what to do, so I turned away. I was aware of my friend saying something but I couldn't understand. Finally, my friend grabbed my hand and dragged me to our next class."

"Here's my side of this story," began Darcy. "I was sitting there reading when this loud discussion at the next table broke my concentration, so I listened to this broad-shouldered girl with long golden hair passionately and brilliantly explicating her points about racism. I was enchanted by her brilliant mind. When she stood up, she seemed to go on forever, reminding me of a picture of a baby giraffe I'd seen once, all ears and eyes and head on a spindly body with loosely connected limbs. A couple of days later I noticed her engrossed in conversation again and sat at a nearby table. This time she was discussing politics and demolishing everyone's arguments. As they were getting up to leave, I waved her over and introduced myself."

"I was so shy I could barely say my name, but I did and she smiled and said 'nice to meet you Victoria' and waved me off." Tori picked up her glass but continued speaking. "About a week later I was studying in the library and someone sat next to me. After a few minutes, my head filled with this sexy perfume. Unable to concentrate, I closed the book I was reading and started to pack my things to move away. Then I saw it was Darcy and she was staring at me. Once again, I turned bright red. She draped an arm over my shoulder, rested a hand on my thigh and leaned in to whisper in my ear. 'Victoria, my love, would you like to pledge Kappa Theta?' I felt a charge through my body that I thought was because of what she was asking, but later I realized her breathing in my ear made me feel that way. Unable to speak, I nodded. She patted my cheek, said, 'Good girl,' and strolled away."

Tori sipped her lemonade. "So I was accepted as a pledge and Darcy took me as her personal slave. By then, I would have licked her muddy boots clean if she'd commanded. But she didn't. In fact, she didn't have me do any of the silly things that the other pledges were asked to do. She did, however, command that we have dinner and study together every night. I was surprised to find the campus playgirl was an intellectual. At dinner we discussed our coursework, politics, world news and everything else under the sun, then we went to her room and studied. Did I say she had a single? Every night she walked me back to my dorm before curfew and we would stand outside under the trees and talk. One night, I impulsively leaned down and kissed her. When I realized what I was doing, I pulled away, afraid of what would happen."

Tori laughed. "Darcy looked up at me. 'What was that?' I started shaking. 'A, um, sorry, kiss. I—' She put a finger over my lips to stop my babbling. 'You're right,' Darcy said. 'It was a sorry kiss.' She pulled my head down and kissed me, at first gently, then she somehow got me to part my lips and allow her tongue into my virginal mouth. After a blissful eternity, Darcy stepped back. 'If you're going to kiss me, you need to do it right. Your assignment for tomorrow is to come prepared to show me you know how to kiss.' She walked away. I was stunned. If someone from the dorm hadn't walked by and reminded me it was almost curfew, I'd probably still be standing there in shock."

Darcy smirked. "See, Andrea, Tori kissed me first."

Tori snorted. "Right. So the next night after dinner we went to her room. Darcy sat at her desk, as she usually did, and I wondered if she'd forgotten my assignment. I cleared my throat. 'Aren't you going to study?' Darcy tossed the question over her shoulder. Relieved, I turned toward the desk she'd added to her room for me. Suddenly, Darcy swiveled and pointed at me, 'Didn't I give you an assignment for tonight?'"

Andrea laughed. "Ah, Darcy, you're cruel."

"It was sweet cruelty, though," Tori said. "Anyway, I fidgeted and blushed and looked every where but at Darcy. 'I'm supposed to show you that I know how to kiss.' Darcy tapped her fingers on the desk. 'And are you ready?'"

"Well I'd spent the whole day reliving Darcy's wonderful kiss and kissing my own arm trying to practice. I nodded."

'I'm going to have to punish you if you don't get this right, Tori, it's one of the most important things you'll learn at college. So proceed.'

"So I sidled over and looked down at Darcy. I was flummoxed about how to accomplish the kiss with her sitting and me towering over her. So the kindly Ms. Silver said, 'Why don't we sit on the bed.'

"We sat. I leaned in and attempted to kiss her without touching her. 'That was terrible, Tori. Put your arms around me and try again.' The second kiss was just as bumbling. Darcy shook her head and pulled away. 'Your punishment for this fiasco is to write, *I must learn to kiss* one hundred times.' Darcy started to get up, then sat again. 'No, that won't work. You have to kiss me one hundred times and I'll guide you so you get it right.'

"By the time Darcy walked me to my dorm that night my panties were soaked, my legs were like rubber and I could barely breathe, but I knew how to kiss. So each night after dinner we'd spend time passionately kissing, until one night I put my hand under Darcy's sweater, touched her breast and came all by myself. I freaked but Darcy held me and reassured me that it was an orgasm, not a seizure. 'It looks like you might be ready to move on to bigger and better things, Tori. We'll discuss it tomorrow night, but for now, just enjoy the feeling.'

"True to her word, Darcy sat me down the next night and talked about sex. What we would do, what it meant to be a lesbian, etc. She gave me a choice. We could kiss but not touch each other, we could try sex, or, if I wanted, she would hand me over to one of the straight girls in the sorority for the remainder of the pledge period. Guess what I chose?"

Darcy smirked. "Can you believe how that beanpole seduced me? There wasn't one curve on her body anywhere but she was very sexy, and a very willing pupil."

"And there you have it, the story of how Darcy seduced me into seducing her." Tori patted Darcy's cheek. "I've always been thankful you were my first. You were so loving, so romantic and so sensual, I think I walked around with my panties soaked most of that year and the next. And you were very kind and gentle in letting me go." Her smile was soft with remembering. She turned to Andrea. "Watch out for her, though. She's slippery as an eel, no one has been able to hold onto her. I hold the record at two years."

Darcy looked like she might say something but stopped when the door to the kitchen swung open.

"And I might add, Darcy also made me aware of how I tried to shrink into myself because I was so much taller than everyone. All my life people had been telling me to stand up straight, but she never did. She made me feel beautiful, made me feel special, made me feel being tall was a gift. She showed me pictures of statuesque African woman warriors, of beautiful models. She kissed my breasts and said it was a shame to hide them behind caved-in shoulders. Being loved by her gave me confidence, made me proud. Then she encouraged me to think about modeling as a possible career." Tori caressed Darcy's face. "You are one of the most important people in my life. I don't know if I'll ever forgive Candace for cutting me out when you needed me."

Darcy's eyes shimmered. Andrea stood and walked behind the wheelchair. "Let's go to the table." While Tori helped Maria move the plates to the table, Andrea helped Darcy blow her nose. "Tori is delightful."

Darcy nodded.

"Hey, Darce, have you gotten religion? I've hardly ever seen you eat anything but steak and fries or, if it's breakfast, bacon and eggs."

She laughed. "Not religion." She glanced at Andrea. "Dr. Trapani. The good doctor put me on a healthy diet and I'm actually enjoying it."

"We all tried, Doctor, but she's a stubborn bitch. We'd all be sitting around the table eating our salads, afraid we'd get fat and she, who never gains weight, would be shoveling in her steak or burgers and fries. She'd eat pork chops and lamb chops, but forget fish or vegetables. And now I'm going to get to see her eat sea bass and salad."

"Ah, Tori, if I'd known it was so important to you, I would have taken a leaf of lettuce now and then. But you have a special treat today. Not only do you get to see me eat fish and enjoy it, but you get to see the lovely doctor feed me."

"Ooh, how sexy."

"Sexy? Are you sick?"

Tori put her hands on her hips, pretending indignation. "You cruel woman. Don't you remember after we made love you used to feed me olives, stuffed grape leaves and cheese, and kiss me after each bite?"

"Well, my dear, you may not have noticed," Darcy's tone was ironic, "but the good doctor and I haven't just made love. And, if you observe very carefully, you'll notice she doesn't kiss me after each bite."

Andrea felt uneasy. All this talk of making love and kissing and feeding each other brought to mind the connection she often felt when Darcy's eyes met hers as she was feeding her.

"Well, I still think it's sexy. It's an intimate connection we don't usually have as adults. And, I can't wait to see you eat fish."

"If you stare at us and say 'sexy' whenever the doctor puts something in my mouth, I'll have you thrown out."

"Don't worry, hon, I'll be concentrating on my own sea bass. It looks fabulous."

Tori was charming and funny and her affection for Darcy was heartwarming. She took the feeding in stride and didn't mention it. But Darcy couldn't resist. "So, are you feeling turned on watching me being fed?"

"No, darling, you know I have my own live-in feeder whenever I desire her, oops, I mean it."

"How does Elle put up with you?"

"She loves me."

"She does. You found a good one, Tori." Her eyes were on Andrea. "We should all be so lucky."

"Is Fire Island out for you this summer? It's always so much fun at the beach with the whole gang, the sun, the sea, good conversation and cocktails on the deck. It would do you good to spend some time there."

"You know I love being at the house, but it doesn't look like I'll make it this summer. I haven't been there since the accident." She looked so wistful it was painful. Andrea wanted to comfort her.

Tori patted Darcy's face. "Patience isn't your strong suit, but you'll get there. And remember, September and October are even nicer because the crowds are gone."

Andrea offered the last bit of sea bass and Darcy opened her mouth. Their eyes met. Andrea smiled and gently wiped Darcy's lips.

Darcy swallowed. "Well, maybe a little sexy."

They all laughed.

Was it sexy? Andrea hadn't thought about it like that but it sure felt intimate, more intimate than most of the sex she'd had in the last few years. Maybe Darcy was right. It was a little sexy.

After dessert and coffee, Andrea excused herself. "I don't want Tori to have to hold back any really sexy stuff to protect my innocent ears, so I'll stroll around the garden and leave you two alone for a little bit." She grinned. "Okay?"

Darcy feigned panic. "Oh, God, no, she'll have me trying to masturbate with my cast."

Tori pressed two fingers to her lips, pretending to consider the idea. "Hmm, I hadn't thought about that. Go on, Doctor, I promise to take good care of her."

They watched Andrea until she turned onto a path that led to the other end of the garden.

Tori wiggled her eyebrows. "So, what's with the lovely Dr. Trapani? Are you in love with her?"

"Yes."

"That explains the glow. She seems into you."

"You think? I don't even know if she's a dyke. And, she thinks my feelings are the result of my vulnerability and will dissipate when I'm stronger. But I know what I'm feeling. Anyway," Darcy's lips quirked, "she wants me to call her doctor, to keep our relationship on a totally professional level, but she's Andrea in my thoughts."

"Ooh, I love dirty secrets. I won't tell."

"Who said my thoughts were dirty?"

"Hmm."

"Oh, you mean sexy? You know I don't consider sex dirty." Damn, her nose was starting to drip. Should she ask Tori or try to wait?

Tori opened her bag and took out a tissue. "Here, let me get that, hon." She wiped Darcy's nose. "Need to blow?"

Darcy shook her head. "Remind me why I let you go."

"You said we loved each other and were great in bed, but we weren't in love." Tori shrugged. "I wasn't so sure about the not being in love part."

"But you went along with it?"

"I loved you, Darcy. And I believed you loved me. It was painful and I could see you were hurting too, but I trusted you had a reason for breaking up."

"I'm so sorry, Tori. It *was* painful. Someday I'll figure it out and explain." Darcy sniffed. "Damn, Andrea's right. I am vulnerable and emotional, I'm so weepy these days."

Tori dried Darcy's eyes and kissed her cheek. "But that's old news, hon. You were telling me about the lovely Andrea."

"When she arrived, I was feeling abandoned by everyone and totally freaked out. Candace had promised to stay with me, to help take care of me, then she disappeared, leaving me with Gerri, whom I had decided to break up with the morning of the accident."

"I'm going to kill Candace, slice her into pieces with my chef's knife…"

"She's drinking again." Darcy hesitated, remembering Candace's recent behavior. "She created quite a drunken scene here a few days ago. She told Gerri I wanted her back and brought her here for dinner, then she told us all if Gerri came back I could get rid of Andrea. She called Andrea a bitch."

"Of course, she's jealous. I felt your connection immediately. But you were telling me about Andrea."

"Right. I was a raving lunatic after the accident. In fact, the morning she appeared, I was in a screaming rage at Gerri who had just announced she was leaving. I was vile, Tori, really vile to Gerri and to Andrea."

"It looks like you didn't scare her away."

"No, in fact she was calm and gentle despite my cursing and screaming. And, with her there, I felt safe. Suddenly I could breathe. A good thing, too, because she thought I was ready to have a stroke on the spot."

"And now?"

"My heart's not so good and bypass surgery is in my future. I'm tired of being an invalid, but I feel calm and happy being with her. We sit in the garden or in my room and she reads to me or we do a crossword puzzle or we talk about things, and I feel connected. For the first time since you, it's not just about sex; it's more, it's deeper. It's strange to say at my age, but I haven't been in love since you."

"I'm so happy for you, Darcy. You're a wonderful woman and I've worried that you'd end up being alone. But, no sex? You're pulling my leg right?"

Darcy smiled. "Of course, it's about sex. But I can't do anything for myself and she's not willing, so, for the time being, all I have is fantasies."

The smirk on Tori's face alerted her.

"Don't even think about asking me to share them."

"Aw, shoot." Tori threw her hands up in surrender. "Do you want me to ask around, try to find out whether she's a lesbian?"

Darcy thought for a second. "No, she'll tell me when she wants me to know. But, I've decided whether she's a lesbian or straight, as long as she's not in a committed relationship, I'll pursue her until I get her."

"Poor thing doesn't know who she's up against. And, speaking of Dr. Trapani, here she comes." Tori stood and kissed Darcy lightly on the lips. "I have to get back to work but I'll see you both soon." She hugged Andrea. "A pleasure to meet you. Give me your phone and I'll put my home number and my private cell number in so you can reach me if you need me to do anything, or even if you just need to vent about Darcy the Terrible."

She keyed in the numbers and handed the phone back to Andrea. "I'll see you both very soon. Now that I know, I'll be underfoot whenever I can get away."

They watched her stroll to the door.

"She's terrific. Are you sorry you let her go?"

"No, my dear. I loved her then and I love her now, but I haven't been in love with her for a long time."

CHAPTER TWENTY

Andrea answered Darcy's phone the next afternoon. "It's Tori. She wants to have a party tonight. Are you up for it?"

"Who?"

Andrea relayed the answer. "The inner circle is anxious to visit and she thought a group visit might be less tiring for you."

Darcy nodded. "Yes, definitely."

Andrea spoke to Tori for a few minutes, then ended the call. "They'll be over around seven. They'll bring everything we need."

"I think I'd better take a nap before dinner, I don't want to doze off in the middle of the party. And when I wake up, I'd like to change into something nice, if that's all right with you?"

Andrea smiled. "No problem."

While Darcy napped, Andrea called Francine and told her to come in around ten, then considered whether she should also change. The scrubs would remind everyone that she was there in her professional role, but since Darcy and her ally Tori would probably tease her anyway, maybe just jeans and her green sweater would do. Darcy seemed to like the way she looked in that color and had commented that the sweater looked sexy. Andrea flushed when she realized where her thoughts were taking her.

When Darcy woke, she requested the deep blue outfit with the plunging neckline. The color was gorgeous and matched her eyes. Once she was dressed, she asked Andrea to retrieve the blue sapphire necklace and earrings that would complement it from the safe in her closet. Andrea was reluctant to know the code for the safe and insisted that she ask Carlo to do it when he delivered dinner.

When Carlo arrived, they shifted Darcy from the bed to the wheelchair. While they were eating, Carlo handed Andrea a blue velvet box. After dinner, she brushed Darcy's hair, then applied eye shadow, lipstick and a dab of Darcy's Perfume #7. She gasped when she lifted the necklace out of the box. It was spectacular, the sapphires a perfect match for Darcy's eyes.

Darcy smiled. "A gift from my parents on my twenty-first birthday."

Andrea moved behind Darcy and draped the necklace around her neck. She stepped in front to put on the earrings, but stopped and stared. The juxtaposition of the sparkling sapphires with the sparkling sapphire blue eyes was stunning. "Christ, you look gorgeous."

"Thank you."

Andrea fastened the earrings, wondering at Darcy's restrained response. Usually, she would have made some smart-assed remark, but, of course, Darcy knew exactly how beautiful she looked and had no need to pretend. "Give me a few minutes to change then we'll go down to the garden to wait for the party to arrive."

Andrea went into her bedroom to change and left the door half-open so she could hear if Darcy called.

* * *

To Darcy's delight, her wheelchair was positioned perfectly in relation to the mirror on the wall in the bedroom and she could see Andrea's reflection as she undressed. When Andrea had stripped to her lacy black bra and black bikini panties, Darcy tried to look away. But despite her honorable intentions, she couldn't help herself. Each time she pried her eyes away, they wandered back to the mirror. Her body clearly thought, if she couldn't touch, she should at least be able to look. She imagined caressing Andrea's muscled and lean runner's body, her fingers tracing the long legs, the sensitive upper thighs, the tight, round ass, the flat stomach, and then burying her face in those surprising full breasts. Feeling warmth trickle down her spine to her groin, Darcy closed her eyes fantasizing—

"Hey you. Falling asleep already?"

Darcy opened her eyes and took a leisurely look at the woman of her fantasy. Andrea knew she loved her in those tight black jeans and the green sweater that displayed her cleavage and brought out the emerald color of her eyes. Could she have dressed for her? One could only hope. Andrea had put on lip gloss, which she didn't wear every day, and her lips looked even more inviting than usual.

* * *

Andrea pinked as Darcy's eyes, naked with desire, swept over her. She stifled a groan as her body responded with a warm surge and an ache of want. She had to get them out of this room into the garden before she did something she would regret. She moved behind the wheelchair to escape those sexy eyes. "Ready?"

"If you are." Darcy's words were more a breathy sigh than a statement.

She pushed the wheelchair into the elevator. Neither spoke. Andrea was glad Darcy's back was to her because she wasn't good at hiding her feelings. The lust in Darcy's eyes combined with the fragrance of her perfume in the enclosed space of the elevator was fueling Andrea's already intense desire to take her to bed. And not for a nap. Shit. Darcy's breath was coming in quick bursts; her pressure was probably sky high. She had to defuse this, pronto.

In the garden, Andrea offered Darcy the iPod but she refused. Andrea could barely breathe. She reached for the medical journal she'd brought with her, hoping to break the sudden sexual connection. What she needed was her emergency room face. She could hear her teacher's voice in her head: "Learn to control your face. Don't let them see your feelings or they'll panic and make it harder to help them."

"Would you mind picking up where we left off in the romance?"

"No." Andrea's voice cracked. She cleared her throat. "I don't mind." She turned to their place and began to read. Thankfully, it wasn't a bedroom scene. She forced herself to keep her eyes on the page and her voice steady but she was aware of Darcy's eyes on her and of Darcy's rapid breathing. What had happened? Different clothes? The sapphires? The makeup and perfume? She didn't know, but she feared they might combust if the party didn't arrive soon.

At last, they heard voices at the side gate to the garden. Andrea let Tori and the women with her flow into the garden, then locked the gate again. She walked back slowly, watching the women surround Darcy and take turns hugging and kissing her. Then Tori started issuing orders. Wine and beer and glasses— glass, not plastic—were placed on the table followed by chips, crudités and dips. Darcy seemed lit from within as she watched her friends assemble the party. Andrea silently cursed Candace for depriving Darcy of this, of the love of the friends Darcy considered her family.

A very tall woman wearing a vivid robe broke away from the activity to sit in the chair that Tori had thoughtfully placed in front of Darcy so she would be on the same level as anyone who came to talk to her. Andrea leaned against a lamppost observing their animated conversation. The woman's posture and her elegance brought thoughts of an African queen, but her hands on Darcy's face and her brushing of Darcy's lips with hers brought pangs of jealousy.

Tori's voice interrupted her fantasy of ripping those hands away. "Is white okay or would you prefer red?"

"White is fine, thank you. And thank you for this." She gestured to the laughing women standing together chatting while they waited for an opportunity to sit and talk with Darcy. She wondered whether Tori had staged it or they understood intuitively that Darcy would be overwhelmed if they descended on her *en masse*. "She really needs it. My heart breaks thinking she felt you all had abandoned her."

"We're here now and you won't get rid of us." Tori put her hand through Andrea's arm. "Come on, she wants to introduce you." Andrea tensed.

Tori patted her hand. "Relax. I doubt she'll put you on the spot tonight. In fact, I think she'll be protective, maybe show you off a little."

"Show me off?"

"Deal with it, woman. She's smitten. She needs to feel good about herself right now and, like it or not, you make her feel good."

Andrea stopped and looked Tori in the eye. "How did you get to be such a wise woman?"

Tori lifted her glass as if to toast Andrea and took a sip. "Like I told you, Darcy taught me everything I know. Ready?"

The tall, bronze-skinned woman had left and the chair facing Darcy was empty but Tori pulled a second chair over and positioned it beside Darcy. As she sat, Andrea said, "How's it going?"

"It's going. I'd like to introduce you, if that's okay? I promise I won't embarrass you."

Andrea patted Darcy's hand. "I'd love to meet your friends." She looked down at their hands. Somehow Darcy had managed to grab her finger. What a devious woman. Rather than get into a pulling match she left her hand there, intending to extract it when Darcy had relaxed a bit.

Andrea looked up. Tori must have given a signal or something because the African queen was back in the chair facing Darcy. "Dr. Trapani, this is Elle, Tori's wife. Elle, my doctor and companion, Dr. Trapani."

Ah, Tori's wife, not, she caught herself about to think, a competitor. Darcy had mentioned that Elle, like Tori, was a model, and that the blond, blue-eyed, porcelain-complexioned Tori and the dark-haired, hazel-eyed, bronze Elle had often been paired in ads. Elle seemed serious, remote, until her face lit up with a smile that warmed Andrea's heart.

"Welcome to our little tribe, Doctor." Elle put a hand on Andrea's arm. "Tori told me all about you." Her eyes dipped to their intertwined fingers. "No, don't blush, it was all good. She likes you, and the opinions of Tori and Darcy go a long way with this group."

"I like her too. We had a fun lunch."

"Yeah, put her and Darcy together and they'll keep you in stitches." She focused on Darcy. "Darcy, love, have I told you that, you look beautiful?"

Tori walked over. "Ready for some wine, Darce?" She extended a glass.

"Love it and" —she glanced at Andrea— "a few chips."

One night of chips and dips and whatever else her friends had brought wouldn't kill Darcy and to tell her what she could and couldn't eat in front of them would embarrass her. Andrea gently extricated her finger and took the glass from Tori. She put her own wine on the table next to her, then plucked a straw from the bag hanging on the back of the wheelchair and put it in Darcy's glass. Tori returned with a small plate of chips. Andrea gave Darcy a sip of wine, then fed her a chip.

"Ah, real food."

Elle laughed. "I heard the doctor put you on a healthy diet. Never thought I'd see the day. Maya's lurking so I'm going to give up my seat now, but don't worry, Tori and I are planning to spend a lot of time with you. And, you too, Doctor."

Maya. Her name made Andrea think of jungles and parrots and exotic foods, but other than her bright red hair, the woman who leaned in to kiss Darcy's cheek didn't match her vision. In fact, she was short and chunky, pleasant-looking but not beautiful, until she spoke.

"Hey, Darcy, my love, you really did it this time, didn't you?" Her voice flowed like warm chocolate, dark and rich, and she crackled with energy and humor and intelligence that had an attractiveness of its own.

"How else is a girl to get the attention of this group?"

Maya frowned. "That didn't work out so good for you did it? I'm going to wring that shrimpy blonde's neck the next time I see her. I've been waiting for you to come back from Italy so we could discuss the latest Teddy Roosevelt biography. And, damn, I find you were here the whole time."

Darcy took a minute to introduce Andrea, then started on the Roosevelt biography. After a few minutes, Tori put a hand on Maya's shoulder. "Sorry to interrupt kiddies, but we have to keep this line moving or we'll overstay our welcome."

Maya stood. "Sorry. I miss talking to you, Darce. And we haven't had a songfest in a while."

Songfest? Darcy was a woman of many talents, a constant surprise.

Darcy glanced at Andrea. "Please come by some afternoon or evening to finish discussing the book. My good doctor reads a lot but you're my only history pal and I miss you." Maya stood and kissed Darcy's cheek again.

Andrea put a chip in Darcy's mouth and followed it up with wine.

The petite woman who sat next wore a chic, scoop-necked jacket with silver embroidered detail over black pants. With her glossy black hair in a French twist, smiling dark eyes, alabaster skin and red lipstick, she was gorgeous. She placed her hands on either side of Darcy's face and kissed her again and again.

"I guess you missed me, eh, Lucia? Have you met my doctor? Dr. Trapani, Lucia; Lucia, Dr. Trapani."

"Oh, Lucia, I love your clothing. Everything you sent for Darcy looks beautiful on her."

Lucia looked pleased. "Thank you, Doctor. I often have Darcy in mind when I'm designing and selecting fabrics." She spoke with a slight accent.

So, another conquest. "Based on what I've seen, she's a great inspiration."

"How's the business going, Lucia?"

Lucia edged forward on the chair and cupped Darcy's face. "Thanks to you, we'll be in Saks in January."

"No, Lucia, thanks to you and your wonderful designs. All I did was arrange a meeting."

"I want to talk to you about expanding."

"Stop by anytime."

"I will. Oops, I have to move on." As Lucia moved away, another chair was dragged over. Two women sat. Darcy introduced them as Beth and Gina, a couple. Beth was small, wiry and surprisingly muscular. With her spiked dark brown hair, large brown eyes, and jaunty smile, she reminded Andrea of a pixie. On the other hand, her partner Gina, a statuesque coffee-colored beauty with lovely greenish eyes and lustrous short black hair with side-swept bangs, had an air of sophistication. Andrea felt a warm vibe emanating from them.

"We figured we could speed things up if we came together."

Darcy raised her eyebrows. "Really, is that how you two get it done?"

Andrea was happy to see that she wasn't the only one always blush-ready. They all laughed.

She could see that Darcy was tiring. She caught Tori's eye, then tilted her head slightly toward Darcy.

Tori studied Darcy for a few seconds then clinked a knife against her glass. "Okay, ladies, we don't want to love our guest of honor to death so no more individual sessions. Everyone pull up a chair."

Tori, Elle, Maya, Stephanie, Monica, Alex and Renee carried chairs over and joined Gina and Beth in a semicircle around Darcy and Andrea.

Darcy cleared her throat and wiggled her fingers but Andrea pretended she hadn't noticed and turned her attention back to the group in front of her. She was aware of the women watching her with interest as she offered the straw to Darcy and held the glass while she sipped her wine, then fed her chips, without being asked. She had no doubt that they all knew about Darcy's interest in her but no one mentioned it or teased them. They were all curious about the accident so Darcy described what had happened and told them about her physical condition. They expressed anger at Candace for not telling them.

Lucia was particularly upset. "I was surprised when she told me she was picking up some things for Darcy and thought she might like wide arms and legs, but I never dreamed she was hiding the fact that Darcy had been in an accident. I'm so angry that she lied by omission."

Everyone dished Candace for another couple of minutes, then the conversation changed and wandered from Fire Island to jobs to who was dating someone new, to vacation plans.

In answer to a question about Andrea's experiences as an emergency room doctor, she described the pressure and the challenges the doctors and nurses faced every day. Then someone asked if she had always been an ER doctor. She told them about her two years with Doctors Without Borders, about delivering babies in an emergency hospital in Afghanistan while bombs exploded in the background, about living in the jungle in the Republic of Congo and loading everything—generators, sophisticated lab equipment, food, water and tents—into primitive boats carved from trees and fitted with motors to go upriver to set up camp where they'd screen and treat entire villages for sleeping sickness, then do the same the next day. Happily, no one asked if she was a lesbian, or why an emergency room doctor was working as a live-in caretaker.

She could feel the power of Darcy's attention as she spoke. When she finished she turned to Darcy. Their eyes met. She shivered at the intensity of the feelings she saw in Darcy's eyes. She knew despite her best intentions, her eyes probably contained the same.

After what seemed like hours, Elle broke the spell. "That's amazing work, Dr. Trapani. Your bravery and generosity are humbling. Thank you for sharing."

Andrea looked away from Darcy. Everyone was grinning. She didn't think her face could get any hotter, but it did. "I—"

Darcy saved her from coming up with a response. "Now I understand why you weren't intimidated by me when I attacked you that first day." Everyone laughed. "Hey ladies, Dr. Trapani is curious about how we know each other."

It turned out that apart from Elle who had met Tori when they were both modeling, and Beth, they had all gone to college together, been in the same sorority and scandalized the campus with their behavior because they didn't look like your stereotypical lesbians. Except Renee who was on the androgynous or butch side, all were ultra-feminine. And every one of them was attractive, personable, witty and playful. Andrea felt totally at ease and accepted by them. The last, she was sure, was based on Darcy's seal of approval.

When they'd arrived, she'd reminded Tori they should leave by about nine thirty, quarter to ten, so as not to exhaust Darcy. And, true to her word, Tori started the cleanup and goodbyes at nine fifteen. The chairs were put back and all traces of the party, including the garbage, were packed up. There were hugs and kisses goodbye for Darcy and for her. At nine forty-five Andrea locked the gate and they were alone.

She wheeled Darcy into the house. She would wait for Francine to put her to bed but she washed Darcy's face to remove the makeup and brushed her teeth. She removed the sapphires and put them in the safe, then replaced the blue top with one of the scrub tops Darcy used for sleeping, removed her pants and covered her with a blanket. When she'd done what she could without help, she sat next to Darcy and brushed her hair back. "Have a good time?"

"A very good time. What about you?"

"Your friends are lovely. How many of them have you been involved with?"

"All but Elle. Tori got there first."

"So, with a rare exception, all your friends are your exes?"

"Jealous?"

"Interested."

She studied Andrea for a minute, maybe seeking signs of jealousy, then shrugged. "It's safe to say that many of my friends are ex-lovers, but not all my ex-lovers are friends. Most of the women in my inner circle are college friends and ex-lovers. Make sense?"

"It's nice that you've managed to maintain connections with so many college friends."

"We were sorority sisters and lovers, not just me but the group with each other and you know lesbians tend to stay friends after the breakup." Darcy stared at Andrea, but she kept her face bland. "Or maybe you don't know."

Andrea smiled but didn't respond. She'd come out with Julie in medical school and had had casual flings since then but her love for Julie had kept her from connecting with other women. Nora had been the last in a string of casual relationships.

"What's this songfest Maya mentioned?"

"Oh, a couple of us get together to sing sometimes. Maya has a beautiful voice."

"You sing?"

"A little."

"Do you play an instrument?"

"Piano, guitar, accordion."

"Accordion?"

She chuckled. "What can I tell you? I grew up in a house full of Italians."

"Hey, ladies, how was the party?" Francine had arrived and they hadn't heard the elevator.

Darcy grinned. "Great. I got to eat potato chips and I learned that my good doctor is a brave doctor."

"Potato chips? You really did have a wild night." Francine turned to Andrea. "May I ask what brave act you performed tonight?"

"Other than daring to meet all of Darcy's friends at once, I talked about the two years or so I worked with Doctors Without Borders."

"Hey, tell her later. I'm beat. Could you two throw me into bed so I can rest after my wild night?"

They lifted Darcy into bed. Andrea helped her with the bedpan. By the time Francine finished checking her vitals, Darcy was asleep. Andrea covered her with a light blanket, put the sides of the bed up and watched her sleep a few minutes. It was getting harder and harder to maintain the distance. She turned to review the chart with Francine.

CHAPTER TWENTY-ONE

Andrea held Darcy's hand in the waiting room, hoping to calm her down. Today was the day the arm casts might come off. She'd been stressing the "might" to Darcy for two days and this morning Darcy had snapped at her.

"I'm not a baby. I understand they might not come off." Then she laughed. "Guess who's being a baby." She stopped complaining but she was still tense.

Finally, they were in the X-ray room waiting for the surgeon to read the X-rays. When Dr. Stern appeared, he sat on a stool and looked at the X-rays in his hand. "So, Ms. Silver—"

"For God's sake, you've probably seen me buck naked, call me Darcy."

He looked up at her, a little taken aback. Then he smiled. "I was going to say I hadn't seen you naked because they cover patients in the operating room. But, actually, I did see you buck naked because you were broken so badly I needed to check every bone in your body. Darcy." His eyes were twinkling. "Now, the cast on your right arm can come off, but I'm afraid the left arm will need a little more time."

Andrea waited for the temper tantrum, but Darcy just exhaled and smiled. "Any relief you can provide is greatly appreciated. One hand is better than none." She looked at Andrea. "How's that for being grown up?"

"Very mature. And soon you can start to feed yourself."

Darcy grinned. "Unfortunately, my dear doctor, I'm left-handed. So you're stuck with me another couple of weeks."

* * *

Darcy was outraged. "What do you mean straighten it?"

Jean Phillips, the physical therapist Andrea had arranged to be at the house after their appointment with the surgeon, repeated what she'd said. "We'll start by straightening your elbow and then we'll move to rotation and strengthening."

"No way. It's been bent for more than six weeks and now you think I can just straighten it? I'm not even sure the damn thing is really my arm. With all that black fur it looks like they transplanted a monkey's arm when I was in surgery. Besides, it refuses to do what I tell it."

Andrea laughed. "Come on, Darcy, don't get your pressure up. Jean is head of the physical therapy department at the hospital. You can trust her."

Jean moved closer. "I'll straighten it for you. It won't hurt."

"What if it breaks again?"

Jean laughed. "Dr. Stern is one of the top orthopedic surgeons in the country. If he says it's healed, it's healed. This is the next step if you want to get the full use of your arm back." She placed her hands on Darcy's arm. "Close your eyes." She ran her hands up and down Darcy's arm and then gently pushed. "Okay?"

"Is it straight yet?"

"Try to relax." With gentle pressure, Jean straightened the elbow a little bit at a time. "How does that feel?"

Darcy peeked. "You didn't break it."

"Now we'll start working on rotation." She gently rotated the arm left, then right, had Darcy rotate it without a weight, then with a one-pound weight. Finally, she did bicep curls with the weight. "Good work. Now comes the reward." She massaged the arm with lotion. Darcy's eyes were closed but her face showed her pleasure.

"Enough for today. Tomorrow we'll work more on rotation and strengthening. Same time tomorrow?"

"Do I have a choice? Wait. I know. If I want to get better, blah, blah, blah."

Andrea laughed. "Sorry, Jean, I forgot to tell you she's a whiner."

"Am not." Darcy stuck her tongue out. "Na, na, na nah."

* * *

Relaxing in the garden after dinner, Darcy seemed to be enjoying the feel of the air on her arm, lifting it from time to time and flexing her fingers. "This is going to be a long haul, isn't it?"

Andrea looked up from her book. "What do you mean?"

"First this arm, then the left. I see they're going to take a while. And the legs will be harder, right?"

Andrea framed her reply carefully. "Yes. I can't say how long, but it won't be as fast as you want. You have to rebuild muscle in all four limbs and learn to walk again. I know you want to be done with all this, Darcy, but even after the casts are off, it will be a while before you go back to your life."

Darcy reached over and touched Andrea's hand. "You'll stay with me, right?"

Andrea nodded. "See, you're already using that hand. I'll be here until you fire me or I decide you're keeping me around just to torture me."

Darcy smiled. But Andrea wasn't fooled. Darcy was struggling. In Darcy's fantasies, it would all be over once the casts were removed. Now, facing reality, she was slipping into a depression, which was really repressed anger, which meant higher blood pressure. Andrea wondered what she could do to head off the heart-wearing blowup that was sure to come.

Later that night, after she helped Francine get Darcy into bed, Andrea went for a run. It was then that the idea came to her. She would take Darcy to Fire Island to pick up her spirits. And she knew just who to call for help.

She showered and as she slipped into pajamas, she could hear Darcy and Francine chatting away and laughing like old friends. Darcy was taking afternoon naps and the result was that she didn't drop off to sleep at eight thirty or nine anymore and often she and Francine hung out together or watched a movie. Sometimes, like tonight, Andrea wanted to stretch out on the bed with Darcy and hang out with the two of them, but she knew it was up to her to keep things clear, so she controlled herself.

Andrea sat in the chair by the window and called Tori. She explained about the cast coming off and Darcy's feeling of hopelessness. "I'd like to take her to Fire Island. Do you think it's possible?"

"If you say she can go, we'll get her there. She'll be ecstatic. I'm ecstatic. What do I have to do?"

"Right now, I need information. How easy would it be to get the wheelchair on and off the ferry?"

"Just a sec." Andrea could hear her repeat the question to Elle. "Elle thinks it won't be a problem but she's going to check it out as we speak. What else?"

"How easy will it be to get from the ferry to Darcy's house?"

"No problem. All the paths are boardwalks so you can easily wheel her from the dock. And the house has a ramp that was built for her grandparents. It allows wheelchair access to the first and second floors."

"What's the house like?"

"The kitchen, dining room, living room and a bathroom are all on the first floor and the five bedrooms and five baths are on the second floor. Darcy's private suite is connected to the first floor and has a large bedroom, a living room and a huge bathroom with a shower and a whirlpool tub."

"Quite a mansion."

"It is. Her grandparents built it years ago."

"So it sounds like we could easily get her there and into the house. What about the beach?"

"The house is right on the beach, you'd just have to wheel her out to the deck facing the ocean or she could sit by her pool which is on the side deck, if she wanted to do that. Oh, wait." Andrea could hear Elle again in the background. "Elle says there's no problem with the wheelchair on the ferry."

"Is there a restaurant that delivers?"

"How about you take care of getting her there and taking care of her while she's there. I'll take care of meals and wine and beer. You just tell me how many people and how many days and I'll prepare menus and run them by you."

"Oh God, Tori, you are truly a wonderful friend. I'm going to go out on a limb here and invite you and Elle to stay with us."

"Tell me when and we'll be there."

"I think I'd better run this by Darcy rather than try to surprise her. Can I call you tomorrow?"

"Call me anytime, my lovely doctor." Tori had pitched her voice to a sexy whisper.

Andrea laughed. "Christ, Tori, you're as big a flirt as Darcy."

"Just emulating the master." Tori snorted. "But seriously, call me after you discuss it with Darcy. I'm hot to trot, as they say."

Really excited, Andrea bolted from the chair, knocked lightly on the door and walked in. Darcy and Francine looked up. Darcy looked shocked, then she pointed with her newly freed hand. "I'm melting, I'm melting. Look at her, isn't she adorable."

Francine grinned.

Andrea stopped short. What the—? She looked down. Oh shit, she had run in wearing her pajamas, a clingy tank top with no bra under it and skimpy cotton shorts that barely covered her crotch. The blood rushed to her face and she turned to go back and put on some clothes.

Darcy was laughing so hard she could barely talk. "You can't put the genie back in the bottle, my lovely doctor. I've already seen those long shapely legs and those sexy muscled arms, not to mention those voluptuous breasts, so come back here."

Andrea put her hands on her hips and spoke in mock indignation. "What. You thought I didn't have legs and arms or breasts?"

Darcy cracked up again, this time taking Francine with her.

When they slowed down, Andrea tried again. "Okay, you guys, I forgot I had my pajamas on. It's not that funny. And, I think you've been watching too many kiddie movies—no more *Wizard of Oz* or *Aladdin* for you."

Darcy snorted.

"Oh, well, I had an exciting propo—," she glared at the two of them, "—an exciting idea I wanted to share with you, about an outing."

Darcy glanced at Francine. "I'd love to out you." They broke up again.

"Geez, have you two been drinking? I'll be in my room when you're ready."

She turned.

"No wait. I'll be good. And, I'll vouch for Francine as long as she doesn't look at me. What outing?"

Andrea took a breath and walked over to the bed. "Would you like to go to Fire Island for a few days?"

Darcy gasped. And, behind her Francine flashed a thumbs-up sign.

"Can I do that?"

"If you want. But I need your help to plan it."

"Tell me what you need."

"First thing, I need to be able to move you in and out of bed. Can you come, Francine?"

Francine's eyes widened. "Yeah, sure."

Darcy could barely contain her excitement. "And you can bring Jennifer, I've been wanting to meet her."

Andrea frowned. "Who's Jennifer?"

"My wife."

Andrea took a long look at Francine.

Francine scowled. "What?"

"So you're a lesbian too. What a coincidence."

"Wrong." Darcy tossed a pillow at Andrea. "It seems that once again Gerri came through for me. Apparently, she insisted I needed lesbian nurses so I could feel comfortable and if the agency couldn't provide them, she'd find another agency."

Andrea caught the pillow. "Wow, you really do owe Gerri, don't you?"

"I do and I'll find some way to make it up to her. But now that I've outed Francine, what else do we need?"

Andrea placed the pillow on the bed. "I'll rent a wheelchair accessible van to get us to and from the ferry. I've spoken to Tori and it seems there won't be a problem getting to the house and the house itself sounds wheelchair accessible."

"It is. And we can stay in my private suite."

"I'll rent a hospital bed and have it delivered out there—"

Darcy put her hand on Andrea's arm. "Since it's only a few nights, can't I just sleep in my own bed? It's a king with a firm mattress."

"What do you think, Francine? Darcy is basically just in bed to sleep these days and there's not much danger of her rolling over."

Francine nodded slowly as she considered the question. "It'll work. We can put some pillows on her side just to be sure and we can use pillows to hike her up if she wants to sit up in bed."

Darcy's eyes were shining with excitement. "What else?"

"I thought we'd give Maria and Carlo a break, so Tori said she would organize the food and beverages and the cooking and cleaning up. Anything else you can think of?"

"I'll call tomorrow and have the house opened for us."

"I hope it's all right, I invited Tori and Elle to stay with us? Is there anyone else you want to come?"

Darcy grinned. "Let me think about it but I'll invite a couple of others to stay as well. Andrea, my love, if you'd let me, I'd give you a big fat kiss on the lips. This is fabulous."

Andrea was so pleased she'd made Darcy happy she leaned over and kissed her lightly on the lips. "You're welcome."

Darcy beamed. "Oh, I just remembered something important."

"Tell me, I'll add it to the list."

"Please pack those pajamas." She started laughing again.

Andrea lightly smacked Darcy's head. "You are so bad. And, I don't know why you're so excited, you've seen me in running tights."

"Yes, but they cover your legs and I could only imagine your creamy, sensitive upper thighs. And, oh, those breasts. Now I can fantasize about the real thing."

Andrea couldn't control the rush of blood to her face or to her barely covered groin, so she turned to Francine. "Let's start a list of things we need so we don't forget anything."

Darcy grinned. "I love it when you blush, sweet Dr. Trapani."

CHAPTER TWENTY-TWO

It had been a feverish few days, with calls back and forth to Tori, planning meals and making shopping lists. Darcy had invited all of the inner circle, other than Candace, but not all of them could make it on such short notice.

At ten o'clock Friday morning, the van was packed and Darcy was ready to board when Maria and Carlo appeared with a basket between them. Maria had prepared sandwiches for lunch and snacks to hold them until the others arrived with the food later in the day. They hugged Darcy and Andrea, then Jennifer started the lift and Darcy slid into the van. Francine helped Andrea secure the wheelchair, then climbed into the front seat with Jennifer, who had volunteered to drive. Andrea sat next to Darcy. They waved to Maria and Carlo as Jennifer backed out of the driveway.

An hour and forty-five minutes later, Francine and Jennifer saw to the loading of their luggage and packages on the ferry and Andrea wheeled Darcy up the ramp. The forecast predicted an unusually warm weekend and if today was any indication, they'd gotten it right for a change: not a cloud in the sky, the sun brilliant and the temperature somewhere in the low eighties. Damn. She hadn't thought to ask about keeping Darcy out of the sun on the ferry. She hesitated, surveying the seating options on the deck, then smiled. Though the front and rear of the ferry had rows of seats open to the sun, the middle had a roof that provided shade for those seated under it. Great. Getting overheated was the last thing Darcy needed. She wheeled Darcy to the shaded area. Francine and Jennifer checked in with them, then settled in the sunny area up front.

A few minutes later, the ferry pulled away from the pier and headed to Fire Island, throwing back a light spray as it sped through the water. Darcy tilted her head toward Francine and Jennifer who were holding hands, faces to the sun, hair whipping in the breeze. "They look happy, don't they?"

Andrea looked up from unfolding the blanket. "They do. Did you know Jennifer was Chinese-American?"

"Actually, Francine never said, but then, why would she? I mean when we talked, it was about how long they've been together, how they met, Jenny's anger about conditions at work, her quitting and her anxiety about finding another job. That kind of thing."

Andrea considered Francine and Jennifer again. "She doesn't look at all like I imagined."

"She's attractive, isn't she? I got the impression from Francine that she's quite strong-minded. I like that in a woman. And I love that slinky black hair. Imagine how sexy it would feel trailing across your body."

"Better not let Francine hear you fantasizing about her wife."

"Not to worry. Jennifer isn't my type. She doesn't meet my height requirement."

"You have a height requirement?"

"Yup. I like my women on the taller side, somewhere in the vicinity of six feet, give or take a couple of inches. And, since you asked, I generally like larger breasts and a little more meat on their lovely bones."

"Jesus, Darcy, flirting is one thing but you are really piggy sometimes. It makes me uncomfortable."

"Sorry, but it's the truth. And to be really clear, you are definitely my type."

Andrea stared at her, not sure how to respond so she tucked the blanket around Darcy. "Are you warm enough?"

"Yes, sweetie."

Andrea stared into impertinent blue eyes that made the blues of the sea and the sky seem pale in comparison. "What am I going to do with you?"

Darcy smirked. "Well, I—"

"Never mind, *sweetie*." Andrea sat on the bench next to Darcy's wheelchair and closed her eyes, hoping to deflect any other innuendos. The drone of the ferry's engine, the squawk of the seagulls swirling above and the kiss of the damp breeze brought images of Trapani, of lying in the warm sun on a deserted beach with Darcy and—

Darcy's hand covered hers. She opened her eyes. Seeing the love on Darcy's face, her heart filled. They gazed at each other for a few seconds, then Andrea broke the connection rather than give in to the impulse to kiss her.

Darcy's thumb moved in gentle circles over Andrea's hand. "I'd like to apologize for being piggy about Jennifer and for being piggy in general. My only excuse is that I'm trapped in this body with my fantasies and no way to satisfy…no outlet."

"I see." Well, she could certainly sympathize with unsatisfied sexual desires. "But I'd feel more comfortable if you kept those kinds of remarks to yourself."

Darcy nodded. She waited but when nothing else was forthcoming, she went on. "You know, the ferry ride is one of the things I love about Fire Island. The minute you get on the ferry you feel as if you're on vacation."

Darcy's thumb was making it difficult to concentrate so Andrea turned her hand palm up and captured the thumb, squeezing it lightly before letting it go. "What else do you love about Fire Island?"

"No cars allowed, so it's a slower, more relaxed pace. And most of all it means friends, being with friends I care about and who care about me."

"Friends are important, aren't they?"

"For me they are. Feeling abandoned by my friends was a good part of why I was so crazy when you came. I don't know if I'll ever forgive Candace for that."

Andrea could see Darcy turning inward. After all the effort that went into planning this weekend the last thing she wanted was for Darcy to be sad. She needed to bring her back to the weekend. "So tell me who's coming to stay with us."

Darcy looked up. "With us. I like that." She grinned. "You've met everybody. Tori and Elle, Gina and Beth, Maya, Renee, Monica and Lucia. The single ones will sort out their sleeping arrangements."

So, bedrooms for Francine and Jennifer, Tori and Elle, Gina and Beth and then two for the four single women. That's five. No room for her. Darcy had arranged it so she'd have to sleep in her suite. She wasn't sure how she felt about that. Well, maybe if she was honest, she liked it. She was finding it harder and harder to deny her feelings, to be professional.

"We're here." Darcy's voice brought Andrea back. The ferry was docking.

Andrea stood. She hadn't realized that the island was so narrow, from the bay she could see the ocean glistening between the buildings. "Is your house far?"

"Nothing is far. It's on the ocean side, just a short walk from here."

Francine and Jennifer came to help them disembark. Gloria, the woman who looked after Darcy's house, was waiting with two wagons to transport their packages. After Gloria exclaimed over Darcy's condition, Darcy introduced everyone to the thin but muscled woman with smiling brown eyes, straw-like hair and the leathery skin of someone who spent too much time in the sun. With a cigarette dangling out of her mouth, Gloria coughed a phlegmy hello, then piled the packages that Francine and Jennifer had reclaimed from the ferry on the wagons.

Gloria and Jennifer each pulled a wagon, Francine pulled their rolling suitcases, and Andrea pushed Darcy along the boardwalk, past houses of various sizes and designs, some with pools, most with people lounging on decks. Everyone they encountered along the boardwalk was wearing a bathing suit. And almost everyone greeted Darcy, asked what had happened, and chatted and joked with her.

It was slow going and by the time they caught up, Gloria, Francine and Jennifer had carried their things into a large beautiful house at the end of the walk facing the ocean. Andrea paused. "Christ, Darcy, your family was into big houses or should I say mansions."

"Well, my sweet doctor, we are wealthy and in the old days we had a large family and entertained a lot. If you take a walk on the beach and check out the oceanfront houses, you'll see that most of them are in the mansion category. It's what people did in those days."

"It's elegant. I love the wraparound decks on two levels."

"Wait until you see the inside. Wheel me in, please."

Darcy was so excited that Andrea thought she might try flapping her arms and legs to speed them along. She put a hand on Darcy's shoulder. "Relax, I'm pushing."

Gloria was just leaving as they entered the foyer. "I opened all the windows, put clean sheets on all the beds and fresh towels in each of the bathrooms. I also put all the perishables Tori shipped over yesterday in the main refrigerator and filled the drinks refrigerator with the wine and beer she sent. I'll meet Tori's ferry tonight and cart whatever else she's bringing. You know how to find me if you need anything else." She turned back at the screen door. "It's really good to see you, Darcy. I hope you have a fabulous weekend."

Darcy flashed a wicked smile. "I intend to, Gloria."

"By the way, I ran into Candace last night in Cherry Grove. She was surprised to hear you were coming out. Actually, she looked a little pissed. I'm sure you'll hear about it from her."

Darcy frowned. "Pissed drunk or pissed angry?"

"Both, I'd say."

Darcy shook her head. "Not good."

"She's been like that whenever I've seen her lately. Pissed drunk, I mean." Gloria shrugged. "You know the drill. Lock up when you leave and I'll come by on Tuesday to clean. See ya."

Andrea wheeled Darcy into the living room. Francine grinned. "Darcy, I've never seen anything as beautiful as this house."

Andrea stopped, taking in the cathedral ceiling, the floor-to-ceiling windows, the glow of the pale pink walls in the sunlight, the hardwood floor, the huge fireplace, the lovely islands of seating with sofas and love seats and comfortable chairs. "It's gorgeous. But somehow, I feel your grandmother didn't have much to do with the décor."

Darcy laughed. "Correct. I redid it two years ago when I had the suite built. I had the ceiling lifted, the skylights put in, the floors redone, and the walls painted, then I bought all new furniture. This house reflects me, my personality. The house in the city and the one in Italy are untouched. So far."

"It's no wonder you love being here. I could learn to love it in another minute or two if I concentrate on it. What about you, Francine?"

Francine giggled. "Nah, I hate roughing it."

Jennifer called from another room. "Come and check out the kitchen and the dining room, guys. Holy shit, the ocean is right there."

"You can leave me alone for a minute," Darcy said. "Go take a look."

When the three of them had inspected the kitchen, the dining room and the five bedrooms and bathrooms upstairs, they returned to the living room.

Andrea knelt in front of Darcy. "I don't think I've ever been in such a beautiful house in such a beautiful setting. No wonder you miss it."

Darcy met her gaze. "I can't believe I'm here." Her voice cracked. "I felt like I'd never see it again."

"Soon all your casts will be off and you'll be walking." Francine patted her shoulder. "Come on, let's have lunch on the deck. We can settle in later." Francine picked up the basket Maria had packed and carried it out to the deck.

Andrea took a deep breath and got to her feet. "Sounds like a plan." She wheeled Darcy out to the deck.

After lunch, Jennifer volunteered to clean up and Andrea and Francine escorted Darcy into her suite. Francine whistled and twirled around. "More nice, Darcy."

Nice? The suite was fabulous. Both the bedroom and the living room had cathedral ceilings with a floor-to-ceiling glass wall, a combination of windows and sliding glass doors that opened onto a deck facing the ocean. Both rooms were huge; both had glossy wooden floors decorated with colorful rugs, wall hangings and cushions, which made them feel warm and welcoming. The king bed was covered with an exquisite green-gray quilt and matching sheets and pillowcases. The living room furniture was a soft blue-green and seemed perfect for the space. Two easy chairs faced the fireplace.

Andrea moved between the rooms. "Really, Darcy, five bedrooms and six baths weren't enough?"

"I love having people around but I also like my privacy when I want it." Darcy's eyes followed Andrea. "You like?"

"I like. Did you decorate this too?"

"I designed it, had it built and decorated it."

"You're a regular Renaissance woman." An intelligent, creative, and talented woman who has yet to find her place in life despite being generous and beautiful and kind.

Francine slid the doors in the living room open, bringing in a breeze, the sound and smell of the ocean and the muted voices of bathers at the ocean's edge. "You did a fabulous job, Darcy. It's gorgeous here."

Andrea wheeled her into the bedroom. "You ready for that nap? There's going to be a lot of excitement tonight as everyone arrives and a nap will give you the energy to stay awake and enjoy being surrounded by your friends."

"Okay. I really don't want to fall asleep in front of them."

"Francine, after you help me get Darcy into bed, you and Jennifer can claim your bedroom and go frolic on the beach. Or wherever you'd like."

"Beach chairs and umbrellas, beach toys, beach towels and suntan lotion are all in the locked room next to the outdoor showers. The key is hanging in the kitchen near the door. Enjoy."

"Thanks."

Once Darcy was comfortable, Andrea sat on the bed next to her. "So Darcy, I realized on the ferry that all five bedrooms are filled. What did you have in mind for me?"

Darcy had the good grace to look embarrassed. "Since I sleep through the night mostly, I thought we could let Francine and Jennifer have the weekend for themselves." She cleared her throat. "And you could sleep with me." She patted the bed. "After all, it's a king, and it's not like I'm able to roll over so you won't have to worry about me attacking you. And, most important, I've already seen you in your sexy sleeping outfit. What do you think?"

"I'll have to think about it." But she had already made up her mind. She stood to leave the room. "Did you plan this?"

"Um, yes." She blew up, trying to get the hair out of her eyes.

Andrea leaned over and brushed the hair off her face. "You are a devious woman."

"You know you look a little tired yourself. Want to take a nap with me, test it out?"

"You're pushing it now. I planned to nap in the other room with the door open so I could hear you."

"The other side of the bed is so far away you might just as well be in the other room. Come on. You can even leave all your clothes on."

Andrea kicked off her sandals and crawled onto the bed, her back to Darcy so Darcy couldn't see the smile on her face.

An hour later Andrea woke and tiptoed into the living room, leaving the door ajar so she could hear Darcy and look in on her to be sure she was okay. When Francine peeked in forty-five minutes later, Andrea put her finger to her lips to signal her to be quiet.

Francine sat close to Andrea and whispered. "So what's the plan? I figured out a little while ago that everybody has a bedroom but you."

"Devious Darcy at work. She's convinced me to sleep in her bed."

"You don't look too broken up about that. But what about me, I mean my shift, if you're there in bed with her?"

"You and Jennifer are to relax and enjoy yourselves. I'll need you to help move her in and out of the wheelchair and maybe stay with her if I decide to run on the beach, but otherwise I'll handle her."

"That's not fair. Why should you do it all? I'm getting paid to take care of her."

"She wants it this way, Francine, and I'm fine with it. Now that she sleeps through the night, she just needs someone with her if she has a problem. And I'll be right there."

"Wowzer, wait until Jennifer hears she has me for the weekend. Darcy is so generous. And, you're wonderful. You make a great couple. When are you going—"

"Hey what's all that whispering out there? I need a bedpan, then I want to get up. Surely, there's someone available to help me out."

Francine and Andrea exchanged a look. "We're coming," they said, in unison, then burst out laughing.

"You won't be laughing if you don't come right in here with that bedpan."

CHAPTER TWENTY-THREE

Sitting on the deck facing the ocean, waiting for their guests to arrive, Darcy talked nonstop. Finally, Andrea took Darcy's hand and rubbed it gently. "Slow down, sweetie, take a deep breath and try to relax. Your heart's working overtime with all the adrenaline you're pumping."

"Well, my lovely doctor, let me remind you that stroking my hand does not slow my heart down. Maybe if you just held it."

They heard shouting from the kitchen. "Okay, where is she?"

"Tori is here," they said simultaneously.

"We need to drink a toast." Tori dashed out to the deck with a bottle of champagne. Francine and Elle and Jennifer followed bearing glasses. Tori kissed Darcy and Andrea. "Here we go." She pointed the bottle toward the other side of the deck, popped the cork, then filled the glasses.

Darcy was able to hold the glass in her right hand, but the wine sloshed over her hand when she tried to lift it. "Doctor, help."

Andrea grasped Darcy's hand with the glass and raised it.

"To friends." Darcy's voice broke. "And a fun-filled weekend." Andrea moved Darcy's hand with the glass to her mouth. They all drank. "Where are the others?"

"On the next ferry. Elle and I are the A team so we're responsible for dinner tonight. We'd appreciate your help Francine and Jennifer, but Darcy and the lovely Andrea are excused. Oh, I love that shade of pink, Andrea."

The four cooks trooped out to the kitchen, leaving Andrea and Darcy alone. "So what's for dinner tonight, my blushing doctor?"

Andrea looked out at the ocean. "Tori said something about tofu."

"Is she grilling it? I can smell charcoal."

"We didn't discuss the specifics of each dish, just the ingredients."

Elle appeared on the deck with a tray of hors d'oeuvres and two glasses of sparkling water. "Compliments of the chef." She pointed to the tray. "Shaved Parmesan cheese on thinly sliced fennel, grape tomatoes stuffed with goat cheese, bacon-wrapped dates, bruschetta with roasted red pepper and pine nuts, bruschetta with spicy tomato salad and grilled lemon tarragon shrimp on lettuce leaves."

"Thanks Elle. Why only two dates, and, I hate to be a grouch, but where's the wine?"

"Tori said the dates are just for tasting. And you can have wine with dinner."

"These hors d'oeuvres look too damn healthy. I knew I shouldn't have let you talk directly to Tori. You've been brainwashing her, haven't you, my lovely doctor?"

Elle smiled and walked away.

"You have to pace yourself, go easy on the wine and the fatty foods. I'd really rather not be catching vomit all night."

"Some caretaker you are. Would you feed me my bacon-wrapped date, please?"

Andrea moved the date toward Darcy's mouth, then pulled it away at the last minute.

"Hey, behave yourself."

"Don't abuse the hand that feeds you, my dear." She teased Darcy's lips with the date, then popped it into her mouth.

Darcy groaned. "Oh, lord, that's almost better than sex. Remember, I said 'almost.'"

"Did I hear somebody mention sex?" Tori ran out to the deck with the tongs in her hand. "The girls just got in. They went upstairs to unpack and wash up. Dinner will be ready in about forty-five minutes. Go easy on the appetizers."

Andrea bumped Darcy's shoulder with hers. "See. Just what I said."

They sat in companionable silence watching the thundering waves roll in and breathing in the briny smell. From time to time Andrea fed Darcy an hors d'oeuvre and ate one herself.

"Why am I always surprised that healthy food tastes good? These hors d'oeuvres are delicious, even the ones that don't have bacon wrapped around them. I smell steak. Is Tori cooking steak?"

She and Tori had discussed the menu for the weekend, striving for a balance between foods that were usually off limits for Darcy, and tasty healthy options. Tonight was the big treat. "Maybe for them. I specifically requested tofu for you and me."

Darcy was outraged. "You mean I'm going to have to watch them eat steak, while I eat tofu?"

Andrea shrugged. "It's for your own good."

She sniffed. "It smells great. You are one mean bitch."

Maya walked onto the deck, greeted them each with a kiss, then did a soft shoe and sang the invitation to dinner. "Okay, ladies, tofu is coming off the grill, food is on the table. Come and eat."

Andrea released the brakes on the wheelchair, then started moving toward the dining room…"Just leave me here," Darcy moaned. "At least I can enjoy the smell of the steak."

"You have to eat." Andrea pushed her into the dining room. "Come on, at least try it."

The other new arrivals greeted Darcy and Andrea as they entered. Andrea parked the wheelchair at the head of the table and took the chair next to it. Darcy's eyes got huge as Elle served them. Each dish held a small darkly crusted steak, a baked potato and a pile of *broccoli di rape*.

"I knew Tori wouldn't make me eat tofu."

Andrea grinned. "Be honest now. You believed she was cooking tofu for you and me."

"Yes, but I knew the wicked doctor must have cast a spell on her."

Andrea cut Darcy a bite of steak and fed it to her. She chewed slowly, moaning softly. Andrea leaned close and spoke into her ear. "This is a special treat for a special occasion. Tomorrow we go back to healthy."

"Yes, my dear, anything you say, just feed me more steak."

Andrea took a bite of steak. "Tori, this is delicious. You are a fabulous cook."

Tori looked at Darcy. "Doesn't she know?"

Andrea was puzzled. "Know what?"

"Elle and I and Darcy own a restaurant. I'm the chef, Elle is the hostess and business manager, and Darcy—"

"Is the official taster. More steak, please, Doctor. Don't get distracted while you're feeding your best patient."

"Sorry." She cut another piece of steak and put it in Darcy's mouth. "What's it called?"

"Café Bonasola."

"That's one of my favorite restaurants. How did you get away for the weekend?"

"Summer weekends are slow with everybody out of town, so we leave our staff in charge." Elle smiled. "Glad you like it."

Andrea hadn't given a minute's thought to what these women did for a living, now she was curious. "So what does everybody else do? Let's go around the table."

"Private duty nurse," Francine said.

Jennifer hesitated. "Physical therapist but I just quit my job."

Beth was next. "Why?"

"They wanted me to handle four patients an hour which means you can't give any patient adequate time. I've been looking but at my salary a lot of places are mills, like the place I quit."

Beth nodded. "I'm a personal trainer. I have my own gym and trainers working for me."

Beth was the bubbly outgoing one in her relationship with Gina. Andrea had wondered at her high energy and impressively muscled arms. Now she understood.

Beth addressed Jennifer. "You should start a therapy practice, so you can do it the way you think it should be done. If you're interested, we could talk over the weekend."

Jennifer grinned. "That would be great. Thanks."

Andrea watched Tori and Darcy exchange a look. She wondered if Darcy had financed Beth's business as well as Tori's and Lucia's.

Gina cleared her throat. "I'm Senior Vice President for Engineering at IBM."

Andrea glanced at Darcy. She was a different woman surrounded by her friends, sweet and kind and even-tempered. The pride and love on her face was adorable. Wait. Had she just used the word adorable in reference to Darcy?

"I hope you're thinking about how to improve this wheelchair, Gina?"

Gina laughed. "Not my kind of engineering but maybe I can work with Beth and Jennifer to come up with a better design for you, Darce. Think about your wish list."

"Got that all ready, Gina. Legs that work."

Gina pretended to scratch her head. "Not so easy, but we'll work on it after we've had a little more wine." She turned to Maya. "Next."

Maya waited for the laughter to die down. "I'm Vice President of Marketing for J. T. Marks. We deal in fine leather goods, clothes, luggage, etc. So if you need a fine leather whip to keep your patient in line, Doctor, just let me know."

Renee finished chewing before she spoke. "I'm a senior partner in Millford, Cooper and Anderson, Management Consulting." Her voice was deep and although she would never be taken for a man, handsome and sexy, was the best way to describe her. She smiled. "It's nice to be here with you again, Darce."

Darcy blew her a kiss. "I'm glad you could make it, Renee. But no date?"

Renee smirked. "Even God rested, Darce."

Everyone laughed.

"I'm on Wall Street, an investment analyst." Monica sipped her wine.

"I work with clothes." Lucia blushed. "Actually, I'm a designer with my own clothing line. And I just got invited into Saks."

Everyone cheered.

"Thanks." Lucia pointed to Darcy. "Darcy's wearing another one of mine today." She smiled shyly.

"My favorite designer. What a powerhouse group." Darcy smiled at her friends. "But be that as it may, I want my dessert."

Andrea tried to picture each of these women with Darcy. Some like Tori, Gina and Renee she could imagine too well for her liking; others didn't seem to fit at all. But based on Tori's story of getting involved with Darcy, it was clear that Darcy appreciated intelligence above looks, and intelligence was something they all shared, as well as kindness, caring and good humor. Darcy had done well in picking her family.

Tori provided a tiny cookie with ice cream and fresh fruit, which like the rest of the dinner was delicious. After everyone had finished, the cleanup team jumped up to clear the table and clean the kitchen, while the A team relaxed with an after-dinner brandy. Darcy and Andrea passed.

The cleanup crew drifted back one by one as they completed their tasks and the storytelling and the teasing and the laughter started. Andrea noted that Francine and Jennifer felt comfortable enough to join in. Darcy was in her element and presided like the grand dame of the evening, all attention on her. Andrea could see why she loved these friends. They were easy, they were giving, they were unpretentious and they were playful. Just like her.

She glanced at her watch. Almost eleven. Darcy put her hand on Andrea's thigh. "In a little while. I'm still okay."

Andrea nodded. Darcy's hand warmed her thigh, then the warmth seeped through her body. She curtailed the impulse to cover Darcy's hand with her own and focused on the conversation.

Maya was in the middle of an hysterical story about an Olivia cruise she'd taken over the winter when Tori bolted upright and stared over the heads of the women sitting opposite her.

Maya stopped talking and followed Tori's gaze to where Candace stood swaying.

"Well, how 'bout that? All my friends together havin' a great ol' time, but they forgot to invite me." Her speech slurred, her makeup smeared, her hair wild, her clothes wrinkled and dirty, Candace was a far cry from her usual, neatly pulled-together self. She was clearly drunk and had been for a while.

"Yes, Candace, just like you forgot to tell us about Darcy's accident." Rage underscored Tori's words.

"Darcy doesn't need any of you." She stumbled toward Darcy, steadied herself, then drank from the almost empty bottle of scotch she was carrying. "When Gloria told me Darcy was coming, I could hardly believe it, all broken like she is. But here she is, havin' a grand time without a thought for Candace. As usual." She swayed. "I figured that bitch of a doctor she thinks she loves was behind it, and sure enough, there she is sitting at the right hand of the goddess. Ya know, Darcy, I found you a cheaper doctor so you can ditch her. I mean I'm the one who loves you, the only one who truly loves you."

No one said anything.

"Didn't you ever wonder why a 'mergency room doctor was available to come and take care of you? It's because she's probably not a real doctor anymore. After all, can you still be a doctor when you just stand and watch your lover die? No wait, did she kill her? I can't remember."

Andrea spoke softly to Darcy. "I won't listen to this. Francine can bring you in when you're ready." She stood and walked out of the room.

Darcy's voice was low and hard. "How dare you come here drunk again and attack me and my guest? Listen carefully, Candace. We will never be lovers. And whether or not I love Andrea is none of your damn business. Now take your drunken ass and get out of my house. You disgust me. I don't want to see your face again until you're sober and ready to face whatever the hell is going on with you." She turned to her dumbfounded friends. "Would a couple of you take her back to her house, please? And since I'm sure she'll conveniently forget all of this, leave a note on her table telling her I want to see her tomorrow, but only if she's sober."

Beth and Gina jumped up, each took an arm and guided Candace out. Darcy took a deep breath. She looked around. "Where did Andrea go?"

Francine stood. "I think she went to the suite. Should I take you there?"

"Please, Francine." She smiled at her friends. "Thank you for a lovely evening. See you in the morning."

"Do you want the pres—"

"Not tonight, Francine. Hold onto it until tomorrow night."

They found Andrea sitting in the middle of the bed against the headboard, her arms wrapped around her knees. The room was dark and quiet except for the rush of the ocean outside.

"Doctor? Are you okay?" Darcy spoke softly in case Andrea was sleeping.

"I'm fine." She rolled off the bed, turned on the bedside lamp, threw the coverlet and sheet back, then smoothed an absorbent pad in place. "Help me get her into bed, Francine, and I'll take over for the night." She kept her tone brisk, hoping to sidetrack questions.

Francine moved to Darcy's side. "Are you sure?"

"I'm sure." They lifted her onto the bed.

Francine left and Andrea began to undress Darcy.

"Can we talk?"

"Let me get you ready for bed, then we can talk if you'd like."

"I would like." Darcy watched Andrea's face as she stripped her, put her on the bedpan, washed her face and brushed her teeth, but her face gave no clue to what Andrea was feeling. Finally, Darcy was ready. "I'd like to sit up, please."

"Put your arm over my shoulder." Andrea pulled her forward and moved pillows behind her, then pulled her up into a sitting position.

"I'm going to change into pajamas. I'll be right back."

Darcy frowned when Andrea came out of the bathroom. "No cute shorts tonight?"

"Maybe tomorrow night if you're good." She climbed onto the bed, crawled to the middle, and propped herself up on some pillows.

Joking. A good sign.

Andrea hugged a pillow to her chest. "Candace was really hurting tonight. I feel bad for her."

"I'm really worried. I thought the drinking was a one-time thing but given what Gloria said, it's been going on for a while. She needs an intervention, maybe even a stay at an alcoholism treatment center. Would you be willing to help her with that, Doctor?"

"I would, but I may not be the best choice, given how she feels about me. But I know someone, a very good friend of mine, a psychotherapist who could help her. I can call tomorrow to ask if she's willing to see Candace."

"You're something, my dear doctor. Candace dumped on you in public tonight and yet you feel for her and want to help."

"That's me, Dr. Pollyanna."

"Sarcasm will get you nowhere. Even though she was drunk and hurt, Andrea, she had no right to attack you or to reveal things about your private life. You did nothing to deserve that. I have no idea what she was talking about and to be frank, I don't care about what happened in your past. But…it would be good for you to talk about it, I think." She sat quietly, giving Andrea time to consider. "Please talk to me, sweet doctor."

Andrea raised her eyes to look at Darcy. "What can I say?"

"You can tell me what happened."

"I can't talk to you."

"Sure you can, you're not my therapist. Besides we talk all the time, but it's usually me who's talking and you're listening. Move closer. Let me hold your hand while you talk."

Andrea laughed. "I think I'd better stay here."

Darcy wondered whether Andrea was afraid of what she, Darcy, would do if they were close, or what she, Andrea, would do. "When did whatever happened occur?"

"A little over five months ago."

"Were you asked to leave your job?"

"No, I left because I was freaked out. I felt like I'd failed Nora."

"Tell me what happened?"

"I met Nora on a hiking trip. She was nice. We both enjoyed outdoor stuff so we started dating. But I was in love with someone else and my relationship with Nora never went beyond friendship for me. When I saw she was getting serious, I broke it off with her. She hadn't expected it and she kept calling and leaving messages, begging me to give us a chance. A week later, I was on duty in the emergency room and the ambulance brought in four people who had been run down by a taxi on Broadway. One of the residents called me over. 'You've got to see this.' The woman had borne the brunt of the collision. She was covered in blood, her arm had been severed and she had been almost sliced in half by the taxi.

"As I opened my mouth to issue orders, the woman spoke. 'Andrea, honey, I'm so happy you're here. Please hold my hand.' It was Nora. I was working fast and hadn't really looked at the woman, so I hadn't recognized her under all the blood and grime. I took her hand but it was the hand on the severed arm. I froze. Someone put my hand in her attached hand. I could see her lips moving but I couldn't hear what she was saying. I couldn't speak. The interns and residents were calling my name but I couldn't do anything, couldn't think, couldn't order an OR. One of the senior nurses, a friend, ran over to see what was happening. She took it in immediately, pushed me out of the way and began issuing orders: 'Call in Dr. Foster,'—he was the other ER doctor—'Get me an OR,' and so on. Nora died before they could get her to an OR. Later the nurse called my best friend who came and took me to her apartment. I never went back."

"Oh, Andrea, what a horrible thing." Darcy stretched her hand toward Andrea, instinctively wanting to touch her. "Do you feel responsible for her death?"

"I...I feel guilty for breaking up with her and causing her so much pain. But there was no way to save her."

"Knowing and believing are two different things, my sweet doctor. Why haven't you gone back to the ER?"

"I was afraid I would freeze again."

"So that's why you were available to take care of me?"

"Yes. Julie, Dr. Castillo, is my best friend. You needed full-time medical care and she thought it would be a good way for me to ease back into medicine." *She didn't tell me I would fall in love with you.* "So, now you know I'm a lesbian."

"You know, Doctor, I would rather have left it a question than for Candace to cause you to suffer like this."

"It's my own fault. If I didn't still feel guilty about breaking up with Nora, then what Candace said wouldn't have hurt and embarrassed me. It's time to come to grips with it, just as Candace needs to come to grips with the fact you don't love her."

"Are you still in love with that other woman?" Darcy's heart was galloping.

"No. I'm over her."

"As your friend said, we can't control matters of the heart." Darcy smirked. "But of course now that I know you're a member of the tribe, I won't give you any peace."

* * *

Andrea woke first, surprised to find herself lying with her head on Darcy's shoulder and an arm thrown over Darcy's chest. Well, she couldn't blame Darcy for this. She tried to move away without waking her, but Darcy's eyes popped open. "You can sneak away but don't think I didn't notice you sleeping on me all night."

Andrea reddened. "Surely not all night?"

"Pretty much the whole night. And, just so you know, Francine peeked in a little while ago to see if we were up."

"Oh no, my reputation is ruined."

"Actually, your reputation is probably enhanced."

Andrea went into business mode. She'd figure out how to handle this later. "Time to get you washed and dressed. Think about what you want to wear while I get organized." She took a deep breath and faced Darcy. "And I don't want to talk about this right now. Okay?"

Darcy nodded.

When they were ready, she called Francine to help move Darcy. Even if Darcy hadn't told her, Francine's expression made it clear that she knew Andrea had slept with Darcy.

CHAPTER TWENTY-FOUR

Andrea hadn't expected the whole group to wait to have breakfast with Darcy, but the table was set with juice, a bowl of fresh fruit and a basket of freshly baked muffins, and the fragrance of griddling buttermilk pancakes and strong coffee drifted from the kitchen. Elle was banging a gong on the deck as they entered, calling anyone who had wandered down to the beach while waiting for breakfast.

Andrea had decided to explain what Candace was referring to, because it was not at all what she had hinted. So when they sat down for breakfast, she described what had actually happened. To her surprise, the women at the table lined up to hug her and thank her for sharing the truth. She felt as if a weight had been lifted from her shoulders. Darcy sought her hand under the table and smiled into her eyes as Andrea fed her.

Everyone lingered over breakfast, then the women drifted out to the beach and Andrea and Darcy went out to the deck on the ocean side with their books and the iPod. Andrea called Karin. After hearing the story, Karin agreed that Candace seemed to be in serious trouble. She suggested that if Candace hadn't come around by about three, they should find her so Darcy could talk to her and get her to call. Karin would talk to her over the phone and then make herself available to meet with her tomorrow.

"How are you feeling, my dear doctor?"

"Actually, I'm feeling terrific. Thank you, Dr. Darcy, for the therapeutic intervention last night."

Darcy cleared her throat. "Do you think that since we're both doctors and since we've already slept together I might call you Andrea?"

Andrea stared into those deep blue eyes, made bluer by the sky and the ocean, then moved to the soft, loving face, and couldn't deny Darcy that intimacy. Truth be told, it thrilled her to hear Darcy say her name in that sexy voice of hers.

"Well, Dr. Darcy, since you have been calling me Andrea more and more, I feel I might as well act as if I have some power in this decision. You have my permission to call me Andrea. But, just so you don't get a big head, I'm going to ask everyone to call me Andrea as well, unless you object."

Lunch was a fun meal prepared by Maya and Renee. A delicious grilled chicken salad stuffed into avocados, served on a bed of greens, with grilled pineapple and a dab of vanilla ice cream for dessert. Wine, beer, iced tea and lemonade were available.

Darcy looked like she'd won the lottery as Andrea fed her. Andrea was aware of the group studying them, as if trying to discern the difference. Then Tori spoke up. "Andrea, why don't we take turns feeding Darcy so you can rest? Give me her fork."

Darcy put her hand up as if to ward off an attack. "No, no, Andrea, please don't give up my fork. They'll kill me. They'll shovel too much in too fast or too slow. You're the only one who knows my rhythm."

"Ah, so you two have rhythm, is that the difference I see, Darce? Have you two found your groove?"

"Wouldn't you love to know? But just what do you think the Pillsbury Doughgirl could do in bed?"

"Ha, I can think of a few things. Let's see, you have one hand and a mouth and Andrea has two hands and a mouth so—"

Elle put a hand over Tori's mouth. "Enough. Leave them alone."

Everyone laughed.

Andrea blushed and glanced at Francine but she shook her head, indicating she hadn't said anything about finding Andrea curled around Darcy this morning. They just sensed a difference in them. Darcy was ecstatic to confirm she was a lesbian and now she could call her Andrea. On the other hand, Andrea was relaxed and feeling more connected to Darcy and to the others as well after having spilled her dirty little secret.

After Darcy's afternoon nap, they were back on the deck and Andrea was reading to Darcy when Candace showed up. Andrea saw her first. "Hello, Candace."

Candace lowered her eyes. She looked like she hadn't slept, she wore no makeup and she had the shakes. She reeked of cigarettes. "I got your note, Darcy." Her voice trembled.

Darcy nodded. "Andrea, would you give us some privacy please?"

Andrea stood. "I'll be at the other end of the deck. Call if you need me." She slipped the paper with Karin's number into the breast pocket of Darcy's shirt, then gathered their things and left. She sat so she could see the two women but not hear their conversation.

Candace sank into the chair Andrea had vacated. "I'm sorry, Darcy."

"You're smoking again. You only do that when you're desperate. Look at me." Darcy waited until she raised her eyes. "I'm hurt and angry that you never told the inner circle about the accident, that you allowed me to feel abandoned by my friends and completely alone at a time when I was so vulnerable. If it wasn't for our history, I would cut you out of my life without a minute's hesitation."

"I'm—"

Darcy put a hand up. "I'm not done. But we do have a history, little sister, and I'm worried about your state of mind, about your out of control drinking. Mom and Dad would never forgive me if I let you become addicted like your birth parents."

Darcy wiggled the fingers of her hand in her lap. "Now hold my hand and tell me what the fuck is going on with you?"

Candace lowered her head. "I don't know. I feel like I'm going crazy. I don't know what to do, where to turn. I feel all alone. I can't eat or sleep. I wish I were dead." She sobbed.

Darcy squeezed her hand. "I could be here for you, Candy, and our friends too, but you've managed to put all of us into such a rage that we'd rather you just go away. No wonder you feel alone. I think you need professional help." She sat quietly and let Candace sob.

When Candace gained control, Darcy spoke. "Move your chair closer, I have limited flexibility so I need you to help me put my arm over your shoulder." Candace did as asked. She sighed.

"Lucia told me what I said and did last night. I'm so sorry, Darcy."

"I can see you're drinking again. What about drugs?"

"No."

"Not yet, anyway. I know you don't want to be like your parents, Candace, but if you continue down this road, you'll be lost to me, to Maria and Carlo and to our friends. Only you can change direction."

Candace reached up and clutched Darcy's fingers. "But I don't know what to do, Darcy, I don't know how to change direction."

"I have the name and number of a psychotherapist who is willing to help you do that. You just have to call her."

"Do you know this psychotherapist?"

Though she hoped Candace wouldn't reject the therapist because Andrea recommended her, Darcy wouldn't lie. "Andrea recommended her. I don't know her."

"Why would she want to help me after I've been so awful to her?"

"Two reasons. One she knows you're important to me. And, two, believe it or not she sees the real you under all the histrionics and she likes you."

Darcy said a silent prayer waiting for Candace to make the decision.

"You promise you'll be my friend if I do this?"

Darcy kissed her temple. "I promise. If you see this therapist and stick with her, I'll always be your friend."

"Give me the information and I'll call later."

"The number is in my shirt pocket. You can sit here or move over there for some privacy but you need to call her now; she's waiting to speak to you."

"She knows about me?" Candace paled. "What will I say?"

"She knows you need help and even though she doesn't work weekends, she's willing to talk to you as a favor to Andrea. Come on, love, you can do this. I'll be right here if you need me. Take the number."

Candace took the slip of paper and moved to the chair Darcy had indicated. She sat for a minute without doing anything, then glanced at Darcy. Darcy smiled and tilted her head toward the phone in Candace's hand. She dried her eyes with the back of her hand then keyed in the number. Darcy heard her say, "Dr. Simons? This is Candace Matthews." Then Darcy waved Andrea over.

"What do you need?"

"The iPod. Please put the earbuds in and turn it on, I want to give Candace privacy."

"Okay, call me if you need anything else." Andrea walked back to the far side of the deck.

Candace and Dr. Simons spoke for more than an hour. During that time, various women wandered onto the deck and either Darcy or Andrea waved them away.

Candace disconnected and slipped the phone into her pocket. She moved back to the chair next to Darcy.

"So how was it?"

"Intense. But I like her. I'm getting an early ferry tomorrow morning so I can meet her at her office at one. She wants to see me every day next week and we'll figure it out from there. I feel…hopeful. Thank you."

"You really should thank Andrea. She set it up for you."

Candace flushed and shifted in her seat. "How can I face her after the awful things I said?"

"She is the gentlest, most compassionate person I've ever met, Candy. Don't be afraid of her. She forgave you last night. She's sitting right over there."

"Oh, Darce, I'm so sorry I didn't tell the gang about the accident. I didn't mean to hurt you, I just…I just wanted you to myself for once, then I couldn't stand seeing you so helpless."

"What's done is done, Candace. You can only change what you do in the future."

Candace nodded and wiped her eyes. "I guess I owe the gang some apologies too."

"I want you here for dinner tonight so get them out of the way. Will it help if I'm with you?"

"I think so."

"You've got me. But remember to release the brakes on the wheelchair before you start pushing. Who do you want to start with?"

Candace looked uneasy. "Are you sure the doctor will talk to me?"

"Positive. Wheel away."

Andrea watched them approach: Darcy smiling, Candace looking frightened. She hadn't heard her conversation with Karin but over the course of the hour-long phone conversation, she'd seen a physical change in Candace. She was happy for Darcy who she knew would be devastated if anything happened to Candace and thrilled for Candace who really needed someone like Karin to pull her out of her private hell. Candace's voice interrupted her thoughts.

"Dr. Trapani, you must be tired of me apologizing and then insulting you again, but I am truly sorry. I was totally out of line talking about things that had nothing to do with me or the quality of care you've been giving Darcy. I gather I also owe you thanks for the referral to Dr. Simons. I'm going to start seeing her tomorrow and hopefully you won't have to put up with my drunken behavior anymore."

"Please call me Andrea." Andrea took Candace's hand in both hers and looked her in the eye. "As I said the last time, it's the negative impact your behavior has on Darcy's health that I find offensive. You're going to have to prove to me that it won't happen again before I let go of that anger."

Darcy cleared her throat.

Andrea continued. "But I will forgive your self-destructive drunkenness and out of control behavior, if you stick with Dr. Simons. So apology partially accepted. Thanks fully accepted. But I owe you some thanks as well. Having the Nora incident thrown in my face hurt, but it forced me to confront it rather than push it back." She dropped Candace's hand. "You're on the right track with Dr. Simons. Good luck."

Candace straightened. "Thank you for being honest, Andrea."

"Andrea, would you tell whoever is in charge of the kitchen tonight that Candace is staying for dinner? Come on, Candace, we need to get to everyone before dinner. Push."

Andrea did as instructed, then feeling at loose ends without Darcy, she went around to the other side of the deck where Tori and Elle were hanging out. She leaned against the railing holding a glass of wine someone had handed her, ostensibly talking, but her full attention was on tracking Darcy.

Elle suddenly hugged her. "Relax, hon, she's fine. We're all keeping an eye on her."

"It's hard to not feel…responsible." And, maybe she felt a little jealous of the attention Darcy was paying Candace. She knew it was stupid, but still…

Elle exchanged a glance with Tori. "Yeah, responsible. Sure."

Tori put a hand on her shoulder "Don't worry, Andrea, Darcy has never been involved with Candace."

She smiled at the two women and spoke softly. "You think jealous is a better word?"

Tori and Elle enclosed her in a group hug. Tori whispered in her ear. "She's yours for the taking, pretty Andrea."

Candace and Darcy made the rounds. Candace apologized to everyone. Andrea marveled again at the gracious and loving nature of this group of women. Tori, though, laced into Candace, letting her know how hurt and angry she was that Candace had kept her and the rest of the inner circle from Darcy when she was in desperate need of them. To Candace's credit, she listened, cried, then begged forgiveness. Tori glanced at Darcy, who was deep in conversation with Lucia, and accepted Candace's apology.

Then it was dinnertime. Andrea brought Darcy to the table and Darcy invited Candace to sit on her other side. Andrea was aware of Candace watching her feed Darcy, then Darcy spoke. "Okay, ladies, last night you were talking about someone other than Andrea having a go at feeding me, so if Candace promises to do it without making choo-choo or airplane sounds, I'll let her have a go at it now." Darcy put her hand on Andrea's thigh and squeezed gently.

"I don't know, Darce, I'm kind of shaky."

"Give it a try."

Andrea handed over Darcy's fork. "It's easy. Just take a forkful, not too much, and give her time to chew." Candace's hand shook and it took several tries to get the food to Darcy's mouth, but as she became more confident and focused, it went more smoothly.

Although she knew Darcy was trying to reassure Candace about their connection, Andrea still felt left out. But the heat of Darcy's hand on her thigh and the occasional caress of her thumb reassured her.

Darcy entertained them with stories from her and Candace's childhood. Once or twice Candace chimed in with a story about one of their escapades. But then she spoke about how she'd come to live with Darcy's family. "Some of you know the story of my hippie, drug-addicted parents dumping me on the Silvers when Darcy and I were three and a half, but bear with me please."

As she recounted her life story, of the Silvers raising her as their own—even to the point of providing an inheritance—Candace broke down. Renee poured her a glass of water, pulled a chair next to her and held her until she regained control. "There's no way I could ever repay Mom and Dad Silver for everything. They would be horrified that I cut you all off from Darcy when she desperately needed your support. I'm ashamed that I did that and ashamed of my behavior last night." She looked around the table. "Most of you helped me through this the last time, in college. I don't deserve a second chance but please help me again."

Everyone was silent. Then Tori got up and hugged Candace. All their friends followed.

It had occurred to Andrea while Candace was talking that she and Candace not only had had the same childhood—abandoned at three and a half years and taken in by good loving people— but they'd also both clung to impossible loves for years.

Lucia lingered, speaking softly with Candace, then stood. "Sorry to abandon you all, but I'm backed up at the office so I'm going to stay with Candace tonight and go back to the city on the early ferry with her. I'll pack and be right down."

So Darcy had made sure Candace had a babysitter tonight and an escort to get her back to the city for her appointment with Karin.

When Lucia returned, Candace turned to Darcy. Her eyes were puffy but she appeared more at ease. "Thank you for not throwing me out on my ass like I deserve." Candace embraced everyone again, then she and Lucia left.

Maya jumped up. "Wow, that was heavy. Who wants to go dancing and work off some energy?"

"Great idea," Darcy said, "but you have to wait until Francine helps Andrea toss me into bed."

Tori snorted. "Maybe we could all toss you and have an orgy on your bed."

"That's a fabulous idea, Tori, but I'm tired. And at best, I'd lie there like a beached whale and you all would have to service me." Darcy's mouth quirked. "Hmm, maybe that would work after all. What do you think, Andrea?"

"I think it's time for me to get you into bed." She didn't need the hoots and whistles to realize what she'd said. She laughed and shouted over the raucous group. "You all are terrible. I meant to say, it's time for me and Francine to get you into bed." She grabbed the wheelchair. "Come on, Francine, let's get her to bed before these wild women decide to ravage her."

Darcy was laughing as Andrea wheeled her away. "Wait, wait, ravaging sounds good."

CHAPTER TWENTY-FIVE

Finally, it was just the two of them and Darcy let her exhaustion show. Andrea hoped Darcy would go right to sleep, so she was silent as she went through their nightly ritual. Now, lying in bed with the lights off, Andrea thought about the day, about waking up next to Darcy this morning, about feeling jealous when she wasn't the focus of Darcy's attention, about how nice Darcy's hand had felt on her leg.

Suddenly Andrea felt anxious. Could Darcy be in love with Candace? No, that was ridiculous. Darcy loved Candace like a sister. Tori had confirmed Darcy and Candace had never been involved and she'd also said Darcy was hers for the taking. Surely, Tori would know. *Why am I so upset by the idea of Darcy and Candace? Am I in love with Darcy?* Andrea's heart skipped. Yes, she was in love with Darcy and Darcy had made it no secret that she was in love with her. So why didn't she say 'I love you' to Darcy? She couldn't explain it, but right now it seemed safer to keep her feelings quiet.

Damn. Why was her love life so complicated? Twenty years of unrequited love and now something she couldn't even define was keeping her from the one she loved. Andrea groaned.

"Are you okay, Andrea? It sounds like you're in pain."

"What are you doing awake?"

"Just thinking."

"You were wonderful tonight, Darcy. You're very sensitive to people's feelings. Have you ever thought about being a therapist?"

"What do you mean?"

"Everything you did tonight, being beside Candace when she apologized to everyone, asking her to feed you, then talking about how she was a part of your family, helped draw Candace back from wherever she's been, to remind her of her connection to you and her friends. And making sure she had someone with her tonight and someone to insure that she gets to her appointment tomorrow was a stroke of genius."

"She's important to me, Andrea. After her breakdown last night, I realized she was freaked out by the accident, thought she'd lost me, and then couldn't deal with me being a raging lump but didn't want anyone else to be there in her place. Then, when she saw me with you, she knew she'd really lost me."

Andrea's heart soared at Darcy's words. But, she reminded herself, she needed to go slowly.

"I missed you feeding me tonight. With Candace, it was eating. With you, it's…intimate."

Andrea smiled, happy that Darcy couldn't see her in the dark. "Candace did a pretty good job once she got over her nervousness and fell into your rhythm." *But I missed it too.*

"It's not the same. And I spent too much time away from you today. Would you consider getting closer and holding my hand?"

Andrea hesitated. Even friends held hands, though. Besides, she'd already shattered the illusion of professionalism last night. She rolled next to Darcy and searched for her hand under the light blanket. Darcy entwined their fingers.

"When your other cast comes off this week, you'll be able to feed yourself."

"Not right away, right?"

"No, not right away." Andrea squeezed Darcy's hand. "Speaking of that, you need to work on strengthening your right arm and you haven't done any arm exercises since Thursday. What do you think of asking Jennifer to work with you tomorrow?"

"That's a great idea. I was thinking of helping her set up her own therapy center but I'd like to know if she's good before I invest in her."

"Do you put all your friends in business?"

"I have the money. I can't think of a better way to use it than helping the women I care about achieve their dreams."

This time Andrea's groan was internal. *So in addition to being beautiful, intelligent, warm, loving, loyal and sensitive, you're generous. How am I supposed to resist?*

"Try her tomorrow. If you like working with her, you could hire her when the other cast comes off."

"What about Jean?"

"She's seeing you as a favor to me. As head of the department, she doesn't do much therapy these days. If you want to work with Jennifer, I'll ask Jean to do a transition session with her."

"Thank you. Let's see how it goes tomorrow." Darcy fiddled with Andrea's fingers. "And have I thanked you for bringing me to Fire Island? Sometimes I forget that I had a life before the accident. But being here reminded me. And it feels wonderful to be surrounded by so much...I don't know what to call it."

"How about love?"

"Yes, love. And being here with everyone made it easier to deal with Candace. Thank you."

"You're welcome but I just had the idea. The others made it a reality. It's actually been a privilege to spend so much time with your friends, to bask in the warmth of the group. I'm amazed that Francine and Jennifer were accepted into the group so easily."

"I thought they would fit right in. At least, Francine. I didn't know Jennifer but I figured if Francine loved her, she was probably okay. It was you I worried about."

"You thought they wouldn't like me?"

"Not them. You're always so held back, even when we're alone, I was afraid you'd withdraw into your doctor persona and not connect with anyone."

"So how did I do?"

"You relaxed and related like the lovely lezzie you are while still managing to take excellent care of me. Everyone loves you. Nobody as much as me, of course."

Andrea didn't have to see Darcy's face to know she was smiling. "Of course."

"Speaking of that, there's something for you in my night table."

"What is it?"

"You'll have to get up and get it."

Andrea rolled out of bed, put the lamp on, opened the drawer and stared at a ring-sized box wrapped in silver paper. Her blood drained. Damn, she wasn't ready for a ring. She climbed into bed and scooted close to Darcy. "How did this get here?"

"Francine brought it with her." Darcy grinned.

"Darcy, I—"

"Open it." Darcy eyed her tense jaw and pale face, and realized they should have put it in a different shaped box. She touched Andrea's arm. "Don't worry."

Andrea carefully tore the wrapping paper, uncovering a blue Tiffany box. She looked at Darcy, then lifted the cover and removed a green velvet box. She snapped it open and gasped at the sparkling tear-shaped emerald pendant nestled on the black velvet liner. She let her breath out. "It's beautiful."

Darcy grinned. "I'd love to put it on you but you'll have to do it."

Andrea fastened the gold chain around her neck, then got to her knees on the bed to look at herself in the mirror. It was the perfect length.

"It matches your eyes. It looks gorgeous."

Andrea's eyes filled. "Oh, Darcy, I can't—"

"You're absolutely right, you can't refuse a gift."

Andrea leaned over and kissed Darcy. She lingered briefly savoring the taste and softness of Darcy's lips, then pulled back before Darcy could respond. "Thank you, I love it."

Darcy's eyebrows shot up. "Whoa, come back here, I almost missed that. Let me reciprocate."

Andrea laughed. "Only one gift allowed at a time." *Besides, if I really kiss you, I won't be able to stop.* "But tell me why and how you got it?"

"I wanted to give you something beautiful because you've been so good to and for me. Francine made the call to Tiffany and I told my sales representative what I wanted. One night when you went out, the rep came over with a box of possibilities. This one seemed perfect."

Right. The night she went on her date with Denise, Karin and Julie's friend. A nice pediatrician, attractive and, some would say, sexy. She'd enjoyed talking to her but there was no spark between them. And now that she knew what sparks felt like, she wasn't ready to compromise. Midway through dinner Andrea had confessed she'd recently realized she was in love with someone. The woman laughed, relieved it wasn't that Andrea found her boring or unattractive. Andrea reassured her and they went on to have an enjoyable evening and agreed to meet again as friends. "You have a Tiffany sales representative?"

"I do."

"It's so extravagant, Darcy." Andrea fingered the pendant. "I don't know what to say."

"Don't say anything." Darcy moved her hand to Andrea's thigh. "Just kiss me again."

"Uh-uh." *I would love to kiss you again. And, ravage you.*

"No dice?"

"I already kissed you. If I kissed you again, I'd have to ravage you and you'd report me to the group tomorrow."

"What if I promise not to say a word?"

"I think that's a great idea. You need to sleep now." She got up and turned off the lamp, then returned to bed. "Good night,

Darcy." Overcome with feelings she couldn't express, Andrea kept her back to Darcy and faced the sliding glass door to the deck. The pendent was just a token of Darcy's appreciation, wasn't it? So why did it feel more like she'd just gotten engaged? Because that's what she wanted. To be committed to Darcy, to act on her love, to announce it to the world.

"Come closer, Andrea. Can we hold hands and sleep together again?"

Andrea hesitated, then rolled to face Darcy. The light from outside on the grounds flickered as the curtains billowed and she could see flashes of Darcy's face, all sharp angles and shadows except for the glittering sapphire eyes. Darcy looked mysterious and sexy and vulnerable and Andrea had to fight the impulse to kiss her. Instead, she moved closer and took Darcy's hand. "Hush. Go to sleep."

CHAPTER TWENTY-SIX

When Andrea woke, she was on her side facing Darcy, still holding her hand with her other arm draped over Darcy's chest. She listened to Darcy's ragged breathing, felt Darcy's breath on her face and took a minute to consider what she was doing. She opened her eyes. Darcy's face was inches away, her blue eyes searched Andrea's green. Neither spoke.

Andrea willed herself to move but her body had other thoughts. At least if she left her hands where they were, she could keep them from touching Darcy in ways a doctor shouldn't think about. Every nerve in her body was throbbing. And what she saw in Darcy's eyes and the feel of Darcy's erect nipples rubbing against her arm was making it impossible to avoid thinking that way. She didn't move for fear of disturbing the moment and losing the contact.

"So, is this what they call a Boston marriage?" Neither had heard Francine enter the suite and it took them a few seconds to separate and enter the real world. Francine stood, hands on hips, eyes narrowed. "Or was there some ravaging going on here after I left you last night?"

"None of your business," they said simultaneously. "Or anybody else's for that matter," Andrea added.

Francine made a turning-the-key motion at her lips. "Your secret is safe with me. But we've been holding breakfast for you and if you don't get up soon the whole group will be in here wanting to see what's going on."

Andrea rolled over and out of bed. "How about you get started with Darcy while I shower and dress?" She felt Darcy's eyes on her but they needed to cool off. A shower would do it for her. Darcy would have to do with Francine's hands and a little separation.

Francine's hand went to Andrea's neck. "The pendant looks lovely, Andrea."

Andrea reached for the emerald. She'd forgotten it. "Thank you." She flushed. "And, thanks for helping Darcy shop for it." She gathered her clothing and headed into the bathroom. Twenty minutes later, they were at the table and she was feeding Darcy eggs and an occasional bite of waffle. She tried to keep it businesslike but their eyes keep meeting and Darcy had a goofy smile on her face. Andrea knew it wouldn't take Tori long to sniff out the sexual tension in the air so she tried to head it off.

"Jennifer, we were wondering if you could help Darcy with her arm exercises this morning? She hasn't done them since Thursday."

"Love to," Jennifer said, after swallowing.

"Is that a new necklace, Andrea?" Elle pointed to the pendant. "It's beautiful."

"Thank you. "It's a gift from Darcy." She tried for nonchalance but couldn't stop the rush of blood to her face.

Gina smiled. It's perfect for you, Andrea. Impeccable taste as usual, Darce."

Had Darcy given expensive gifts of jewelry to other lovers? Maybe it wasn't so special if she'd given gifts like this to the women in her inner circle when they were lovers. Christ. Other lovers? What was she thinking? She and Darcy weren't lovers.

Darcy put her hand on Andrea's thigh.

Maybe they weren't technically lovers, but after waking and drowning in those eyes Andrea had to admit her connection with Darcy felt intensely sexual and profoundly intimate. It sure felt like they were lovers. Had she ever felt this way with Julie?

As they were eating, Tori cleared her throat, her smile mischievous. "So, as we were saying about ravaging…" She wiggled her eyebrows at Darcy.

"Who was saying? I don't remember any mention of ravaging." Darcy nodded toward her glass of juice and Andrea lifted it to her lips.

"Gee, weren't we just talking about ravaging? Oh, right, that was last night." Tori's glance included the table. "I think there was a lot of ravaging going on around here last night."

"Really?" Darcy tried to keep a straight face. "Speak for yourself, Tori. I wasn't that lucky. No ravaging at all in my bed last night."

Andrea avoided looking at Tori, but didn't miss the smile on Francine's face as she watched Tori and Darcy fence.

"Oh, Darcy, giving lovely ladies gorgeous emerald pendants usually follows ravaging. I'm sure I smell ravaged this morning and it seems to be wafting down from your end of the table."

Darcy started laughing. "Oh, God, Tori, would that you were right. Unfortunately, it's been a very long time since I've been ravaged."

"Hmm, I think I need to have a conversation with Dr. Trapani, who's awfully quiet this morning and looks, I don't know, ravaged."

Andrea burst out laughing. "Given what Darcy just reported, are you insinuating that I ravaged myself?"

The whole table broke into laughter. Tori managed to snort out, "We all do what we have to, Andrea."

Elle punched Tori in the arm. "You are relentless. Leave them alone, you beast."

Tori raised her hands in a helpless gesture. "Just making breakfast conversation."

* * *

Elle sat next to Andrea watching Jennifer work with Darcy. "Tori's in the kitchen where she belongs, preparing breakfast, lunch and dinner for tomorrow so you don't have to think about it. I hope that makes amends for her relentless teasing."

"Actually, the teasing makes me feel part of the group. And, Tori is so witty and funny that it's hard to take offense. Darcy is lucky to have such wonderful friends."

"We're lucky to have Darcy. And I know I speak for the others, we hope you'll consider us your friends as well."

"Thanks, Elle. I do. Especially you and Tori."

After the physical therapy session, Elle and Jennifer drifted out to the kitchen to assist. The others were on the beach. Andrea and Darcy sat in a sunny spot on the deck facing the ocean, enjoying the sunlight and the breeze. Andrea was careful to monitor Darcy's time in the sun to avoid overheating her arm and legs in their casts. A couple more weeks and Darcy would be cast-free. What would she, Andrea, do? About Darcy? About work? About her life?

"Why so quiet? Thinking about your non-ravaging?"

Andrea kicked her cast lightly. "Don't you start." She waved her arm, indicating the beach and the house. "I love it here. I'm savoring it. You're lucky to have this, Darcy."

"I am, aren't I? Share it with me?" Darcy knew she was pushing it. She'd vowed to go as slowly as Andrea needed, and if she doubted they were moving closer, this morning clinched it. But she'd waited so long for the right one and she was impatient. Damn, she didn't want to frighten her away. "I hope Tori's teasing didn't upset you."

She answered the easy question. "No, it didn't upset me at all. She's fun. I enjoy seeing you two together." Her fingers found the pendant. Share it with me felt like a marriage proposal. She wanted to shout yes. Yes, I want you, yes, I want to share your life, yes, I want to be with you forever, but she had vowed to stand back, let things unfold as they may. It was getting harder and harder but she was disciplined, had twenty years' practice, if nothing else. A voice in her head said, oh, was that discipline in bed this morning?

"Tell me about the house, Darcy, I'm curious about this place."

"Well, my grandparents picked the perfect location to build the house. The Pines and Cherry Grove, the epicenter of the gay and lesbian action on Fire Island, are just a short walk," she pointed, "in that direction. The women in the family used to spend the whole summer here and the men came on the weekends."

"Has it changed much?"

"Some. It was originally only the big houses on the beach but over the years, smaller houses have been built. It's pretty exclusive."

Someone banged the gong and the women straggled in from the beach. The air was redolent with coconut oil and almost everyone had that wonderful sun-drenched, bedraggled look of people after a day at the beach. Despite sunburned noses and shoulders, spirits were high as they gathered around the table on the deck to eat the delicious seafood salad prepared by Renee with the assistance of Francine and Maya, who had stepped in for Lucia.

Darcy's phone rang and Andrea held it to her ear. She spoke for a few minutes. "You can turn it off, Andrea." She turned to the group. "Lucia just deposited Candace at Dr. Simons' office and arranged to meet her after the session to hang out and have dinner." Darcy breathed a sigh of relief. "Now it's up to Candace and Dr. Simons."

Darcy napped for an hour after lunch, then they spent the rest of the afternoon socializing on the deck as the women trickled back from the beach to shower and pack to return to the city later.

At five thirty they sat down to the dinner prepared by Tori and her assistants—thinly sliced chicken breast sautéed with marinated artichoke hearts, Greek olives, cherry tomatoes and white wine, accompanied by a quinoa pilaf and broccoli with a lemon butter dressing. With the weekend winding down, Lucia in the city, and Maya having dinner with a woman she'd met last night, the conversation was more low-key than the previous two nights, but still lively and filled with laughter.

Francine and Jennifer volunteered to clean up. Darcy and Andrea walked Tori, Elle, Beth, Gina, Monica and Renee to the dock to catch the seven o'clock ferry. As they waited, Darcy asked Tori, "So how much do I owe you for everything?"

"Nada. The eight of us chipped in to treat you and your medical team." Tori grabbed Darcy's face and kissed her on the lips. "Next time, my sweets, you can share the cost as usual."

"Thanks. I had a wonderful time...even if I didn't get ravaged."

Elle stepped over. "Please don't get her started on that again, Darcy."

There were hugs and kisses all around as the ferry docked and started to board. Tori whispered as she hugged Andrea. "You have my permission to ravage her." Then she followed Elle onto the ferry and waved innocently.

Andrea smiled and shook her head as she waved back.

They watched the ferry pull away then turned toward the house. Except for dealing with Candace, it had been a laughter-filled weekend. Darcy had spent enough time with her friends to reconnect and feel the love and support she had missed because of Candace's jealousy. The next month or so promised to be difficult physically and emotionally and Andrea hoped Darcy's friends and the glimpse of her old life would get her through it without stressing her heart. As they rolled along, Andrea put her hand on Darcy's shoulder. "You all right?"

"Sad they're leaving, happy to have you to myself."

Not quite. When they got back to the house, Francine and Jennifer were sitting on the deck talking. Darcy and Andrea joined them. It was the first time since Friday that the four of them were alone.

Darcy waved her hand at Jennifer and Francine. "So, ladies, did you enjoy yourselves?"

Jennifer and Francine exchanged a look but Jennifer spoke. "I love your friends, Darcy, and I think Francine does too. I'm usually shy in groups, but I felt welcome. And, seen. Everyone was connected and so...kind, so caring. I enjoyed it tremendously. Thank you for including us."

"It's a special group and you two fit right in." Her phone rang. "It's Candace." She addressed Andrea. "Please turn on my speaker phone and move me to the other side of the deck so we can talk privately."

Andrea rejoined Francine and Jennifer. "So what did you two think was the best thing about the weekend?"

"That's easy." Jennifer laughed. "Having my woman to myself in this fabulous place."

"That," Francine giggled, "and I thought Tori's riff on ravaging was hysterical." She looked at Andrea. "I can't thank you enough for doing my job so I could be with Jennifer."

"My pleasure."

"Hey, could someone come and get me?" Darcy called from across the deck.

"Coming." Andrea stood.

"What about you, what did you think was best?"

"Just between us," she said, throwing the words over her shoulder, "being forced to sleep in the room with Darcy."

Darcy was grinning. "Candace is in love with Dr. Simons, couldn't stop talking about her. Dr. Simons said this and Dr. Simons said that. If Lucia wasn't with her, I would have assumed she'd been drinking. One of the many wise things Dr. Simons said is that Candace shouldn't be alone, that she's in a very fragile place and needs someone to watch over her. So Lucia invited her to move in. Temporarily."

"That's wonderful."

"Thanks to you, Andrea, she's found Dr. Simons."

"And, thanks to you, she may have found Lucia."

"Lucia is pretty quiet but I always sensed interest and a spark when Candace was near. It would be great if they connected. Dr. Simons also suggested that Candace call her friends and set up a schedule so she has someone to go with her to two AA meetings every day for the first few weeks."

Jennifer pulled her hair into a ponytail. "Since I'm not working I'm happy to go with her or just be a backup in case she needs someone."

"Great, I'll give her your number. Not to change the subject, Jennifer, but I was wondering if you would consider coming on board as my physical therapist?"

Jennifer glanced at Francine. "Are you kidding? I would love to. But I thought you had a therapist."

"I do, but she only comes as a favor to Andrea. I'll ask her to do a joint session with you to pass the baton, so to speak. Hopefully, my arm cast will come off this week. Andrea tells me that the stronger my arms are, the easier it will be when the leg casts come off. Can you handle legs?"

"Sure. I worked at a veteran's hospital for a couple of years and I got lots of experience with legs. With everything actually. When do we start?"

"Jean is scheduled for the day after tomorrow in the afternoon. If you're free, Andrea will give her a call tomorrow and arrange it."

"Whenever you need me, I'll be there."

"I don't know what we pay Jean but I'll find out. Once we decide on the rate you can talk to Candace about the paperwork."

"Thanks for the opportunity." Jennifer kissed Darcy on the cheek. "And, thanks for the weekend." She took Francine's hand. "I can't remember the last time I enjoyed myself so much."

They chatted some more about the weekend, then Darcy yawned.

"While I'm thinking of it," Andrea said, "I'd like to run on the beach tomorrow morning. Can you come in early to take care of Darcy?"

"Sure. And, since it's our last night, I'd like to take another walk on the beach with Jennifer. What time should I get back to help you into bed, Darcy?"

"If it's all right with Andrea, I'd like to do it now."

"Sure let's go."

CHAPTER TWENTY-SEVEN

Francine poked her head in early to wash and dress Darcy so Andrea could run on the beach while it was still relatively cool. "Don't I get to have an opinion on this? It is my body you two are talking about."

"Come on, grumpy, you and Andrea have been together twenty-four-seven since Friday morning, surely you don't begrudge her an hour to herself."

"Ah, but that's where you're wrong, Francine. I'm an egocentric bitch and twenty-four-seven sounds exactly right to me."

"Yeah, yeah, yeah."

Andrea came out of the bathroom in her running shorts, tank top and sneakers. Darcy whistled softly. "Very nice, my beautiful Andrea."

"Don't be piggy, Darcy."

"Me piggy? I was expressing my appreciation."

"That's what they all say." Interesting. Now that she'd let herself feel her love for Darcy, she wasn't put off by the sexual comments. But the woman did need to control those flip remarks.

"Wave goodbye to the nice doctor and let's get on with your morning ablutions so when she gets back you'll be ready to get in the wheelchair."

Forty-five minutes later, a sweaty Andrea ran on to the deck, surprised to find Darcy already working with Jennifer. "Ah, good, you didn't waste time waiting for me. What smells so good?"

Darcy looked up from her bicep curls. "Francine's baking the vegetarian strata that Tori left us for breakfast. It should be ready in about fifteen minutes."

"God bless Tori. I'm going to jump in the shower. Be out in ten."

Breakfast with just the four of them was relaxed but Andrea missed the animated give-and-take at the weekend meals. Without it, her mind wandered as she fed Darcy and she was overcome with sadness. In a few days, Darcy's arm cast would be gone and not too long after that Darcy would be able to feed herself. Darcy was unusually quiet, maybe thinking the same thoughts, maybe not.

Andrea was aware of Francine's eyes on her. Francine was the only one who knew for sure that she was in love with Darcy and it seemed to puzzle her that Andrea didn't declare herself to Darcy, especially since Darcy made no secret of her feelings for Andrea. She wondered why herself. Yes, professionalism, but she'd gone way beyond those boundaries already, holding hands, sleeping with Darcy. Darcy's vulnerability, yes as well, but in her heart she believed Darcy knew her own feelings and Tori had confirmed them. Fear? Hmm, interesting. She hadn't considered that before. But fear of what? Of loving someone who wanted her? Of letting go of Julie who'd been her ostensible reason for never letting anyone touch her heart. Of loving and losing that love as had happened before. All of the above?

Darcy touched Andrea. "Hey there, dreamy girl, remember me? I'm hungry."

She was holding Darcy's fork in the air but she hadn't moved it close to her mouth. Maybe that's why Francine was staring at her. "Sorry, I seem to have wandered off."

Darcy swallowed. "Dreaming about your girlfriend?"

"As a matter of fact." Andrea knew her smile was mischievous, but she couldn't hide it.

"Oh, ready to share?"

"Not yet." It had occurred to her while she was running that Karin might tell Candace to fight for what she wanted and that Candace would launch a campaign to win Darcy. Andrea resolved to fight for her, aware she needed to figure this out sooner rather than later if she wanted Darcy.

They had a low-key day, talking, enjoying the ocean breezes, reading, doing puzzles and dozing in the fresh air. They caught a late ferry and while Jennifer and Darcy were in a serious discussion about boats, Andrea took the opportunity to tell Francine that she would stay with Darcy tonight and she could have another night off.

"Hey, you're not trying to steal my job, are you?"

Andrea laughed. "Not at all. It'll be late when we get back. I'm sure once we get her into bed, Darcy will go right to sleep. Take the night to get some rest and we'll go back on our regular schedule tomorrow."

"Are you going to sleep with her again?"

"Of course I'll be in her room with her all night."

That's not what I asked, Andrea. Are you going to sleep in that narrow hospital bed with her?"

Andrea blushed. "Busted." *I'm not ready to separate. I love her, want to hold her close forever. And narrow is better, easier to justify sleeping on top of her.*

"Is it all right with Darcy?"

Andrea raised her eyebrows.

"Duh. Of course, Darcy would want you all to herself another night. So when are you going to tell—" Andrea put a finger on Francine's lips to prevent her from asking the question.

"You're right, Andrea, it's none of my business, but you're obviously in love with her and it hurts me to see her yearning for you."

"I'm doing the best I can, Francine." But she needed to figure this out. Why she couldn't say the words but acted as if she'd said them when it pleased her, then pretended she wasn't in love with Darcy.

CHAPTER TWENTY-EIGHT

Since returning from Fire Island two days ago, Darcy and Andrea had existed in a warm bubble of connection, sitting in the garden or in Darcy's room talking, reading, doing a puzzle, listening to music together. They'd interacted with Maria and Carlo and Gregg around meals and Jennifer around physical therapy, then slipped back into their comfortable world.

But Darcy wasn't serene and content this morning. Instead, from the minute she'd opened her eyes Darcy had vacillated between crabbiness and withdrawal. Francine had left a note in the chart for Andrea. *She wouldn't say but I think she's worried about the doctor's appointment today.*

Now, in the examining room waiting for Dr. Stern to review the X-ray of her left arm, Darcy looked miserable. Andrea held her hand and tried to get her to talk about what was bothering her, but she just shook her head.

A grinning Dr. Stern burst into the room. "The arm looks great, Darcy. It'll take a couple of minutes to remove the cast, then you're good to go. Pick up a prescription for therapy at the front desk and I'll see you in two weeks to hopefully get these leg casts off."

Darcy glanced at Andrea but didn't say anything.

The doctor frowned. "Hey, what's this? I thought you'd be ecstatic."

"I am ecstatic, Doctor." Darcy attempted a smile. "In a couple of days I should be able to do most things for myself, right?"

"Yes, if you work the arm in therapy."

Jennifer was sitting in the van outside the doctor's office waiting for them. She jumped out to help Andrea get Darcy into the van but her smile faltered when she noticed Darcy's hunched shoulders and downcast face. Behind Darcy's back, Andrea lifted her shoulders in answer to Jennifer's questioning look.

They drove home in silence. When they rolled Darcy out, she spoke for the first time since leaving the doctor's office. "I'd prefer to start working tomorrow morning, Jennifer, so you don't need to come back after you return the van."

"Are you sure? I could just massage the arm, if you'd like."

Darcy shook her head. "Let's start fresh tomorrow, about eleven."

Andrea took Darcy up to her room, then called down to let Maria know they'd have dinner inside tonight. She sat facing Darcy. "Would you like me to massage your arms?"

Darcy nodded.

Andrea washed her hands, warmed Darcy's lotion between them and gently rubbed the newly freed arm. Darcy closed her eyes.

In a couple of days, Darcy would be able to feed herself, a major milestone in her recovery. But rather than the elation Andrea had expected at this significant progress toward independence, it felt like a loss. She was positive that Darcy's mood had soured because she was anticipating the loss as well. She needed to do something to shift Darcy's mood—and her own, of course. She switched to the other arm and thought about what to do.

Later, after she forked the last of Darcy's dinner into her mouth, Andrea gave her a sip of iced tea, then wiped her lips.

"Would you like to take a long walk with me tomorrow, then have dinner out?"

Darcy's breath caught. "Are you asking me for a date, my lovely Andrea?"

Andrea blushed. "A celebration of sorts. Just the two of us enjoying dinner out."

Andrea considered the unspoken question between them. Well, she'd opened the door and she owed it to Darcy to be honest. "Before you begin to feed yourself."

"Andrea, I…"

"Something wrong, Darcy?"

"Uh, no. Where should we go?"

"It's a surprise."

Jennifer visibly relaxed when she found Darcy smiling and in a better mood the next morning. She used one- and two-pound weights to begin to strengthen and rotate the left arm, then switched to heavier weights for the right. She enjoyed Darcy's obvious pleasure as she massaged both arms at the end of the session. "You're very resilient, Darcy. You'll regain your full strength quickly so by the time the casts come off your legs your arms will be strong enough to support you."

The three of them had lunch together and before leaving Jennifer helped Andrea move Darcy into bed for a nap. At three Gregg and Andrea put her back into the wheelchair and at three thirty Andrea rolled her out to the wheelchair-accessible van waiting in the driveway. She'd already stowed a bag with books, crosswords, the iPod, the bedpan and other necessities. Now she loaded Darcy and strapped her in.

"We need to talk, Andrea."

"Can it wait until we get settled?"

Darcy shrugged.

Andrea focused on driving from the east side to West 68th Street and Riverside Boulevard. It took about twenty minutes and the handicapped license plate allowed her to park at the entrance to Riverside Park. Darcy's eyes lit up when she saw the Hudson River. "I haven't been to Riverside Park in years."

Andrea unloaded them and their bag and wheeled Darcy over to the little street level park. "The path along the water now runs the length of Manhattan. I thought we'd walk uptown for a while then head back here to eat at Pier 1, the outdoor restaurant right below us in the park."

"Sounds good." Darcy pointed to the steep path down to the park. "Are you going to be able to keep my wheelchair from running away down that path?"

"Trust me."

"I do. But it's still scary."

Andrea put her hand on Darcy's shoulder. "If you'd rather, we can sit here and I'll get the food and bring it up."

Darcy covered Andrea's hand. "What's another broken bone or two? Let's go."

They made it down the hill with no problem and headed uptown toward the George Washington Bridge, which seemed to float in the air over the river in the distance.

Darcy relaxed. Being near the water spoke to her soul: the briny smell, the steady rise and fall of the tide, the sound of it. Maybe she was a mermaid, or, more likely, a shark, in a previous life. Whatever the reason, it felt wonderful to be here. She reached back for Andrea's hand and miraculously it was there. Maybe they would be able to maintain the intimacy without her having to be fed for the rest of her life. She certainly didn't want to be in that position.

When they hit the 79th Street Boat Basin, Andrea stopped to rest on a bench. "Have you ever dreamed of living on a boat?"

"A big boat in the tropics, maybe." Darcy stared at the boats bobbing on the water. "Living on a boat in the middle of Manhattan has its appeal, but it would be a mite too claustrophobic for me. Besides, I'll bet it's freezing in the winter."

"Probably. A few boats moor here year-round but most leave when it gets cold." Andrea stood. "Shall we?" She pushed Darcy a little way, then veered right, through a short tunnel and up a steep incline.

"Why are we going here rather than along the water?"

"Did you see the movie, *You've Got Mail*?"

"The one with Tom Hanks and Meg Ryan, about his big bookstore driving her small one out of business?"

"That's the one." She stopped. "These flower gardens are where they meet at the end."

Andrea took a slug of water. "Drink. I don't want you to get dehydrated." As she moved the bottle toward Darcy's mouth, it slipped.

Without thinking, Darcy caught the bottle in her right hand.

Andrea's jaw dropped. They both stared at the water bottle clutched in her right hand.

"You're not left-handed, are you Darcy?"

"That's what I wanted to talk to you about."

"Really? To confess that you lied to me?"

"I didn't mean to. The day the cast came off, you remarked I'd be feeding myself in a couple of days. Smartass that I am, I said I was left-handed as a joke. But once I said it, I realized I didn't want to lose the intimacy of you feeding me." She shrugged. "And it was only for a week or two."

"And all this time you've been pretending?" Andrea wheeled Darcy to a bench facing the garden and sat with the wheelchair at her side. "So this little celebration of ours is kind of a farce, isn't it?" Andrea leaned over, elbows on her knees, head in her hands. "Is this why you were upset yesterday?"

"Yes. I didn't know how to tell you." Darcy put her hand on Andrea's thigh. "I was stupid, but please don't be angry, Andrea. Until the weekend on Fire Island it was the main way we connected and the thought of losing it was scary." Darcy rubbed Andrea's thigh. She flinched but didn't move away. "Please don't punish me for wanting you…needing to be close to you."

Andrea lifted her head and stared straight ahead at the garden. She didn't speak. After what seemed like an eternity, she sighed. "I'm hurt that you lied, that you couldn't just ask for what you wanted."

"Until this weekend when you chose to sleep with me, it seemed you were intent on pushing me away so I went with the lie to stay close."

Andrea nodded, considering what Darcy said. "I'm sorry I've made it difficult for you."

"I'll forgive you, if you forgive me and allow us to have our celebratory dinner."

Andrea turned and met Darcy's eyes. "You're forgiven. I think." She touched Darcy's face. "But no more lies."

Relief flooded Darcy. "No more lies." Fighting the impulse to kiss Andrea she shifted her eyes to the riot of color in the gardens and took a deep breath. "Who are the people digging around in there?"

"Volunteers. They plant and maintain the gardens."

Darcy drank some water. "Is this where you run when you're not living with me?"

"Yes." Andrea looked around with a smile on her face. "It's nice, isn't it?"

"I love running on the beach. This would be a great substitute, if I ever run again."

"You will, Darcy. It's going to take time and hard work and maybe heart surgery before you get there, but with your spirit and a lot of sweat and some pain, I believe you'll run again, wherever you want."

They watched the gardeners for a while. "Do you live near here?"

"Not too far."

"Could I visit your apartment?" Darcy wanted to know as much as possible about Andrea; maybe her apartment would give up some of her secrets.

"Let's see how we feel after dinner. If not tonight, another time."

Hmm. She probably doesn't live with anybody. That's a good sign. "Is it a brownstone?"

"No. One of the Upper West Side prewar buildings. I grew up there and my parents bought it when it converted to condos."

"You live with your parents?"

Andrea laughed. "No. I left New York after high school to go to Harvard. I also went to medical school there, then did my internship and residency in Chicago. Right after I came back to New York about six years ago, they gave me the apartment and moved back to Sicily."

"Were your parents here for work?"

"We came to New York City because my dad was offered a tenured professorship at Columbia University."

Darcy leaned forward, her excitement palpable. "Is your dad Gaetano Trapani?"

"Yes. I wondered if you'd read him."

Darcy was practically levitating out of her wheelchair. "Not only read him, I took classes with him. I have all his books. He's a great historian and a fabulous teacher."

"Do you think he'd remember you?"

Darcy shrugged. "It was a long time ago. He encouraged me to get a PhD but I doubt he'd remember me. Is your mother a professor as well?"

"She's a physician. She gave up practicing medicine to come here with him. But she did medical research and, in fact, invented a number of medical procedures and devices that made her wealthy. More wealthy, actually."

"So you come from money and you're not after mine?"

"No, not your money."

"And medicine is in your veins?"

"Not exactly. I'm adopted so I don't have her blood in my veins, but she is in my heart." Andrea looked at her hands. "I wanted to be like her, make her proud."

"I'll bet you have. So they saw this adorable little thing and plucked you out of the orphanage? How old were you?"

"About three and a half. And it didn't happen that way. My parents were living in Milan but were in Trapani for the holidays. Christmas Eve my mother went to the church of St. Andreas for midnight mass. On the way out, she noticed a woman in a back pew clutching an adorable little girl asleep in her arms. The woman looked so distraught my mom started to approach her but she averted her eyes and made no move to leave as the church emptied so Mom figured the woman was waiting for someone.

"Mom didn't think much about it until she went out for her early morning walk at six thirty the next morning and noticed me asleep on a blanket, on the steps, alone except for a rag doll I was clutching. A small suitcase was next to me. My mom sat nearby waiting for the woman to return so she could give her a piece of her mind but when the little girl woke and started crying for her mama, she figured out I'd been there all night waiting for my birth mother to come back for me. She took me home." Andrea took the bottle of water from Darcy and took a long drink, then handed it back.

"My birth certificate and a note addressed to them was pinned inside my jacket and the same note was in the suitcase along with some pictures of me with my birth mama, her with my birth father, and some clothes.

"The note said she'd had an affair with my father, a married man, while he was in Italy working on a short-term assignment. She found out she was pregnant six weeks after he went home to America but they hadn't exchanged last names or contact information and she didn't have any idea how to find him. Now almost four years later she had cancer and was dying and hoped her daughter would be adopted by Professor and Dr. Trapani. By the time they located her, she was dead."

"Wow, seems like fate."

"The church is right across the street from our *palazzo* so most anyone who found me would probably have brought me to my parents but it did seem serendipitous that it was my mom who found me."

"And is Andrea your birth name?" Darcy wanted to know everything about this woman.

"No. It was Claudia, but they changed it to honor St. Andreas, the patron of the church where I was found."

"Andrea suits you." Darcy was silent for a minute. "Your father is a count or something and the town is named after your family, right?"

"Yes. In fact, my mother is a Trapani, as well. Mom and Dad are second cousins so when they married, they agreed not to have children. Having me dropped into their lives seemed like a miracle to them."

Though her story was well known in Trapani, here in the US only Karin and Julie had heard it. For some reason, she'd never shared it with any of her other American friends or casual lovers, like Nora. And now, here she was babbling to Darcy. But Darcy was special.

"Hey, are you in there?" Darcy tapped lightly on Andrea's head. "I didn't mean to upset you. Come back to me, please."

Andrea smiled. "You didn't upset me. I was just wondering why I told you all that. Only my two best friends know the story."

"Maybe we're getting close? Maybe you love me. Or maybe, you just felt like talking today? We'll never know, but I feel privileged to learn something only people special to you know." Darcy picked up Andrea's hand and kissed her palm. "I like being special to you."

Andrea's body fired up instantaneously. Her feelings were escalating, yet she was unable to say 'I love you.' No wonder Darcy felt she had to lie, she must feel like a yoyo in Andrea's hands. She laughed to cover her feelings and got to her feet. "It's past our dinnertime. Are you getting hungry?"

"Are you afraid of me, Andrea?"

Andrea sat again. "What do you mean?"

"I feel so connected to you. I can't believe you don't feel it too."

"I feel it, Darcy. And, no I'm not afraid of you." *I don't know what I'm afraid of.* She avoided Darcy's eyes. "How about we walk back to the restaurant?"

Darcy studied her for a minute. "Sure. That's why we're here, isn't it?"

Yes. A celebratory dinner to mourn the loss of intimacy through feeding. She found them a table and placed the wheelchair so they were facing the water, then she went up to the counter to select and order their dinners. Mahi-mahi tacos for her, quinoa salad with grilled shrimp for Darcy, two beers.

She brought the beers back and sat with Darcy waiting for the buzzer thing they'd given her to flash so she could pick up their dinners. Darcy enjoyed people watching, making up stories for people she felt were interesting. They both jumped when the thing buzzed. They laughed, and Andrea went to get their dinners.

With all the conversations around them and so many people walking by, it was hard to feel the usual intense connection.

Maybe it was the lie or maybe they'd both already let it go and the eating was just business as usual.

"Andrea?"

Andrea looked at Darcy. "What do you need?"

Darcy held Andrea's eyes, picked up a shrimp with her fingers, and fed it to her.

Andrea felt a surge of warmth, felt as if she was falling into the sapphire-blue eyes, felt surrounded by love.

Darcy touched her face gently. "Am I forgiven?"

She chewed slowly. "Yes."

Darcy smiled and put another shrimp into Andrea's mouth.

As she chewed, Andrea fed Darcy some mahi-mahi.

And so it went. In the midst of hundreds of people, they were alone in an erotic cocoon. Andrea felt as if Darcy was touching her and her body burned with desire.

When they were finished feeding each other, they each dabbed at the other's mouth with their napkins. Darcy took Andrea's hand and kissed her palm, then broke eye contact. They sat holding hands without speaking and stared at the river.

"Time to go home. Francine will be arriving soon." Andrea had planned to use this evening to ease the loss of the intimacy the feeding had provided but somehow, it hadn't been like that. It felt like they'd made love, just the opposite of what she'd meant to happen. Or was it?

"Okay."

Andrea tossed their garbage and gathered their things. She yearned to talk about what had just happened, about her feelings, but once she opened that Pandora's box there would be no going back.

As she knelt to strap Darcy's wheelchair into the van, she looked up and Darcy captured her eyes again. They both leaned forward as if to kiss, then Andrea caught herself and stood. She climbed into the driver's seat and with her back to Darcy said, "Big day tomorrow, you need to go right to bed when we get back." They were quiet on the crosstown trip and Andrea was relieved to see Francine sitting on the front steps waiting for them.

* * *

The inner circle came over the next evening to celebrate the unveiling of Darcy's left arm. Jennifer stayed late and Francine came early for the popping of the champagne.

Andrea circulated and talked with everyone. Darcy was celebrating but despite their outing yesterday was still mourning the loss of what she considered their most intimate connection. Darcy's face lit up when Candace arrived looking considerably better than the last time they'd seen her and they sat holding hands and talking for a long time. Darcy gave Candace her full attention but every once in a while her eyes found Andrea's and held them briefly.

"Jealous?" Andrea jumped. Elle had come up behind her and spoken softly into her ear. Andrea started to deny it, but then shrugged. "Is it so obvious?"

"To everyone but Darcy. She's still not sure. What's the problem, Andrea? A wife and four kids somewhere? A girlfriend? Or, I don't know, you just hate nice, beautiful, intelligent, wealthy dykes?"

Andrea smiled. "What if I hurt her, Elle?"

Elle studied her. "What if she hurts you? There's always that risk when you love someone." Elle put an arm over Andrea's shoulders. "Trust your heart, Andrea, and get your mind out of the way. She's worth it." Elle kissed her cheek. "And you two are wonderful together. Call me if you want to talk, but right now I think she needs you."

Andrea followed Elle's nod. Darcy was staring at the two of them. Andrea smiled and mouthed, "Coming."

"Enjoying your party?"

"Sorta."

"Are you tired?"

"Sorta."

"Feeling decisive tonight?"

"Sorta."

Andrea bent and looked into her eyes. "Sorta, doesn't sound like the Darcy I know. What can I do for you, sweetie?"

Darcy closed her eyes. "Stay with me."

Andrea was afraid to ask whether she meant now or forever, so she pulled a chair over and sat. Darcy put her hand on Andrea's arm. As always, Darcy's touch set her on fire. Why didn't she just tell her? God help her, she was giving Darcy such mixed signals that she probably had no idea what to make of her. It was time to talk to Karin, to try to cut through the shit in her head.

CHAPTER TWENTY-NINE

While Darcy was napping the next afternoon, Andrea took a deep breath and made the call. "Karin, I need help sorting out my feelings. I want to schedule an appointment to see you."

Karin was silent. "You know, Andrea, if I see you as a client it's going to screw up our friendship and I don't want that."

"I don't either but you're the best person I know, the best therapist."

"Tell you what. Let's meet and talk as friends in that fabulous garden I've heard so much about from Julie. If you need someone beyond that, I'll refer you to a therapist I trust. If that's okay, I can be there by nine thirty this evening."

* * *

Andrea led Karin through the house and into the garden. She'd picked up a bottle of sauvignon blanc and two glasses in the kitchen, and after they strolled through the garden, they sat side by side on a bench sipping the chilled wine.

"Ah, this is so much better than sitting in my office." Karin tipped her glass toward Andrea. "So, what's up?"

"I'm in love with Darcy."

"And?"

"I can't bring myself to tell her. I move toward her but as soon as I start to feel loving, I pull back. I'm making the two of us crazy. In the beginning I convinced myself that Darcy didn't know what she was feeling, that it was because she was vulnerable and needy. Now I feel if she knew I loved her, she would disappear."

Karin sipped her wine. "Do you think you deserve to be loved?"

"Of course." Andrea looked away. "Maybe."

Karin touched Andrea's arm. "As I recall, when you were a little over three you spent all night alone on the steps of the cathedral waiting for your birth mother to come for you."

Andrea stood and faced Karin. "What has that got to do—"

Karin raised a hand to cut her off, then patted the bench next to her. Andrea sat again. "When you're three, Andrea, and you cry for your mommy for hours in the dark and cold, and she doesn't come, it's a life-changing experience that makes it hard to believe that anyone will ever be there for you."

"But that was thirty-eight years ago and I was lucky to be adopted by wonderful people who I love and who love me with all their hearts."

Karin nodded. "But other than them? You've only let yourself love Julie. Yes?"

"Yes."

"And you've loved Julie since you met her, but she didn't love you, at least not in the way that you wanted. True?"

"Did Julie tell you I continued to love her even after she broke up with me?"

"No, honey, I told her." Karin took Andrea's hand. "I only bring it up because you waited almost twenty years for Julie to come back and you didn't let yourself love anyone else or let anyone close enough to love you."

"I never expected Julie to leave you."

"We're not talking reality here, Andrea. That three-year-old is alive and well inside you and she knows when you love someone, they abandon you. That's what your birth mother did. And that's what Julie did. You opened your heart and let her in and she left you. And until Darcy, three-year-old Andrea was waiting for her to come back. It's hard for three-year-old Andrea to believe Darcy will love her and not abandon her."

Andrea sobbed. Karin pulled her close and held her until she caught her breath. "This is a good thing, Andrea. Confronting these feelings, of expecting to be left, of not trusting that anyone will be there when you call, will enable you to begin to put them behind you."

Andrea pulled back from Karin to see her face. "I don't understand. My parents loved, love me."

"I've seen you with them. They adore you. But that three-year-old inside knows when you love someone they abandon you."

"You think that's why I move close to Darcy then pull away?'

"What do you think?"

Andrea wiped her eyes on her sleeve. She nodded. "But how do I change the way I feel?"

"Do you think Darcy loves you?"

"She thinks she does. Her friends think so. Francine thinks so."

"And what do you think?"

"I think she loves me."

"Good." Karin smiled. "Opening your heart, putting your feelings out there, is always a risk because you never truly know what the other person feels. You could get hurt if you declare yourself and Darcy doesn't feel the same way. Only you can decide, Andrea, but if you don't risk it you'll always be that three-year-old waiting for your mommy to come back for you."

"Do you think I need to see a therapist?"

"I'll leave that up to you. I'd be happy to recommend someone if you'd like. Think about it. We can meet again to talk, if you want. But I'd better go, I have a long day tomorrow."

"Come upstairs with me before you leave. I have a couple of books I think you and Julie will enjoy."

Andrea didn't turn on the light in the room because she'd left the connecting door to Darcy's room open earlier, but there was enough light from the full moon and the nightlight in Darcy's room to see the package. Karin followed her in. Andrea turned to Karin and hugged her tightly. She spoke softly so she wouldn't wake Darcy. "Thank you so much for tonight and for being there for me all these years, Karin." She kissed Karin lightly on the lips, then leaned back. "I don't know what I would have done without you and Julie." Karin brushed Andrea's lips with hers. "That's what friends are for, hon. Now, I really have to go. Give me the package and get me out of here before we wake your patient."

* * *

Darcy opened her eyes at the whispering. She blinked. She could see Andrea in the mirror, in her bedroom kissing a small woman with flowing blond hair. She must be dreaming. She blinked again. No, she wasn't asleep. Now the woman kissed Andrea. *So she has a girlfriend.* That's why she'd been jerking her around, teasing, flirting, coming close, then pulling away.

Darcy moaned softly but not so softly that Francine didn't hear. Francine stood and put her knitting down. Darcy closed her eyes and felt the air shift as Francine passed her. When she opened her eyes again the door was closed. She wondered whether they were in there having sex, but then she heard the creak of the elevator going down. The woman must be leaving. Maybe they'd already had sex while she was sleeping.

She lay there in pained silence. She'd been sure that Andrea was attracted to her, if not in love with her, but she'd sworn not to pursue Andrea if she was in a relationship. It would be too painful seeing her every day knowing there was no hope. And, how embarrassing that she'd told all her friends she was in love with Andrea and they would be together. She would stay cool and not let on that she knew, but as soon as she could, she would ease Andrea out. Chalk up another failure for Ms. Darcy Silver, world's biggest fuck-up.

CHAPTER THIRTY

Andrea dashed out of Central Park and ran toward the house, bemoaning the loss of the sense of peace and calm that running used to bring. Nowadays rather than clearing her mind, it left her brain free to obsess about Darcy's thrusting her aside and anticipate another lonely day filled with tension and angst. For the thousandth time in the last two weeks she tried to figure out what had changed between her and Darcy. It was as if the minute she decided to tell Darcy she was in love with her, she'd pulled away and had continued to be distant. When Darcy was like that, there was no talking to her.

They were rarely alone anymore. Darcy's days and evenings were crowded with visits from the inner circle and other friends Andrea hadn't met before. Almost every morning and afternoon one or more women appeared to discuss books or politics or music, and almost every day there were guests for lunch and dinner. What really hurt was that Darcy subtly excluded her so that she ate alone or sat off to the side like the hired help she was. In the little time they spent by themselves, Darcy listened to music or read a book. When Andrea tried to talk about it,

Darcy cut her off, saying she wasn't feeling so vulnerable and needy anymore and Andrea must be reacting to her feeling stronger and more independent. How could she argue with that? Hadn't she been the one to say that Darcy's feelings for her weren't real? Yet, she felt sure that wasn't true but really she had no idea what the truth was.

Karin encouraged her to declare her love to Darcy, pointing out that otherwise she was condemning herself to the same unrequited love she'd suffered with Julie. But Darcy had indicated clearly that she wasn't interested in hearing what Andrea had to say and became cruel and cutting whenever Andrea tried to broach the subject.

Today was the big day. Unless there was some unforeseen problem, Darcy would be cast-free and the hard work of strengthening her legs and learning to walk again would begin. She'd promised Darcy she would stay until she didn't need her or she fired her. She would give it another few days but this hostile environment was too painful and if nothing changed, she'd leave.

Andrea showered and dressed, took a deep breath, then knocked and walked into Darcy's room. For the last two weeks, Francine had been washing and dressing Darcy and now that her arms were stronger, she needed only one person to move her, so she was already in the wheelchair. Andrea told herself it made more sense for Francine to wash and dress her because Francine was a nurse. But she knew it had nothing to do with more sense and everything to do with Darcy pushing her away. "Good morning, ladies." It was becoming more and more difficult to remain upbeat.

Darcy cleared her throat. "Since Jennifer's the one who's going to woman-handle my legs once the casts come off, I've asked her to go with me to Dr. Stern's office this morning. You're welcome to come or stay here, if you prefer."

"I'm going to run along now. See you two tonight. Good luck today, Darcy." Francine ducked out.

Darcy's words sliced through Andrea. Struggling for control, she turned to look at the chart. Francine had left a note:

Andrea, what the hell is going on. Darcy's not sleeping and if she does drop off she wakes up crying. She doesn't talk to Jennifer and she barely talks to me. She won't say what's wrong. Have you two had a fight?

She added a note to the chart for Francine.

She won't talk to me either. I wish I knew what was going on. If things don't get better in a couple of days, I'll leave.

Then she turned her attention to the numbers. Darcy's pressure had been creeping back up. She took a breath. "Your pressure is higher again this morning. I'd like to listen to your heart." Without waiting for approval, she lifted Darcy's blouse and put the stethoscope over her heart. She felt Darcy's breath on her face and inhaled her spicy fragrance. If only she could see what was in this heart. Very sluggish. She would have to let Julie know. She avoided Darcy's eyes as she straightened up. "Not so good, Darcy. I think the blockage is worse." Her eyes went to the birds flying in and out of the feeders Carlo had finally gotten someone to hang outside the windows several weeks ago, then she turned to face Darcy. "Would you rather I didn't come with you this morning?"

Darcy shrugged. "Totally up to you."

"Please tell me what's wrong, Darcy? Did I do something to hurt you? What's happened to us?"

Darcy laughed. "Us?"

Andrea recognized that harsh laugh, that anger pushing away hurt laugh. "Yes, us."

Darcy's lip curled into a snarl. "There is no us. I've told you, just as you predicted, as soon as I felt stronger and more independent, I realized I wasn't in love with you. It was all an illusion."

"I don't believe you."

Darcy avoided her eyes. "Too bad. I guess it's nice to feel wanted, huh? You know, I've been thinking that Francine could do what you do and cheaper too. So maybe it's time I let you go." She laughed, that harsh sound again. "What is it you said? Oh, right, you would stay until I was strong or I fired you."

"You want me to leave?" Andrea fingered the emerald pendant she wore under her shirt.

Darcy's eyes sparked. "It's time, don't you think?"

"No. But you've become hateful and the atmosphere is toxic so maybe it is time. Would it be all right if I come to Dr. Stern's office with you and then leave?"

"I'm not that independent yet. Could you stay until Francine comes back tonight? I'll give her a call later and make sure she and Jennifer are willing to move in for a few weeks."

"Whatever you want, Darcy. I won't leave until I'm sure you have somebody with you. Oh, there's the breakfast cart. Do you want me to eat in the other room? I'll leave the door open." Andrea needed to escape. She couldn't believe this was happening.

Darcy flashed her killer smile. "No, let's have our meals together today, if that's okay."

Andrea's heart leapt at the sight of that smile. Maybe she'd change her mind.

CHAPTER THIRTY-ONE

What should have been a day of celebration was depressing and sad. The X-rays looked good and the casts came off. Darcy insisted on trying to stand and got quiet when her legs couldn't hold her. She looked away as Andrea tried to comfort her, to explain that it would take time. When Darcy reached for Jennifer's hand, Andrea struggled to keep from breaking down.

The three of them were eating lunch in the garden when Darcy told Jennifer that Andrea was leaving and she hoped she and Francine would move in until she was back on her feet.

Jennifer paled. "Why—"

Darcy put her hand up. "It's time, that's why."

Jennifer's head swiveled between Darcy and Andrea trying to understand what was going on. The ensuing silence was rife with tension and they avoided looking at each other. Jennifer excused herself to go to the bathroom. When she returned, the three of them went upstairs so Jennifer could begin working on Darcy's legs. This time there was no joking as Jennifer gently manipulated Darcy's knees to bend them. Darcy moaned and looked ready to cry. Andrea longed to comfort her but feared she'd be attacked if she dared offer encouragement, so she miserably watched Darcy miserably endure the therapy, which a totally confused Jennifer miserably performed. All three sighed with relief at the end of the session. Jennifer departed immediately.

Andrea and Darcy were in the garden not relating at all when Francine called. Darcy told her Andrea was leaving and asked if she and Jennifer could move in for a few weeks. There was a long discussion with Darcy grunting 'yes,' 'no,' 'okay,' 'I'll ask,' then she hung up. She stared at Andrea for a minute. "They need a couple of days to get things together before they can move in. Are you able to stay or should I call the agency?"

Andrea considered saying 'fuck you,' but really she didn't want to leave without trying to straighten this out with Darcy. "I'll stay as long as you want me."

They ate dinner in morose silence. Andrea stacked the dishes on the cart and wheeled it into the kitchen. When she returned to the garden, Darcy spoke. "Dr. Trapani, would you mind helping me get ready for bed? Francine can't get here until eleven tonight."

"Certainly, if you like." She used her doctor voice and her doctor face to cover her pain.

Darcy nodded and looked away.

At nine thirty, she wheeled Darcy upstairs. The ritual that used to feel connected and pleasurable was now painful for Andrea. Not only was Darcy much more independent, but she was also cold and distant. Helping Darcy with the most intimate things, Andrea felt invisible, unseen, as if she was a servant and of no consequence. The loss was devastating. Using the nightlight, Andrea made notes in the chart. Darcy's blood pressure was higher again tonight and her heart continued to sound labored.

"Dr. Trapani?"

There it was again, back to being formal, no teasing, no flirting, just someone to make life easier for her.

"Please sit with me until Francine gets here. I'm used to having someone with me."

"Sure." *But I feel so alone sitting near you, unable to touch you.*

"Not behind me, next to the bed where I can see you."

Andrea moved her chair around to the side of the bed and faced Darcy. It was difficult to see in the dim light of the nightlight but she thought Darcy was staring at her.

"Thank you. We had a good time while it lasted, didn't we?"

"Yes, but—"

"Please...Dr. Trapani, I can't explain it any better than I have."

She sounded so bereft Andrea was ready to forgive all but there'd been no mention of wanting her to stay. So be it. She'd get through these next few days the best she could and then move on. The best she could.

Darcy's breathing deepened into sleep, though it was ragged, as if her heart was working hard. She woke once and cried out. "Andrea, please." Andrea put a hand on her chest. "I'm here, Darcy." Her eyes opened. Andrea caressed her face. "It's only a dream, sweetie, relax and try to sleep." Darcy closed her eyes and in a few minutes was asleep again.

Around eleven, Francine beckoned her out into the hall.

"Is Darcy out of her freaking mind? How can you leave?"

"To be frank, I can't tolerate this toxic atmosphere much longer." Andrea raised her shoulders. "Besides, she wants me to go. She said you can do what I do so she doesn't need me anymore. You *can* do what I'm doing for sure, but there's something she's not saying. She seems to be struggling."

"You think maybe her brain isn't getting enough oxygen because her heart is not pumping enough?"

Andrea shook her head. "I don't know."

"I told her we need a couple of days. I'm hoping that's enough time for you to knock some sense into her."

"How did you know?"

"Jennifer called me from the bathroom after Darcy told her."

Andrea hugged Francine. "You guys are the best. I doubt I can change her mind but I'll try."

They both turned at the sound of Darcy moaning.

"She's been like this every night for the last couple of weeks. In an hour or two she'll be unable to fall back to sleep."

"Go to her, Francine."

Andrea stood in the doorway where Darcy couldn't see her. Francine sat on the bed and took Darcy in her arms. "It's all right, honey, it's just a bad dream."

"Where's Andrea?"

"In her room. I'll get her."

"No, don't wake her."

"You agreed I could use my judgment about whether to call her when you're feeling bad. And, I'm going to do that now."

"No, Francine, please don't. It will only make it worse." She broke down.

"Make what worse?" Francine held her. "Talk to me, baby. Nothing is so bad it can't be fixed."

"Please come to live with me, Francine. I can't have Andrea."

Darcy was in pain and she was part of whatever was causing it. The last thing Andrea wanted was to be a source of pain for the woman she loved. As soon as Francine settled Darcy down, she would ask her to wrap things up and move in.

Later that night, she convinced Francine it would be better for Darcy if she left. They agreed she would call Julie in the morning and tell her Francine would be taking over as of the day after tomorrow. Andrea would work tomorrow day and also take Francine's night shift. The next morning, Francine and Jennifer would move in and Andrea would move out.

Andrea spent the night listening to Darcy wake up time after time sobbing or screaming and the murmur of Francine comforting her. From time to time, Andrea dozed but she woke each time Darcy did, feeling her pain and her own pain at the loss of the one she loved. Again.

CHAPTER THIRTY-TWO

After she showered and dressed the next morning, she and Francine told Darcy the plan they had worked out. Pale and drawn, Darcy looked ready to snap. She didn't speak, just nodded. After Francine left, Andrea read the note she'd left in the chart:

She's been awake since four a.m. She's killing herself.

Andrea wrote a note that Francine would see in the morning:

Francine, call Tori and Elle and tell them what's happening. They need to intervene, try to figure out what's going on with her. ASAP.

"You had a rough night, I hear." Andrea sat facing Darcy over breakfast. Both their trays contained croissants.

"I guess."

"Hmm, Maria seems to have gotten our breakfast order mixed up. I'm going to call her and ask for cereal and fruit. Would you like some or are you going to eat that?"

"I'll eat this."

Andrea nodded but walked over to the intercom to ask Maria to send up cereal and fruit for her. While she waited, she watched Darcy pick at her croissant. "Can I convince you to not go back to eating badly?"

Darcy smirked. "What do you care?"

Andrea flipped. "What do you mean what do I care? I care a lot and if you can't see that you're fucking blind and full of self-pity and whatever bullshit has gotten into you these past few weeks. I can't stand to see you like this. What can I do? Tell me what you want?" She was so angry, so frustrated.

"The plan you and Francine worked out is what I want. Francine and Jennifer move in tomorrow morning and you go back to your real life instead of wasting your talents caring for me." She took a bite of her croissant. "By the way, you really shouldn't talk to your employer that way."

"Go fuck yourself, Darcy." Andrea walked into her room, leaving the door open and Darcy to her breakfast. She sat in the chair by the window and glanced at the mirror opposite. Darcy was watching her. She picked up a book and read the same paragraph over and over.

Maria walked into Darcy's room and kissed her. She glanced at Andrea, then spoke to Darcy. Francine had probably told her. Although their voices were low, she could see that Maria was agitated, talking a lot with her hands. After a few minutes, Maria stormed out shaking her head. Darcy reached for a tissue and dabbed her eyes, then looked in the mirror. Despite her anger, when their eyes connected, Andrea felt the usual jolt.

When Jennifer arrived, she spoke to Darcy, then moved into the doorway of Andrea's room. "Andrea, could you come down to the garden in about an hour and a half, to help me with Darcy's therapy? It will be safer with two of us holding her when she stands."

Darcy spoke from the other room. "I'd like her to come now."

"Of course." She took the banana off the tray that Gregg had brought up for her and followed them to the elevator.

Jennifer had created a therapy area under a tent in the garden with a massage table, weights and other equipment. Now she'd added portable six-foot long parallel bars to help Darcy support herself as she learned to walk again.

Jennifer started with a half-hour massage then a half-hour of strengthening exercises like leg lifts and marching in a seated position. The three of them barely spoke. After a half-hour of rest, Jennifer encouraged her to use her arms to push herself up as close to standing as she could. They lowered her into the wheelchair, let her rest and then repeated the exercise. Each time they did it, they let Darcy take more of her own weight. After a few times, Jennifer said it was time to rest, but Darcy insisted she could go on. Finally, pale and sweating, she teetered toward Andrea and collapsed into her arms. Andrea held her close, inhaling her sweat laced with her perfume. Except for last night, they hadn't touched in weeks and she could have held her forever. But Darcy was wheezing so she eased her into the wheelchair. Without giving her an option, she wheeled her to the elevator and with Jennifer's assistance put her in bed. Darcy watched Andrea move around the room, then drifted off to sleep.

When Jennifer came back to see how Darcy was doing, Andrea waved her out to the hall. Jennifer's eyes were huge. "I don't understand why she's doing this to you."

Andrea hugged Jennifer. "Neither do I, but she is, so all we can do is go on from here. In any case, she's had more than enough for today. Why don't you go home? If she asks, I'll tell her you went home to help Francine get ready for the move."

Andrea sat watching Darcy sleep, wondering how they'd come to this place. She knew Francine and Jennifer would take good care of her, but she wanted to be the one beside her as she got back on her feet, and for the rest of their lives. When a sob nearly escaped, she got up and washed her face. Enough wallowing.

She sat again, and lulled by Darcy's ragged breathing, dozed off. When she woke, Darcy was staring at her. They gazed at each other for a long time, before Darcy spoke. "Did I do all right, Doctor?" The familiar lopsided grin tugged at Andrea's heart.

"You did great, Darcy. It won't be long before you're walking. But you need to be careful. Don't do too much too soon."

"Still worried about me despite," her voice broke, she turned away, "despite everything."

"Not despite, Darcy. Because of everything." Andrea spoke softly, "Darcy, can't we—"

"Oh, well, I guess that's what I pay you the big bucks for, isn't it Dr. Trapani?" The bitterness and anger were back.

Andrea tensed. She knew it came out of fear and loss but she hated the cruel part of Darcy. When Carlo brought their lunches, he looked from one to the other. "Everything okay?"

"*Si, zio*, everything is peachy. But I'm not hungry so you can take my tray away."

"Leave it, Carlo," Andrea commanded.

He looked at Andrea and nodded. "I take it later if you don't finish. I see you later, *cara*."

"You going to eat two lunches?" Darcy's smirk was mocking. "Stocking up."

"No, my dear Ms. Silver. As long as you pay me to take care of you, you will eat. Even if I have to force feed you."

"Is that a threat?"

"A promise. Now, you get to pick whether you eat in the bed, the recliner, or the wheelchair." Andrea stood, hands on hips and waited. "If you don't choose, I will."

"Well, well, Mistress Trapani. Do you have a nice nippy leather whip hidden somewhere?"

"Maybe. Where?"

"Bed."

She raised the hospital bed so Darcy was sitting up, then pushed the bed tray close. "Eat."

"Or what? You'll feed me?"

"Is that what you'd like?"

Darcy lifted her shoulders. She looked out the window at the birds swooping to and from the feeders.

Andrea pushed her own tray aside and scooted closer to the bed. She tucked Darcy's napkin under her chin and swung the tray over so she could cut the sole. She picked up a forkful and held her breath as she moved it toward Darcy's mouth.

Her eyes on the window, Darcy took the food from Andrea and chewed slowly. "I'll always think of you when I eat something other than steak. On the rare occasion I do, that is."

Andrea gave Darcy a sip of iced tea, followed by a forkful of rice. "I gather you're feeling suicidal."

"Does it matter?"

"Christ, Darcy, of course it matters. You sound like you've given up. Tell me what's going on?"

Those startling blue orbs focused on Andrea. "No."

There was nothing more to be said about that, so Andrea concentrated on feeding her and avoiding her eyes. But when their eyes did accidentally meet, the electricity was still there, and they both seemed to have trouble breathing. She was sure Darcy was in love with her. Maybe she just needed time.

Darcy ate everything and at the end closed her eyes while Andrea patted her lips. Andrea was tempted to take advantage and kiss her, but she didn't want to jeopardize the flimsy harmony they'd achieved. Darcy slept again, this time with a small smile on her face. Andrea thought about packing while Darcy slept, but she could do that tonight or tomorrow in about fifteen minutes. She didn't feel like reading, so after she moved the dishes out to the cart she sat in the chair again watching Darcy sleep. Her sleep today seemed more restful than it had been at night these last couple of weeks.

Pale, drawn, thin and wretchedly unhappy, Darcy was still beautiful, could still melt her with a smile, turn her on with her eyes and reduce her to jelly with her deep, flirting voice. Despite everything, she still longed to touch Darcy, to make love to her. She'd never felt this deeply about anyone, not even Julie. How could it not be right?

When Darcy woke, she smiled sweetly. "Would you read to me? Not a romance though, do we have anything else?"

"Do you want to get out of bed?"

"No, I'm still tired."

"I have a mystery, just a second." Andrea retrieved the mystery she'd been reading and showed it to Darcy. "*Point of Betrayal*, the fourth in Ann Roberts' Ari Adams series. Have you read it?"

"Looks good." Her phone rang and Andrea retrieved it for her.

"Darcy." She glanced at Andrea. "Yes, she's here. Not now, Candace, she's busy. I was going to call you anyway to cancel this evening. The therapy is exhausting and I want to rest. Come for dinner tomorrow." She hung up.

"Why didn't you let me speak to Candace?"

"It was something about your paychecks being missing. I'll straighten her out when she comes over tomorrow. Don't worry, she'll send the last check to your apartment."

"You didn't answer my question. Why didn't you let me talk to her?"

"Because I didn't want to deal with her shit."

"Does she know I'm leaving tomorrow?"

Darcy closed her eyes. "No."

"What about Tori and Elle? The others?"

"No."

"Why, Darcy?" She couldn't keep the anguish out of her voice. "Why?"

"It's easier for me, Andrea. Please try to understand. I know I'm being a bitch but it's easier for me this way." Darcy's voice was so low and so full of pain that Andrea could barely make out what she said.

Thinking only to comfort her, Andrea took her hand and brought it to her lips. Darcy turned away and began to sob. Andrea slid onto the bed and pulled Darcy into her arms. They cried together, then lay quietly, released somehow. When they heard the elevator grinding slowly up with their dinner, Andrea slipped off the bed and washed both their faces.

A melancholy tenderness replaced the tension between them. They ate in silence, Darcy feeding herself, but maintaining constant eye contact with Andrea. After dinner, Andrea read aloud but when Darcy started yawning, she helped her undress and put on her pajamas, then wheeled her into the bathroom so she could wash and brush her teeth.

When Darcy had finished in the bathroom, she handed Andrea the hairbrush. "Would you mind?"

"Of course not." Andrea moved behind Darcy, happy to be able to touch her, happy Darcy couldn't see her crying. She dragged the brushing out as long as she could, then helped Darcy into bed and turned off the lights.

"Andrea, I know I have no right to ask this, given how I'm treating you, but would you sleep with me tonight? On the bed with me, I mean?"

Andrea froze. It would be unbearable being so close knowing she was leaving tomorrow, but it was her last chance to have the closeness with Darcy she craved and maybe she would feel okay walking away tomorrow. She went back and forth a few minutes, then admitted to herself that she wanted to do it. "Okay."

After washing and changing into pajamas, she climbed on the bed, on top of the blanket. Without the casts, she was able to get close. She rolled to her side, facing Darcy in the dark, trying to figure out where to put her arm when Darcy took her hand, kissed it, then pulled Andrea so she was half-draped over her. She held Andrea's hand to her heart.

"Do you want the pendant back?"

Darcy's body jerked. "What?"

"Given the circumstances, I thought—"

"That was a gift. I hope you'll wear it always and remember me."

"I'll never forget you, Darcy."

She kissed Andrea's hand again and settled down.

Andrea was almost asleep when Darcy whispered, "And I'll always love you, my lovely doctor. Please forgive me."

CHAPTER THIRTY-THREE

Andrea woke at six as usual. Darcy had slept through the night with no nightmares. They were face to face with Darcy's arm holding her close, her face soft, her lips parted slightly, her breathing raspy. She felt a surge of love. It didn't matter that Darcy had treated her badly these last couple of weeks, she knew the loving Darcy was in there behind whatever was scaring her.

She must have dozed again because soft kisses on her eyes, her nose, her lips, a hand on her breast, woke her. She groaned and rolled onto Darcy, then realizing what was happening, she pulled back. They couldn't do this. It wasn't right. She pushed onto her elbows, met Darcy's lust-darkened eyes. "No, Darcy, I don't want this. I can't. Please stop."

Darcy blinked, seeming to come awake. "Sorry, I was dreaming. About you, Andrea." Then, a jaunty smile. "It was a very nice dream."

Andrea rolled off Darcy. When her racing heart stilled, she got out of bed. "Let me help you wash and dress. When Francine gets here, I'll shower and dress, then pack."

Darcy started to cry. Andrea held her again, brushed the hair off her face, and kissed her forehead. "I'm glad you don't hate me and I'm glad this is hard for you too, but I wish I understood what was going on."

"It's just less painful this way. It will be after, anyway. You'll see."

"I doubt that I'll see, but I guess I'll have to wait to find out." She lifted Darcy's chin. "We need to get moving." As she helped Darcy wash the body she'd hope to make love to someday, she chatted to keep both of them from getting maudlin. If they were going to do this, they needed to get on with it.

They were finishing breakfast when Francine and Jennifer arrived. Francine, sensitive to the mood as usual, picked up the connection and the lack of tension in the room. "You two have a nice evening?"

"Better than expected." Andrea stood. "I'm going to get ready and pack, then I'll be out of your hair." She knew her voice was too chirpy and bright but she wanted to keep it light this morning, to leave with some dignity.

She moved through her shower, brushed her teeth and dressed in a fog. Darcy loved her, in spite of asking her to leave, she'd said and shown it again last night. Francine had corroborated it. Andrea felt it. Surely this must be a nightmare.

Checking herself in the mirror as she combed her hair, she realized she'd put on the jeans and green sweater that Darcy admired on her. The emerald pendant nestled just above her cleavage. She thought about changing but everything else was packed and ready to go. Darcy would just have to deal with it, a reminder of what she's throwing away. She picked up the books she was leaving for Darcy and went to say goodbye.

"Well, I'll be off. It's been wonderful working with you all." She hugged Jennifer and whispered, "Go easy on her."

"And it's been nice working with you." Andrea leaned over the recliner, touched Darcy's face and kissed her lightly on the lips. She spoke softly into Darcy's ear. "Thank you for a lovely day and evening yesterday, it's made it a little easier to leave you. Remember, I love you and you'll always have a special place in my heart." She straightened. "Walk me out, Francine."

In the elevator, she collapsed against the wall. "Oh, God, leaving is hard."

"You both look so miserable."

Andrea's eyes filled. "I'm thankful she let me see that my leaving is as hard for her as for me. When she thought I was asleep last night, she said she loved me. But if that's true, why is she sending me away?"

"I wish I knew. She seems to be in a lot of pain but can't or won't say why."

They hugged. "Take care of her, Francine. Her heart sounds bad. Call Julie, maybe she can convince her to have that angiogram."

CHAPTER THIRTY-FOUR

It was done. Andrea was gone. And with her, Darcy's heart. Incapable of dealing with questions from Francine and Jennifer she put the recliner back and closed her eyes. She knew they could see she was crying, but she'd just sent the love of her life away and she couldn't stop. Was this how Candace felt about her? Poor baby. And selfish Darcy hadn't even noticed. At least Andrea knew she was suffering, knew she loved her. And, part of her felt Andrea loved her, or at least was sexually attracted, but she was committed to someone else and she'd sworn to not pursue her if she was already committed. They'd come close to making love this morning. Darcy admired Andrea for stopping them, for not cheating on her lover, but she still wanted Andrea, could still smell that perfume or soap or whatever it was that was so tantalizing. She had considered telling Andrea she didn't want to wash so she could hold on to her fragrance but the need to be touched by her won out.

What was she supposed to do now? Live alone, date placeholder women and pretend she was happy? Been there, done that, as they say. At least before she'd had hopes of meeting the one destined for her, but now she'd found her and lost her. There was no future for her. Living without Andrea was unthinkable.

CHAPTER THIRTY-FIVE

Andrea spent the first day and night in bed crying. She did the same the second day until Julie and Karin showed up after they'd finished working, then she spent the night crying in the arms of one or the other of them. The following day was Saturday. Her pillow was soaked when she woke. At ten a.m., Karin and Julie used their key to get in, made her dress, took her for a long walk and then out for brunch. They spent the rest of the day together, at the movies, dinner out and watching TV until late. She cried off and on throughout the day and the night.

By the time Karin and Julie arrived Sunday morning, New York Times and bagels in hand, Andrea was exhausted from crying and lack of sleep so the three of them spent a quiet day. Julie and Karin read the papers and the books they'd brought with them while Andrea slept on the sofa with her head in one or the other of their laps.

Monday morning Andrea intended to get up and run as she'd promised Karin and Julie she would, but she couldn't get Darcy out of her head and she cried until she fell asleep again. When the insistent ringing of the doorbell woke her, she stumbled to the door and peered through the peephole. Tori and Elle were standing there. Her heart flipped. Maybe Darcy was with them. But they were alone. She tried to smile but thought it probably came out as a grimace. "Hi."

Elle looked her up and down. "Get dressed, Andrea, we're going out for breakfast." Andrea opened her mouth to protest but Elle put her hand up. "Get going."

She took a quick shower, threw on jeans and the sweater Darcy loved on her, then collapsed on the bed. Elle and Tori pulled her up into a group hug. After a few minutes, Tori kissed her forehead. "Come, lovely Andrea, let's get some food into you."

Edgar's Café was busy but they were seated right away.

Andrea pushed the menu aside. "Just coffee for me."

"Uh-uh." Tori took her hand. "How about the gruyere, arugula and roasted red pepper scramble, Andrea?"

"I can't—"

Tori squeezed her hand. "Yes, you can."

She didn't have the strength to fight. "Okay, with multigrain toast, no butter." She drank some coffee. "How's Darcy?"

"About the same as you. A total mess," Elle said. "She won't talk about it, even to Tori, which is a first. She's not eating or sleeping much. We've spoken to Julie and Karin and they, the inner circle, and Francine and Jennifer are extremely worried about the two of you. What's going on?"

Andrea stared into her coffee cup, trying to avoid crying. "I don't know. I finally got up my nerve to tell her I was in love with her but that morning when I went into her room she was distant and angry and wouldn't say what was wrong. Later that day, she told me I was right, she'd mistaken being dependent and vulnerable and needy, for love."

"Do you believe her?" Elle took Andrea's hand and rubbed it between hers.

"No. In fact, the night before I left she asked me to sleep on the bed with her and when she thought I was asleep she whispered that she loved me."

"Why then—"

"I don't know why, Tori." Her voice was filled with anguish. "She would only repeat that she didn't love me. She wouldn't tell me what had changed, or answer any questions or explain. Then she got cold and nasty, which usually means she's feeling afraid, but I can't imagine what she's afraid of."

"Oh, honey. I'm so sorry she's doing this to you and I'm worried sick about her. She's hardly eating. Jennifer says her legs are getting stronger but she's getting weaker." Tori rubbed her eyes. "I don't know how to reach her. Francine is the only one she'll let near her. She pretends to be asleep when anyone else comes in the room, even Maria and Carlo. And she refused to participate in a therapeutic intervention with the inner circle. It's almost as if she's trying to kill herself."

The three of them walked along the water in Riverside Park for another hour, they talked and cried some more, then Tori and Elle left Andrea to go visit Darcy. Andrea sat on a bench facing the boat basin, crying, not caring that people stared as they passed. By evening, she felt numb and went home to bed.

The next day she woke and realized she wanted to be alone. She went to the park and spent the day sitting or walking by the water, remembering. She didn't answer her phone but she did call Karin and Julie periodically during the day to reassure them she was all right.

After another day spent mourning in the park, she woke thinking she was wallowing. She'd survived disease-infected villages in remote jungles, faced down a medicine man who threatened to stick his spear in her throat, delivered babies with bombs falling around her, fought off meth crazies in the emergency room, and spent the night alone on the steps of a church when she was little more than three years old. She could survive this pain. She could survive this loss. She could make a fulfilling life for herself helping people in need. She pulled on her running clothes and sneakers, and went to the park to run.

It was as if a fever had broken. After one of the loneliest and most painful weeks of her life, she invited Karin and Julie to join her for dinner at Fred's, a favorite neighborhood restaurant.

Julie studied Andrea for a moment, then reached across the table and took her hand. "How are you feeling?"

"Better. Well, not totally, but I'm not wallowing and I'm not paralyzed. I've started eating, as you'll witness when we order. And I've decided to go home to Sicily to get some TLC from my parents. When I feel up to it, I'll sign on for a tour with Doctors Without Borders. I'm not sure when I'll come back to New York City."

The day after her dinner with Julie and Karin, she stopped by Bonasola for lunch to say goodbye to Tori and Elle and to ask about Darcy. "Not well," Elle said. "Actually, awful."

It pained her to hear it and she was tempted to stop in to try to talk to Darcy, but she reminded herself that Darcy didn't want her. She did, however, run in for a few minutes to say goodbye to Maria and Carlo. The three of them had a good cry. Later that night she called Francine to let her know her plans and give her the address in Sicily.

Five days later, Andrea was sitting in the Alitalia lounge in JFK, staring unseeing out the windows at planes taking off and landing. In two hours, she would board the flight to Sicily. She'd gone there to reassemble the pieces of her heart after Julie had broken up with her. She doubted her heart would heal this time, but the tranquility of Trapani and the love of her parents and family would help her move on with her life.

"Dr. Andrea Trapani, please report to the Alitalia desk. Dr. Andrea Trapani please report to the Alitalia desk. Call for Dr. Andrea Trapani."

Hearing her name startled her. She'd left her cell phone with Julie and Karin since it wouldn't work in Sicily and one of them was probably calling to make sure she'd made it to the airport. She identified herself at the desk and took the phone.

"Dr. Trapani."

"Dr. Trapani, it's Marion from Dr. Castillo's office. Karin asked me to call you. Dr. Castillo has an emergency and is asking for you."

"Is Julie all right?"

"I'm not sure what the situation is. All I know is Karin said Dr. Castillo needs you and you should get to the hospital as soon as possible. I've arranged for a police car to bring you there. It should be waiting outside."

"Oh, my God. Tell her I'm on my way." She grabbed her carry-on and ran out to the waiting police car. Siren blasting, they made it into the city in record time. Andrea prayed Julie was all right.

CHAPTER THIRTY-SIX

Karin was standing at the emergency entrance of New York Presbyterian when the police car pulled up. Andrea thanked them and jumped out. She ran into Karin's arms. "Is Julie all right? What happened?"

"Come." Karin dragged her inside and into the elevator. "Julie is fine. She has Darcy on the table and she's losing her. She thinks you can give her a reason to live but she didn't think you'd come if she told you that."

"You lied?" Andrea pulled away from Karin. "Don't you get that Darcy doesn't want me? Or do you two think having the pleasure of watching her die will help me forget I love her?" She paced in the cramped elevator, trying to control her anger. "I'll never forgive either of you for bringing me here to watch her die."

Karin touched her face gently. "The important thing is, will you ever forgive yourself for not trying to save her?"

The elevator door slid open.

Andrea glared at Karin, then her shoulders slumped. "No."

"Then go scrub in." Karin pushed her toward the OR.

A nurse was waiting with a pair of Julie's scrubs. Andrea changed and washed up, then entered the OR. She couldn't see Darcy on the table but she could see the monitor. Karin hadn't exaggerated. They were losing her.

Julie smiled as she entered. "Hey, there's Dr. Trapani. See Darcy, I told you Andrea was coming. She's here now and she'll tell you herself that she's in love with you and wants to spend the rest of her life with you."

All eyes swiveled to her. She flushed from her toes to her scalp. What now?

"Make room for Dr. Trapani at Darcy's head, she has a lot to say to Darcy. Most of it is private and we don't want her to have to scream it across the room. Don't be shy, Andrea, just pretend we're not here."

Andrea knew the playful tone was for Darcy but she was embarrassed. What was she supposed to do, pour her heart out in a room full of doctors, residents, interns and nurses? She moved through the crowd to Darcy. She looked awful—bloodless, with tubes and drips and wires—and beautiful. And she was dying right in front of her. "Darcy sweetie," she spoke softly, "it's Andrea."

"Speak up, Andrea, we want to be sure Darcy hears you. And, somebody get Darcy's hand free from the blanket and let Andrea hold it, so Darcy knows we're not playing a recording of her voice."

Andrea entwined her fingers with Darcy's and ran her thumb back and forth. She glanced at the monitor. Darcy's pressure was dropping. She forgot about the room full of people. "Oh, God, Darcy, please don't leave me. I am so in love with you and I know you feel the same. I don't know what the problem is but I've never loved anyone as much as I love you. Please don't give up."

"Look at that spike. Keep going Andrea."

Andrea glanced up at the monitor. Things were looking better. "Almost from the moment we met, well you were vile when we met, but not too long after, I was falling for you and your flirtatious ways. I've never met anyone who could make love with her eyes. Some of the most intimate times I've ever had in my life were our meals together, feeding you, seeing the love and the want in those gorgeous sapphire eyes of yours. Please, Darcy, don't give up. I need you to live." A sob escaped. "I don't know if I can go on without you."

"Yes."

She looked up at Julie's shout. The monitor displayed normal readings. There wasn't a dry eye in the OR.

"Hey, somebody dry the surgeon's eyes before she screws this up." Julie's voice was hoarse with emotion. A nurse leaned in and dabbed Julie's eyes. "Keep talking, Andrea."

Andrea looked around. Everyone was nodding. What the hell. If exposing her feelings would keep Darcy alive, so be it. She kissed Darcy's forehead, her eyes, her cheeks, her palm. "Come on, love. Eye sex is great but you owe me some real sex." She looked up at the laugh. The monitor had spiked. "Please forgive me, sweetie, for not telling you I was in love with you. I was afraid, not because of you, but because of old stuff that Karin helped me work out. I'll tell you about that when you wake up. Some things are too personal to talk about in front of a roomful of colleagues."

"When you asked me to share your house in Fire Island, it felt like a marriage proposal. I wanted to say yes, I'll share your house. I'll share your life. I didn't say it then but I'm saying it now. If you live, I'll never leave you again."

"And, when you set me up so I had to sleep in the king-sized bed with you in Fire Island and I woke up draped over you, you were polite enough to not point out that despite what I had said about professional distance, I was the one who had rolled across this gigantic space and wrapped my arm around you. I don't know how somebody whose arms and legs are in casts, whose body is bruised, who can hardly move, could be so sexy. And that last morning, I don't know where I found the strength to get out of bed without making love. Or why, actually."

"Fight, sweetie, fight for us, we have a wonderful future ahead of us." She talked for more than three hours, going over the things they did, the things they would do, how much she loved her, how important it was that she live. She said it in English, repeated it in Italian, then said it in English again.

"Okay, let's sew her up." Julie stepped aside. "Josh, you have the steadiest and finest hand, let's see how small a scar we can leave. She stood behind Andrea and wrapped her arms around her. "Darcy, we're almost done here. Everything looks good. I'm sending you and Andrea to the cardiac intensive care unit. You still have some work to do but Andrea will be there to take care of you. I'm going to insist on no sex of any kind in the CICU, kissing and hand holding will have to suffice."

She kissed Andrea's cheek. "I'm going to keep her sedated to give her time to rest. Then, if she can breathe on her own, I'll remove the breathing tube while she's asleep to minimize her stress when she wakes up."

She turned to address the room. "Ladies and gentlemen, you were privileged this evening to hear some very personal and intimate details from our colleague, Dr. Trapani. If I learn that anyone has repeated anything Dr. Trapani unselfishly shared to save our patient, you will pay dearly. Now, if, on the other hand, any of you want to go home and have eye sex or any other sex with a spouse or partner, you have my permission. I think I'll try the feeding thing, myself."

Andrea punched her in the arm. "So how did you get a police car to drive me here?"

Julie laughed. "Special privileges granted to the surgeon who saved the life of a very important police chief."

Andrea followed Darcy into the CICU and once they had her hooked up to the various machines and feeds, held her hand, touched her face and watched the monitors. Darcy's vitals continued to look good. Within an hour, it was clear that while they may not have known the details, every nurse in the recovery room, every nurse and doctor who peeked in, and, many did, knew the gist of what had happened in the OR and how much she loved Darcy.

But did Darcy know? No question Darcy had responded to her voice but did the words and the feelings seep into her unconscious brain? And, even if they had and she now knew Andrea loved her, did that change her feelings? Andrea would never regret exposing her love to give Darcy a reason to fight. But what if Darcy didn't love her or worse, what if she did love her but still didn't want her in her life? Rather than welcome Andrea back, Darcy might ask her to leave. Again. After all, it was Julie, not Darcy, who'd invited her into the OR.

Realizing she was depressing herself, she started talking again, telling Darcy all about their future together, where they would go, what they would do. After a while, she dozed off, still holding Darcy's hand.

CHAPTER THIRTY-SEVEN

Darcy came to consciousness slowly, puzzling over the whooshing and beeping sounds and her aching body. She was too exhausted to open her eyes. Besides, if she did she would lose the feelings from her dreams. In her dreams, Andrea had been with her in a hospital. In her dreams, Andrea told her repeatedly that she was in love with her and wanted to be with her forever. In her dreams, she'd been happy.

She had been so sure that Andrea loved her, had felt it deep in her heart. Yet, she'd let herself doubt it, let herself believe that at the same time the ever-professional Andrea had chosen to sleep with her, at the same time she could see the love in Andrea's eyes and feel the sizzling sexual tension between them, Andrea had a secret lover. Secret from her at least. But would the woman she loved, the kind, compassionate, sweet, generous, loving Andrea be so duplicitous? And, why? Andrea could easily have said so in the beginning to put an end to Darcy's piggy comments and constant sexual innuendo. Could she have been mistaken about Andrea having a lover? Why hadn't she talked to Andrea, asked her about it? Why had she thrust Andrea out of her life? Had she done what she always did, fight up to a point then give up? Why hadn't she fought for her? Oh, God, had she thrown away the love of her life through cowardice and paranoia and insecurity?

She wasn't the only one who thought Andrea was in love with her. For sure, all her friends did. So why couldn't she talk to any of them about her feelings? What was behind the shame? Was it just the fear of rejection or was there something deep inside that made her so ready to doubt that Andrea could love her? She'd walked away from Tori before Tori could reject her and now she'd done the same with Andrea.

Maybe it wasn't too late. Starting today she would mount a campaign to win Andrea. She would get her number from Francine. Where the hell was Francine this morning? Usually she materialized as soon as Darcy came to consciousness, even before she opened her eyes.

She opened her eyes. And gasped. She was looking into the gorgeous green eyes of the woman of her dreams, eyes filled with love. Was she still dreaming? Where were they? What was all that noise? She tried to ask but she had no voice. Grunting, she struggled to get up, pulling at the wires tying her down. Andrea grabbed her hands and kissed her forehead.

"Don't be frightened, sweetie. You had emergency bypass surgery and you're in the hospital. Your throat is probably sore because you had a breathing tube in, but Dr. Castillo removed it a while ago." She kissed Darcy's eyes and stroked her cheek.

Darcy relaxed, attempted a smile and dozed off.

The next time Darcy woke Andrea was gripping her hand but she was asleep, her head cradled on one arm on the bed. Was she real? Darcy watched her for a while, then reached out and ran her fingers through her hair. She woke and smiled. A loving smile. Darcy's heart flipped. Maybe it hadn't been a dream. She waved her hand around, then raised her eyebrows hoping Andrea would tell her what was going on.

Andrea spoke over the bleats and beeps of the machines. "You were rushed to the hospital yesterday and Dr. Castillo did an emergency quadruple bypass. It's hard for you to talk because you were hooked to a ventilator and had a breathing tube in your throat."

Darcy's hand went to her throat.

"Dr. Castillo removed it while you were still sedated. Are you in pain? Do you need pain medication? Squeeze my hand once for yes, twice for no."

Darcy squeezed Andrea's hand once. Andrea waved the nurse over. "She's awake and says she's in pain. Can you give her something?"

The nurse asked Darcy a few questions then injected medication into one of the IVs they'd inserted into her arms. In a few minutes, she was asleep again. "Dr. Castillo asked me to let her know when you woke up. I'll give her a call."

"Tell her to bring me coffee." She checked her watch. Six a.m. Julie must be sleeping somewhere close.

Julie arrived fifteen minutes later. "I hear she woke up." She handed Andrea a sandwich and a bottle of water. "No hospital sludge for you, Andrea, you need to eat and stay hydrated."

The sandwich was warm. She breathed in its tantalizing fragrance and took a bite. Egg, cheese and bacon on a croissant, not the healthiest but delicious, and Darcy was still asleep so she didn't have to worry about tempting her. "She woke twice, for a few minutes. She was confused but I think she was happy to see me. Roberta gave her something for the pain."

Julie drew up a chair. "I apologize. First, for lying to get you here. But, I was losing her and I knew you would feel you had to obey her wishes. And second, for asking you to expose yourself. What you did saved her life. Do you hate me?"

She reached over and squeezed Julie's hand. "No, I love you, but don't expect a public declaration of why or what we did or anything close to that. And, as for your little threatening talk about what happens in the OR stays in the OR, everyone on staff knows what happened, even if they don't know all the details. I've had more hugs and pats on the back since we got to the CICU than in all the years I worked in the ER."

"Oh, Andrea, I'm so sorry. I'll find out who gossiped and make their life miserable."

"Forget it, Julie. Everybody knows more intimate details than I would ever share, but it was worth it. Who cares if they know how much I love Darcy? I would do it again if necessary."

"Karin was ecstatic to hear the details." Julie smirked. "I mean that you were able to talk Darcy back."

"You are so bad, Julie. You'll never change. I hope. So are you and Karin really going to try the feeding-eye sex thing? I highly recommend it. Ah, good, you're blushing." She drank some water. "Do you know what happened? Why Francine brought her in?"

"Francine texted me in the late morning yesterday. Darcy's heartbeat was too slow, she could barely stand and she was sleeping more and more. I was going into the OR to do an angioplasty so I told her to bring her to the hospital in two hours. I had just finished when she arrived in the ambulance with Darcy. She collapsed when Francine was transferring her from the bed to the wheelchair to bring her in. She'd stopped breathing so Jennifer called 911 and Francine gave her mouth-to-mouth until the EMTs got there."

"So Francine saved her life?"

Julie grinned. "You bet she did. She was still a wreck when I went out to talk to Darcy's family and friends after the surgery. The others were freaked about Darcy's heart stopping, grateful to Francine for saving her life, and grateful to you for getting her to fight to live, thereby saving her life again. Her aunt and uncle were quite agitated, so I ran them in for a quick look while you were both asleep."

"Shit, was I sleeping with my mouth open?"

"No, my dear, you looked beautiful as always, maybe even more beautiful now that you're in love with someone who will make you happy rather than sad."

"You're so poetic, Julie. But I still don't know if she wants me in her life." She brushed Darcy's hair back and kissed her forehead.

Julie yawned. "I want her to rest today so no visitors until seven tonight and only two at a time for ten minutes, every hour. My office will let Francine know and she'll coordinate with the others. Send for me if she needs me." She glanced at her wristwatch. "Karin will bring your hospital ID and fresh scrubs for both of us sometime in the early evening when she has a break."

She stood and hugged Julie. "Whatever the outcome, you and Karin were right. I would never have forgiven myself if Darcy had died and I hadn't tried to save her."

Darcy slept most of the day. They brought Andrea a tray around five. She dozed after she ate. The nurse was bustling around and Darcy was staring at her when she woke at six thirty. For a second or two she thought Darcy was angry, but then she smiled. She seemed more alert than she had the last couple of times she'd woken. Andrea smiled and leaned over her to brush her lips.

The nurse looked up from typing something into the computer at Darcy's bedside. "Ah, good evening, Dr. Trapani, she's been waiting for you to wake up."

Andrea checked the monitor. "Everything still good?"

The nurse nodded. "What's your level of pain on a scale of one to ten, Darcy?"

Darcy held up three fingers. "Good. You're probably feeling the discomfort of the chest tube and the wounds in your legs where the doctor took the veins. I'll inform Dr. Castillo you're awake again. Let me know if the pain gets worse. And don't forget to use the pad."

Darcy nodded, then wrote something on a pad and turned it so Andrea could read it. "I dreamed you said you're in love with me."

"You didn't dream it. I repeated it over and over to you in the OR in front of a cardiothoracic surgery team of fifteen or more of my colleagues."

Darcy appeared puzzled. She wrote, "Why am I here? Why was I in the OR? And, how did you get there?"

She knew Darcy would probably not remember much the first day in the CICU so she kept the story brief, then smiled into those gorgeous blue eyes and kissed Darcy's palm.

Darcy pulled her hand away, wrote something, then turned the page toward her. "You're in love with me?"

"Absolutely."

Darcy smiled, then frowned and flushed. She said something. Andrea couldn't understand the words but the pain in Darcy's face pierced her heart. "Are you in pain? Don't try to speak. Write it down, sweetie." She ran her hand over Darcy's arm.

Darcy shook her hand off, made a note and flashed the page. "What about your lover?"

"What? I don't have a lover. You're the only one for me."

Darcy stared at something behind Andrea. Puzzled, she turned and followed Darcy's eyes. Karin had arrived with clean scrubs.

Andrea looked from Karin to Darcy. "I don't understand."

Darcy wrote again. "Saw you in mirror, hugging and kissing. Looked like post-sex."

"Christ, Darcy, I don't know what…? Oh, my God. Karin?" She waved Karin closer. "Darcy, this is Dr. Karin Simons, Dr. Castillo's wife."

Darcy's eyebrows shot up. She looked from Andrea to Karin and back. She wrote and turned the page toward them. "And you two were…"

"No, no." Andrea was shaking her head. "Karin is one of my closest friends. I asked her for help because the mixed signals I was sending were making us both crazy. We'd been talking in the garden and she came up to my room to get some books. We did hug and, I guess we kissed, but a friendly kiss, not a lover's. I planned to tell you in the morning I was in love with you." Andrea stared at Darcy. "You thought we were lovers? Is that why you withdrew from me and became cold and hostile?"

Darcy nodded.

Was it that simple? Had Darcy almost ruined their lives over a shadowy kiss? Andrea fought to control the rage. Darcy needed her strength to heal and this was not the time to attack her. "Dammit. Why didn't you trust me enough to ask before banishing me?"

Darcy's eyes bounced back and forth between the two women, then she wrote on the pad. "Stupid pride. Shame. Almost lost you."

"Stupid is right. I swear I'll kill you, if you ever try that again." Andrea glared at Darcy. "We're not done with this Darcy; we'll talk about it later. But I'm here now and you're okay."

Darcy colored. She held up a note: *Hello Karin, nice to c u again.*

Karin smiled. "Yes, nice to see you too. Sorry about the mix-up but you know lesbian friends are always kissing."

Andrea felt a hand on her shoulder. "Hey, Dr. Trapani, you're upsetting my patient. I just saved her life so you're not allowed to kill her." Julie pulled Karin close and kissed her cheek. "I see you've met my wife, Darcy."

Darcy wrote and flashed a note: *Not upset. Happy. Thanks 2 you, Doc.*

"My pleasure, Darcy. I detest it when my friends are miserable and I really hate it when my patients die. Not that it ever happens. Now let me check you out." She checked the incision, then listened to Darcy's heart, lungs, pulses. "You can have two visitors for ten minutes every hour starting at seven."

Darcy gave her a thumbs-up, then fell back to sleep.

After Karin and Julie left, Andrea watched Darcy sleep. Such a bundle of contradictions. Aggressive and confident and, yes, proud, but shame? She didn't understand it. Maybe she'd talk to Karin. Maybe Darcy should be in therapy. In any case, she'd be vigilant from now on to ensure nothing came between them again.

Andrea woke Darcy when Maria and Carlo, the first of her visitors, arrived. She reminded her that she should avoid talking, but Darcy croaked a few words out for the benefit of her aunt and uncle. They hugged and kissed Darcy as best they could, given her hookups and her wounds and they vigorously hugged and kissed Andrea. "Don't worry," Andrea said, "I'm not leaving her. She'll be home in a few days."

Darcy dozed off as soon as they left. Andrea caressed her hand and her face. Periodically, Darcy woke, eyes widened to see Andrea, then smiled, her face radiant with love.

It turned out that the group had made a schedule before leaving the night before so everyone could come in for their ten-minute visit rather than spend the night waiting to see Darcy. Even at ten minutes each hour, Darcy was exhausted and slept between visits.

CHAPTER THIRTY-EIGHT

Darcy had felt terrific when she came home from the hospital. No more hospital beds for her. She wanted to sleep in her own king-sized bed with Andrea beside her. So while still in the hospital she'd asked Carlo to bring in painters and movers and convert the room she'd used as her hospital room back to her sitting room. When she arrived home, it looked the way it had originally. Everything was great.

Then, Andrea stopped the OxyContin and she began to feel anxious, so she'd started taking the pills on her own. But she was worried because the prescription was running low and it was not renewable. She took two and as she was counting to see how many she had left; the walker fell against the table.

Andrea opened her eyes. "Are you in pain, Darcy?"

Damn walker, now Andrea was awake. "Not at this moment. I have no pain at all. In fact, I feel terrific."

Andrea sat up in bed. "What are you doing with the OxyContin?"

"You're spying on me?"

"Darcy?"

She shrugged. "Counting them." *Hopefully, she'll write a prescription.* "I'm afraid I'll run out."

"I'll bet you are."

"What's with the sarcasm? Can't you just prescribe more?"

Andrea swung her legs over the side of the bed. "Sweetheart, those pills are addictive. I stopped them to keep you from getting dependent. When did you start taking them on your own?"

"A couple of days ago."

"Were you in pain?"

Darcy turned the walker toward the window. "No. Just anxious. I feel better when I take them."

Andrea followed her, wrapped her arms around her and nuzzled her neck. "Do you want to get addicted?"

Darcy stared out the window. What kind of stupid question was that?

"I didn't hear your answer."

"No, damn it, of course I don't want to get addicted, but I need them—"

Andrea put her hand over Darcy's mouth. "You have to stop now."

She knew Andrea was right, was only protecting her, but she needed these pills. "I already took two this morning."

"Well, enjoy today, because the party is over." She turned Darcy, kissed her forehead, then clasped her shoulder. "Come with me." She picked up the bottle of OxyContin and led Darcy into the bathroom.

Darcy panicked. "You're not going to flush them, are you?"

Andrea hugged her, careful as always not to put too much pressure on her wound. "No, sweetie. You are. Here."

Darcy moaned. "I can't. I need them."

Andrea nodded and handed the bottle to Darcy. "Trust me, sweetie, you need to do this."

Darcy looked at Andrea and seeing the love on her face, knew she would do anything to not lose her again. She took a breath, then removed the cap and turned the bottle upside down over the toilet. When it was empty, she handed it to Andrea.

"Flush the toilet, Darcy."

She turned into Andrea's arms, sobbing. "I don't want to feel bad."

"Oh, sweetie, the last thing I want is for you to feel bad. But I've just got you back and I won't lose you to drugs. I'll be here to help you through it but you have to tell me what you're feeling. I'll give you non-addictive pain meds if you need them and something for the anxiety. Go on. Flush it."

Darcy depressed the lever and watched the precious pills circle and disappear.

"Come." Andrea hugged her again, then brushed her lips over Darcy's. "Let's get ready for breakfast." Since they'd come home from the hospital they'd been taking meals in the garden or the kitchen or the dining room. If Darcy was feeling weak, they could eat in the bedroom or the sitting room. But that hadn't been necessary. Yet.

Feeling Andrea against her, the softness of her breasts without a bra, the smell of her, the feel of skin on skin, Darcy's body responded. She nuzzled Andrea's neck, then slipped her hands under Andrea's pajama top, caressing her breasts, her nipples. The walker pressed against Andrea's hips as Darcy moved to her mouth, running her tongue over her lips, teasing them to open. Andrea pulled back. "No Darcy. You know we can't have sex for another three to six weeks."

One of Darcy's hands pulled at the waistband of Andrea's pajamas the other slid down and kneaded her butt. "Sure we can. I feel great."

Andrea grabbed Darcy's arms. "That's the pills talking, Darcy." Her breath was coming in short bursts. "Please stop."

Darcy looked up, confused. "The pills?"

"Yes. They make you feel euphoric, exhilarated, but your body isn't ready for it. You need to be taking it easy." Andrea hugged her. "I love you and want you, but we have to wait. Take a deep breath, then let's get dressed."

Andrea led Darcy into the bedroom and helped her dress, then, as usual, she went into the bathroom to dress herself. Maybe some food and sitting in the garden would help calm her until the pills wore off. Damn, why hadn't she noticed that Darcy was taking the OxyContin on her own? She was going to have to be vigilant.

Darcy seemed fine the rest of the day. Of course she was still experiencing the high of the last two pills. Andrea hoped she hadn't already taken enough to experience withdrawal pains.

* * *

A few days later, she noticed Darcy getting agitated as it got close to bedtime.

She claimed she wasn't sleepy but she dozed and jerked awake continuously, then started spending nights in the sitting room with all the lights on, staring wide-eyed at the dark windows. Sensing Darcy's fear, Andrea held her all night to keep her calm. Once it started getting light outside, she was able to get Darcy into bed and they would sleep for a few hours.

She knew what was going on, but she needed Darcy to talk to her about it. So far, Darcy had deflected her questions by saying nothing was wrong, other than Andrea making her stop taking the OxyContin. It looked like she was going to have to force the issue to get Darcy to voice her fear.

One afternoon, they were sitting in the garden with Candace and Darcy asked about her therapy. "I've worked through my feelings for you, Darcy. I'd confused being in love with wanting to be close, to needing our family connection, and I was afraid you would abandon me if you loved someone." She smiled shyly. "Lucia and I have started dating."

Andrea turned to Darcy "Isn't that great?" But Darcy was asleep. She signaled Candace to follow her.

"What's going on, Andrea? She's never fallen asleep in the middle of a conversation. She seemed stronger in the hospital. Now she looks exhausted, has dark circles under her eyes and she's lost weight. Is this normal?"

"Don't be upset with her." Andrea took Candace's hand. "She's so stubborn, Candace. She's not sleeping and barely eating but she denies it. Until she admits there's a problem, we can't address it."

"Is there anything I can do?"

She squeezed Candace's hand. "Just keep coming, even if she does fall asleep on you. I'm going to wake her now and tell her you're leaving. Could you make a joke about her falling asleep on you? Maybe if she's embarrassed, she'll talk to me."

Andrea rubbed Darcy's shoulder. "Sweetie, Candace is leaving."

Darcy woke with a start. "Oh, sorry, I closed my eyes for a second."

Candace took Darcy's hand. "Uh-uh, my friend. You fell asleep while I was baring my soul. Is the fact that Lucia and I are dating that boring?"

"I heard you. I wasn't asleep."

"Hey, I know snoring when I hear it. Poor Andrea, I never realized you made such a racket. Maybe it's old age."

"You lie. I don't snore. And I'm only three months older than you so you can't say old age."

Andrea watched them banter. It was nice to see Darcy being more like herself.

"I'm leaving now, but next time I come I'm bringing a whistle and if you fall asleep on me I'll blow it in your ear." Candace kissed them both goodbye and sauntered out of the garden.

Darcy took Andrea's hand and kissed her palm. "I don't snore, do I, love?"

Andrea turned her hand so they were palm to palm, and entwined her fingers with Darcy's. "You don't sleep long enough these days to snore."

"What does that mean?"

With her free hand, she tilted Darcy's face up, so they were eye to eye. "It means when you start to fall asleep in front of your friends, I really worry."

Darcy tried to turn away but Andrea held her chin in place. She closed her eyes. "What do you want me to say?"

"Please don't hide from me, Darcy. I'm not blind. I see you're not sleeping and barely eating. Tell me what's going on. Whatever the problem, we can fix it."

Darcy struggled to turn her face away, but Andrea held on. She kissed each of Darcy's eyes. "Please talk to me. You're pushing me so far away I might as well be in Sicily." She let go of Darcy's face and took her in her arms. She listened to the *thump, thump, thump* of Darcy's heart. "Your heart is so strong I can hear it without a stethoscope." She felt Darcy's body contort, trying to hold back the sobs. "It's just a matter now of letting your chest heal and building your strength. You need to sleep and eat and exercise to do that."

Darcy tensed. "I'm afraid if I fall asleep, I won't wake up. When I wake up in the dark, I panic, thinking I must be dead. I didn't want to live without you, Andrea, now I'm afraid I'm going to die."

Andrea held her until she began to relax, then pulled away so Darcy could see her face. "Trust me. There is no way in hell that I'm going to let you die. We'll sleep with the lights on and I'll hold you all night so I can feel you breathing, feel your heart. We can get through this together, Darcy." She placed Darcy's hand over her own heart. "Can you feel how strong your heart is, Darcy? Before surgery, I could barely feel it."

"It does feel strong."

"I have one other thing we need to discuss. Why aren't you eating? Wait, let me rephrase that. I notice you're eating lettuce with no dressing and nothing else. Why?"

Darcy shrugged.

"Darcy?"

"I'm afraid I'll clog my arteries again and I'll have another heart attack."

"Do you remember that one of the first things I did when I came to take care of you was insist you eat a heart healthy diet?"

Darcy smiled. "How could I forget?"

"I promise, I won't let you eat anything that will hurt you. But you need to eat what I serve you."

"I'll try."

"No. You will eat." She considered Darcy for a minute. "Could I feed you for a few days? I'd like to do it."

"No choo-choos or airplanes?"

"You know I don't do choo-choos or airplanes." Her mouth quirked. "Maybe just a little eye sex."

"How come you always bring up sex?"

"Hmm, could it be because I'm madly, wildly in love with you and looking forward to the day when we have permission?"

Darcy picked up Andrea's hand and kissed her palm. "I would love for you to feed me."

Andrea took her hand back and kissed Darcy on the lips. "I promise to keep you safe."

CHAPTER THIRTY-NINE

Having confessed her fear of sleeping to Andrea, Darcy was more relaxed than she'd been in days. Now if she could get Darcy eating, she would be on the road to recovery. But they'd forgotten that Tori and Elle were coming for lunch and hadn't discussed whether it was all right for Andrea to feed Darcy in front of them. Andrea watched Darcy push her food around on the plate while joking with her friends, and considered whether she'd be doing more harm than good if she attempted to feed her.

With her eyes on Darcy, Andrea put some fish on her fork and lifted it. Preparing herself for an angry attack, she moved the fork toward Darcy who was speaking. Darcy finished her statement, turned to Andrea, opened her mouth to receive the food, then pushed her plate over to Andrea. Andrea let her breath out, and followed immediately with another forkful from Darcy's plate. Elle, she knew, would be cool but she chanced a glance at Tori, not sure how Darcy would deal with a joke. Tori seemed intent on her lunch.

"So aren't you going to comment, Tori?"

"On what, Darce?" Tori looked up. "I was just trying to figure out if Elle would feed me if I asked nicely. You know how I feel about being fed." She winked. "Sexy."

Darcy laughed. The other three followed.

It was slow going getting her to eat, she chewed each bite thoroughly, then took her time swallowing. The others were drinking coffee and Darcy had only eaten half her lunch when she put her hand up to stop the next forkful. "Enough. I'm stuffed."

Andrea knew to pick her battles and this was not the time, but it was a beginning. She put the fork down.

Darcy suddenly got serious. "There's something I wanted to discuss with you three." She looked at each of them, then grinned. "I'd like to make a plan for another weekend in Fire Island. Can you two do it?"

With Darcy's attention on Tori, Elle turned to Andrea with a question on her face. Andrea shook her head. She hoped Elle would take the lead and be the bad guy on this one.

Elle touched Darcy's hand to get her attention. "Isn't it a little too soon to go traipsing off to the wilds of Fire Island? I know you think you're superwoman but you did just have major surgery."

Darcy frowned. "No, I can…" She turned to Andrea. "Can't I?"

"Julie will probably clear you in a few weeks, I think. Focusing on cardio rehab, eating and sleeping in the meantime will speed the healing process."

Darcy shot Andrea a look of betrayal. "But I thought—"

"Mid-August is still summer. Let me know when you're ready to discuss details." Tori took Darcy's hand. "And speaking of Fire Island, I've been wondering about the ravaging. How's it going?"

Darcy's eyes swung to Andrea, asking permission.

She nodded. Bless you, Tori, for changing the subject. The last thing Darcy needed was a temper tantrum.

"Actually, it's not. Dr. Castillo says we have to wait another three or four weeks."

Tori rocked back in her chair and stared at them. "Shit. But, hey, you guys seemed to manage before you actually got together."

Darcy looked puzzled. "What do you mean manage? We've never made love." She blushed.

"Well, I don't know what you were doing but you two were positively glowing all that weekend. Right, Elle?"

"Yes, they were, but this conversation is intrusive, Tori."

Andrea was burning with embarrassment. Darcy took her hand, held her eyes for a second, then the burning became sexual. "It's all right, Elle. You were seeing our feelings for each other, our love, unspoken by my lovely doctor, but acknowledged in other ways. Nothing to do with ravaging, everything to do with proximity and electricity between us. I'll bet lust can make you rosy-cheeked and starry-eyed. Right, Tori?"

Tori laughed. "I suggest you have a fire extinguisher nearby when you finally get to it."

Elle smacked her on the arm and they all laughed.

Andrea looked at Elle. "Is she like this all the time, or is it just with Darcy?"

"Mainly, just Darcy. But in Tori's defense, Darcy did this to us when we first got together."

"Ah, now I see. The old tit for tat."

Darcy cleared her throat. "Um, don't get her started on tits, Andrea."

They all laughed.

Andrea loved spending time with Tori and Elle. The conversation was always interesting, she always felt their love, and Tori always made Darcy laugh and that was good for her spirits and her recuperation.

As they were leaving, Tori whispered an apology for grossing her out. Andrea kissed her cheek. "You didn't gross me out. I'm sure you've noticed I blush easily. Thank you for pulling Darcy back from the precipice of a screaming rage."

Tori pulled Andrea into a hug and squeezed her hand. "She often seems on the edge these days and it can't be good for her heart."

"She's pretty fragile but we're working on it. The better she feels the less anxious she'll be." Andrea pulled away. "You are by far the best medicine I can think of for her, so please visit as often as you can."

"Hey, what's all that whispering?" Darcy glared at them. "Bad enough you got to Elle first, now you're after Andrea's heart?"

"Ah, Darcy, would that I could steal her heart but she's already given it to you. But now that I know her body is avail—"

This time it was Andrea who punched her shoulder. "Oh no you don't."

Tori shrugged. "My loss." She kissed Darcy. "Keep up the good work, Darce, you're looking fabulous. I'll see you for lunch in a day or so. Take care of my girl, Andrea."

CHAPTER FORTY

They could have come to Fire Island in mid-August rather than the weekend after Labor Day, but the stronger Darcy got, the more vigorously she brushed aside suggestions of a weekend in Fire Island. This puzzled Andrea, but when Jenny casually mentioned how well Darcy was doing in cardio rehab and that she had been climbing four to six flights of stairs with no problems, she had an aha moment. The ability to climb stairs without getting out of breath was a measure of readiness for sex and she was sure Darcy was afraid she'd die if they had sex. In fact, she realized, she harbored the same fear. So she'd asked Julie to do some tests, including a treadmill stress test to reassure both of them, then she had enlisted Tori and Elle to prod Darcy into making the trip.

Although Andrea hadn't broached the subject with Darcy, sex loomed large in her mind on the silent drive to the Fire Island ferry. They loved each other, their sexual connection flared with just eye contact or a kiss, and there was no physical reason they couldn't make love. It was time. She resolved to confront the issue of their making love whether or not Darcy had a meltdown. The good news was Darcy's heart now could withstand the rush of sex and/or a meltdown. It would work out, wouldn't it?

Once they boarded the late afternoon ferry, they both relaxed. Darcy reached for her hand and caressed it while chatting with other passengers who stopped to say how happy they were to see her looking so well.

"Welcome back." Gloria greeted them with a big smile as they walked off the ferry. "You look like your old self, Darcy."

"Thanks, Gloria, I feel like my old self. Better, actually." Thanks to Andrea and three times a week in cardio rehab and at home exercising with Jenny, she was sleeping better, eating more, gaining weight, building muscle, and no longer needed assistance walking.

Andrea pointed out their suitcase and packages and helped Gloria stack them on her wagon. "Your groceries arrived on the early ferry and I stashed everything in the fridge and the closet."

Darcy squeezed Gloria's shoulder. "Efficient, as always."

Gloria smiled. "Flatterer." She turned and pulled the wagon toward the house.

Andrea slipped her arm through Darcy's and pulled her close. "It must feel good to be here sans wheelchair and casts."

Darcy nodded but Andrea felt her tense. Damn, this wasn't supposed to be stressful. She supposed Darcy was remembering the feelings between them the last time they were here and getting anxious. Well, she was anxious too, but she wasn't willing to go on this way. She didn't look forward to Darcy's rage when she confronted her about their sex life or lack thereof but there was no reason they couldn't consummate the relationship. She smiled at the thought.

"What are you smiling about?" Darcy sounded annoyed.

"Just remembering what a nice time we had the last time we were here."

"Maybe we should have waited to come with the others tomorrow. I mean we always have a lot of laughs when we're all together."

"We had a pretty good time all by ourselves the last time. I'm sure we'll be fine."

At the house, Gloria placed their suitcase in the suite and the package with their dinner in the kitchen, then took off. Before heading into the suite, Andrea hugged Darcy. "Relax on the deck while I settle in, then we can eat dinner."

The curtains billowed in the gentle breeze and early evening sunlight and the fishy tang of the sea filled the room as Andrea unpacked their clothing and cosmetics, and the candles she lit at night so Darcy wouldn't have to sleep in the dark. She turned down the bed. Unlike their last visit, there would be no pretense of not sleeping together tonight. And, hopefully, they would make love for the first time. She felt confident having sex wouldn't kill Darcy, now all she had to do was convince Darcy.

Andrea joined Darcy on the deck with a glass of wine for each of them. "How do you feel about what Julie said this morning?"

"Great. It's good to know that it's all healing as it should."

"Uh-huh." She kissed her temple. *Then why do you sound like you're about to walk the plank?* She patted Darcy's hand. *Better to discuss it later, when we're in bed.* Andrea closed her eyes, enjoying the freshness of the ocean air, the sound of the squawking seagulls and the taste of salt on the light spray carried to the deck by the gentle wind that ruffled her hair. But above all else, she was aware, in every cell of her body, of Darcy, of her beauty, of her scent, of her anxiety.

They didn't speak much as they ate at the table on the deck but the silence was comfortable and the fact that occasionally their eyes met and sparked before Darcy could break the connection encouraged Andrea to go ahead with her plan.

Darcy cleared the dishes while Andrea marinated the chicken for tomorrow's dinner, then Andrea suggested they sit on the deck off the bedroom or get into bed to read. Darcy went right into the shower. Andrea considered joining her but thought that might be too aggressive.

When Darcy came out of the bathroom with just a towel wrapped around her, Andrea nearly tossed her on the bed and ravaged her, as Tori had advised, but at this point, Darcy required more delicacy than the cavewoman approach afforded. Maybe next time. Prickling all over with desire, Andrea moved to Darcy, trailed a finger along the part of the scar visible above the towel, then planted a kiss on it. "You're healing really well." Darcy shivered and turned away.

Andrea stepped into the shower and allowed her fantasies to run wild, thinking about Darcy's newly muscled legs and arms, her flat stomach, the soft mounds of her breasts, and her ass, as firm and beautiful as the first time she saw it. After drying herself, she pulled on the pajamas that Darcy had swooned over months ago, cotton shorts that barely covered her crotch and a skintight tank top without a bra.

Darcy was reading in bed, as close to the edge as she could get without falling off. When Andrea walked into the room, she looked up. Her flashing sapphire eyes widened and darkened and she made a small sound. Andrea hoped it was a moan of desire, not anger. She pretended she hadn't heard it but her heart was beating so fast it seemed to be turning inside out. Wouldn't it be ironic if *she* had a heart attack?

She lit all the candles, then climbed onto the bed and ran her hand over Darcy's body. Darcy shivered. She whispered in Darcy's ear. "I love you, Darcy Silver, and I'm dying to make love to you."

Darcy pulled her head away. "I'm not ready."

"You don't have to do anything. I'll stop if you feel uncomfortable."

"Maybe we should wait until tomorrow, you know, when Julie and Francine are here, in case something happens."

At least she hasn't mentioned having an emergency helicopter standing by. Andrea put a hand on Darcy's shoulder. *How can I help my poor sweetie get past her fear?* "I was afraid that your heart would give out too but the tests and Julie reassured me that your heart is stronger than ever."

"I can't believe you talked to Julie about us having sex."

"Who else would I talk to, Darcy? She's my best friend and your cardiothoracic surgeon. She said there's no medical reason we can't have sex."

"I'd feel better if we waited until tomorrow night." Darcy turned to put her book on the night table next to the bed, turned the lamp off and lay with her back to Andrea.

Andrea stroked Darcy's back. "Don't turn away from me, sweetie. I'll wait as long as you want, but I won't tolerate being cut off from you."

* * *

Darcy rolled toward Andrea and felt a stab of pain at the love she saw on her face. She kissed Andrea's lips gently to reassure her, then pulled back and, without meaning to, was eye to eye with her. As usual, the connection between them burned through her body and throbbed in her groin like a hunger she could never satisfy. She'd wanted to make love to Andrea, had desired her from the first day they met and had dreamed and fantasized about her ever since.

Not trusting Andrea, not trusting herself, and being afraid to risk fighting for her love, had resulted in them almost losing each other. And now she was doing it again, letting her fear keep them apart. When had she become a coward? Her surgeon had cleared her for sex. Jennifer and her cardio rehab therapist had congratulated her when she'd passed the marker for having sex weeks ago. If necessary, Andrea would administer CPR until she herself dropped dead. How many guarantees did she need? And what better way to die, if she had to die, than making love to the woman she adored?

She caressed Andrea's face. "I love you." She gazed into Andrea's eyes. "And I want to make love to you."

Andrea's eyes widened. "Are you sure?"

The fear was gone, replaced by the gnawing need. "I've never been surer of anything." Still gazing into Andrea's eyes, her finger traced Andrea's face, trailed down her neck to the valley between her breasts, circled each breast through her tank top, moved over her stomach, stopped to explore her belly button, then slipped between her legs, pressing on the material bunched in her crotch. Andrea shivered. Darcy's sweet, soft kiss quickly deepened into raw passion.

Ever since she'd surreptitiously watched Andrea undress in the mirror she'd fantasized about her generous breasts. As they kissed, Darcy cupped a breast.

CHAPTER FORTY-ONE

Andrea put an arm under Darcy and pulled her closer, then placed a hand on Darcy's chest to avoid too much pressure. Her breath caught when Darcy's mouth covered her breast and her finger slipped under the leg of her shorts and slowly stroked her. Her skin on fire, her head fuzzy, her breath coming in short bursts, she tensed as she climbed higher and higher, then swung over the precipice, and tumbled. She rode the waves of pleasure in Darcy's arms, with Darcy planting gentle kisses on her face and chest. "Christ, Darcy, I'm so sorry. I usually take forever to come so I didn't expect it would happen so fast."

"I came too, sweetheart." Darcy took Andrea's face in her hands. "Kissing you and having my way with those lovely breasts of yours did it for me. And don't apologize, we're just getting started."

"I don't know, Darcy, I don't…I mean one orgasm is all I can manage."

"I don't care about orgasms; I need to touch you. Is that okay?"

Andrea smiled. "I'm all yours, sweetie."

Darcy grinned. "As you should be."

Side by side, eye to eye, Andrea floated on waves of sweet pleasure as Darcy caressed her. When a finger slid under the leg of her shorts into the wetness, Andrea arched and moaned. Darcy leaned in to kiss her again. She threw her arm over Darcy and cupped her ass, but Darcy shifted and tossed Andrea onto her back. She partially covered Andrea and pinned one of her arms to her side and the other between their bodies.

"Open your legs for me, my sweet doctor," Darcy breathed into her ear.

It took a minute for her brain to interpret the words, then she obeyed. As Darcy slid one finger, then another inside her, Andrea's whole body tingled with exquisite ecstasy, her breath came in short bursts, her knees came up and her body followed. Darcy's tongue slid from Andrea's ear to her mouth, but her fingers didn't miss a beat even when Andrea screamed her name.

With her fingers still inside Andrea, Darcy raised herself on her elbow and gazed at her. After a few minutes, Andrea opened her eyes. Darcy grinned mischievously. "What happened, sweetie?" She wiggled her fingers.

"You took advantage of me. I've never—"

"Should I apologize?"

Andrea smiled. "You should kiss me."

"First I want you naked."

A surge of heat pulsed through Andrea. She started to sit up but Darcy pushed her down. "I'll do it." She got to her knees, pulled Andrea's tank top over her head, stopping to kiss each breast and her neck, then slipped Andrea's shorts over her hips and down her legs. She threw them to the other side of the king bed, then sat back on her heels. Her eyes raked Andrea's naked body and, as it had that first day, Andrea's body responded with a flush and a gush of wetness. Darcy leaned down and gently kissed the soft skin just inside Andrea's hip bones, one side then the other, then buried her face in the triangle of honey-colored hair. She inhaled, then looked up. "You're even lovelier than my fantasies."

Andrea grinned. "You fantasized about me?"

"Don't play innocent. You fantasized about me too but you were at least able to touch me even if you pretended you didn't want to make love." Darcy stripped her own pajamas off, tossed them on the floor, then crawled on top of Andrea.

Andrea caught herself about to ask Darcy if her chest hurt, then realizing that Darcy could take care of herself, she answered Darcy's question. "Yes." She'd imagined being skin to skin with Darcy so often when washing her that it almost felt familiar. She ran her hands up and down Darcy's nicely sculpted back and over her buttocks. Every inch, every pore, of Andrea's body felt alive as her burning skin merged with Darcy's heat. Maybe Tori was right, maybe they'd combust now that they were finally having sex.

"Yes, you fantasized?"

"Yes, your body feels wonderful. Yes, I fantasized big-time. And, yes, I was dying to make love to you." Her fingers traced gentle circles on the silky sides of Darcy's breasts. "But feeding you, looking into your eyes, touching you was enough to bring me close to orgasm. I took a lot of cold showers."

Darcy raised herself to her elbows. Keeping her eyes on Andrea's, she brought one of Andrea's hands to her lips, kissed the palm then placed it over her heart. She did the same with Andrea's other hand, then held them there. "My heart beats for you." She released Andrea's hands, stroked her face and lowered herself to maximize skin contact. Her voice was huskier than usual as she whispered in Andrea's ear. "I'm not done toying with you, my sweets."

The words turned Andrea to jelly. She flushed as another surge of pleasure shot through her.

Darcy placed a hand on her stomach and pressed. "Stay."

Andrea gasped. Either Darcy's finger or her tongue was generating ripples of pleasure through her body. Her head fell back onto the pillow, her hips lifted to meet Darcy's thrusts, until she tumbled down and down and down, breathing Darcy's name again and again.

Andrea tried to pull Darcy up but Darcy had other plans. She pleaded with Darcy to stop. She'd laughed and cried and moaned and screamed, had multiple orgasms and now she needed time to recoup. "I've unleashed a sex monster. A wonderful, loving sex monster but you're going to kill me if you don't stop. Please come here and hold me."

CHAPTER FORTY-TWO

Andrea woke first. Her head was on Darcy's chest and she listened to the comforting thumping of her heart. She marveled at how Darcy had vaulted from wanting to defer sex until a surgeon, an emergency room doctor and a nurse were in the house, to letting loose the aggressive and wonderful lover barricaded behind the fear. Just as she'd imagined, Darcy was a sensitive and passionate lover. But Andrea was flabbergasted by Darcy's ability to break through the protective walls she'd built, unleash her eroticism and passion and awaken a hidden playfulness. She'd had good sex over the years but she'd never felt so free, come so frequently, experienced so deeply.

She shifted her position, wanting to watch Darcy sleep, but it turned out Darcy was watching her. Neither spoke. Then Andrea noticed Darcy's arm moving. She grabbed it. "Oh, sweetie, I'm so sorry I fell asleep. You don't have to do that; I want to make love to you."

"I'm okay." Darcy's eyes slid away. "I don't...I can't...it's better for me if I..."

Andrea froze. "If you what? You're joking right?" She pushed herself up onto her elbow so she could see Darcy's face better in the flickering light of the candles and dim light from the bathroom. "I don't understand."

Darcy looked miserable.

Judging by the look on Darcy's face, this wasn't a joke. Andrea suddenly remembered Gerri's angry words that first day: *I have great sex but it's all about you giving, you don't let me touch you.* Not an exact quote but something like that. She felt as if she'd been kicked in the stomach. "You don't want me to make love to you? You'd rather masturbate?" Never in her wildest dreams would she have imagined this would be a problem.

Darcy's eyes skittered around the room as if seeking an escape. "It doesn't mean I don't love you."

Andrea could hear the pain in Darcy's voice but she couldn't get past her rage. "Fuck you, Darcy, if you think I'm going to live like, like, I don't even know what to call it. You think I should just lie back and let you service me? You think that's a relationship?"

Darcy turned to face Andrea. "It's who I am. Take me or leave me."

Did she mean that? Andrea studied Darcy. Of course not. She could see the fear in Darcy's eyes. "It's not who you are. Not based on my experience of you, not based on the way Tori talks about you. Talk to me."

"What do you want me to say?"

She could see how difficult this was for Darcy. She needed to calm down and get to the bottom of the issue. "I know you love me. And I want to be able to make you feel the way you made me feel. If you don't let me in to love you, then what are we?" She sat up and pulled Darcy into her arms. She kissed her temple and entwined their fingers. "Please tell me why?"

Darcy lay in her arms, her breath labored. Andrea hugged her and from time to time kissed her temple or her palm. "You know, I almost lost you because I was afraid if I loved you I would lose you. The mind does stupid things. Talking, bringing things into the light, helps to expose the fallacy, the magical thinking we use to hide our fears."

Darcy shifted to gaze into Andrea's eyes, her fingers traced Andrea's face, her lips brushed Andrea's. "A couple of years after we graduated from college, Candace and I were hanging out, watching TV. She suggested we drop some LSD she'd scored. I don't do drugs so I was reluctant but she knew, knows, how to push my buttons and I did it. After a while, the air seemed to change, I thought I could count the atoms, the movie seemed hysterical. Then Candace started kissing and touching me. The drug magnified every feeling but even in my drugged state it felt wrong, like incest, and I pushed her away.

"She became enraged. She slapped and punched me, bit my lips, my breasts, and my thighs while screaming that I belonged with her. She became this gigantic mouth, looming over me. I thought she was going to devour me, that she would suck everything out of me, swallow me and there would be no me, just her." Darcy's arms tightened around Andrea. "And since then I've been afraid to let anyone…"

"Whoa." Andrea couldn't control her reaction. "Sounds like a bad trip mixed in with some unfinished business between you and Candace. Did you have sex? Did you ever talk about what happened?"

"No, we never discussed it. And though we didn't have sex, the next time I was with a woman, I felt she was going to devour me and I freaked." She twisted around so she was in Andrea's lap with her head on Andrea's shoulder. "Stay with me, please."

"I'm not going anywhere without you, ever." Andrea rocked her.

Darcy dozed. Looking at her, Andrea was filled with love. How alike they were, both structuring their lives so they couldn't love or be loved. She kissed Darcy's forehead. She didn't know whether she and Darcy would be able to work through these feelings without some professional help. Perhaps Karin could recommend someone they could see. In any case, she would be patient, try not to pressure Darcy or make her feel bad.

Darcy woke with a jolt. "Andrea?"

"I'm here. It's late, let's sleep. We'll talk in the morning."

* * *

Darcy woke wrapped in Andrea's arms. She felt safe and loved. Why hadn't she talked to Andrea about her fear of being made love to before? She'd been so focused on wanting to make love to Andrea that she hadn't given any thought to Andrea making love to her. No, that wasn't true. She desperately wanted Andrea to make love to her. It was magical thinking. She'd hoped it would just go away despite fifteen years and other women when it hadn't. Andrea was adamant about wanting a mutually loving, equal relationship. And she wanted that too. Over the years, she'd often thought about Tori, about how easy the loving and the sex had been between them, about the mistake she'd made breaking up with her because Tori was growing independent and she feared she would eventually break up with her. Now that she thought about it, hadn't Candace fanned her insecurities about losing Tori, saying once Darcy left school Tori would find someone else?

Did Candace have any idea of what she'd done? Of the pain walking away from Tori had caused her? Of the damage caused by that LSD trip? Probably not. Andrea was too important, she needed her too much to let that LSD trip be a destructive force in their relationship. She would do whatever was necessary to get back to being the sexual being she had been with Tori.

Maybe now that Andrea knew her dirty secret they could… maybe she could desensitize herself. She would do anything not to lose Andrea.

"I hear someone thinking." Andrea's voice was gentle and Darcy could tell she was smiling.

Darcy opened her eyes to bright sunlight. "How do you know I'm not sleeping?"

"The grinding of the gears in your head. And your breathing."

She kissed Andrea's nose. "I've been thinking…about my problem."

"Our problem, you mean?"

Darcy's breath caught. "Yes, that one. I want it to go away. Maybe try and see if I freak?"

"Sounds good to me." Andrea tightened her arms around Darcy. "What about we just take our time? Kissing seems to be okay and maybe some touching, nothing too intense, and when you feel scared, you tell me to stop. Would that do it, you think?"

"Can we try now, I'm still…I still want you from last night."

Candace had loomed over Darcy so Andrea stretched out next to her, not on her. "I spent months trying not to be sexual when I was touching you. Tell me what you want."

"Just touch me."

Andrea took her time stroking Darcy, maintaining contact with her at all times through kissing or looking in her eyes. In whispered Italian, she told Darcy how much she loved her, loved being with her, wanted to be with her for all time. Darcy's gasps of pleasure encouraged her to continue. "Is there anything else you want, sweetie?"

Darcy took her hand and moved it lower, through the tight black curls, to her groin, over each of the sensitive inner thighs. She broke away from their kiss. "Now you."

Andrea slid a little lower. She gently tugged Darcy's pubic hair, then cupped her crotch. Her instinct was to spread Darcy's legs and use her mouth, but she controlled herself. She breathed into Darcy's ear. "Spread your legs for me, Darcy."

Darcy tensed but did as asked.

"Good," Andrea breathed into Darcy's ear again. She ran her fingers up and down Darcy's inner thighs, then into the wetness. Darcy sucked in her breath. Andrea kissed Darcy's eyes, her cheeks, her lips. Darcy kissed her back, then her lips separated and her tongue teased Andrea's lips.

Andrea smiled. Her lips parted and her tongue welcomed Darcy. It didn't take long for their bodies to heat and become slippery with sweat. Andrea was having a hard time concentrating on what she was supposed to do, or not do. One hand strayed back to Darcy's breasts, circling and squeezing. Darcy moaned and pushed Andrea's hand down.

"Tell me what you want, Darcy."

"Inside." Darcy's voice was hoarse.

"You want me inside you?" Andrea wanted to be sure she understood.

"Yes."

Andrea slipped a finger in. Darcy sighed. Andrea slid her free arm under Darcy, pulled her closer and slid a second finger in. Darcy moaned, her eyes darkened. She could feel Darcy's excitement, her heart was pounding, she was rising to meet every thrust, then she closed her eyes. Andrea slowed down. "Open your eyes, Darcy, look at me. Say my name."

Darcy's eyes were almost black when she opened them. "Andrea."

"Keep those gorgeous blue eyes open for me, sweetie. And I want to hear my name when you come." Andrea picked up the tempo and the force of the thrusts.

Darcy rocked to meet her. She chanted *Andrea, Andrea, Andrea.* Her voice rose as she climbed, then her vagina tightened around Andrea's fingers and wave after wave held them until Darcy relaxed. Andrea left her fingers inside.

Darcy crawled on top of Andrea and nestled her face into Andrea's neck. The only sound was the pounding of their hearts, their rapid breathing, and the rhythmic ebb and flow of the crashing ocean. They dozed.

Darcy lifted her head. Andrea was awake, staring out the sliding glass doors. Darcy touched her cheek and turned Andrea's head so she could see her face. "Thank you. You are a wonderful lover." She grinned. "I'm looking forward to the time when there are no restrictions on what you can do."

"I loved what we did just now and anything else will be a bonus. Frankly, I was surprised you were able to tolerate even that given what you described."

"Since that LSD trip I've only had a few sexual partners and I've been afraid to let them touch me. Physically or emotionally. You're the first I've been in love with, the first I've trusted." Darcy smiled. She took Andrea's hand and kissed each finger, then the palm. "I love you."

Andrea brushed the hair off Darcy's forehead. "I love you too."

Darcy rolled to the side of the bed. "Come into the shower with me and maybe I'll let you show me how much you love me."

Andrea grabbed Darcy's rear end as she rolled away. "You mean I'm going to have to pay you back for all those orgasms last night?"

Darcy's grin was mischievous. "Hey, remember we do tit for tat."

CHAPTER FORTY-THREE

Much later they were sitting on the deck waiting for their weekend guests to appear. The group would cook together over the weekend but they were responsible for dinner tonight. Andrea was making her specialty, *pasta con le Sarde*, a Sicilian dish with sardines, fennel, pine nuts and breadcrumbs. In addition, the chicken they'd marinated overnight was ready for the grill, a huge salad was prepped and the *broccoli di rape* was ready to be sautéed with oil and garlic. The fresh fruit salad for dessert was chilling. Andrea smiled. They were a good team in the kitchen as well as the bedroom.

Andrea thought they must be glowing and she fully expected Tori to immediately launch into a weekend tease. They were in for it but she didn't give a damn. She squeezed Darcy's hand. She was thrilled that Darcy had come so far so fast. She'd made love to Darcy several times this morning. Darcy hadn't been able to give up control but Andrea was confident that would change. But it hadn't been as one-sided as Darcy had hinted when she invited Andrea into the shower. She'd made love to Andrea again.

Darcy cleared her throat. "I haven't mentioned marriage before because it means honeymoon and that means sex and I was scared out of my mind that I would die if we had sex."

"Hmm."

Darcy slid off the chair onto one knee. "I don't have a ring but will you marry me and share my life forever?"

"Yes." Andrea took Darcy's face in her hands and kissed her. "Yes, I will." She reached up to finger the emerald pendant. "And I don't need a ring."

Darcy grinned. "Let's pick a date and place."

Andrea pulled Darcy to her feet. "What about here? I love this house."

"I was hoping you'd say that. But we have to do it soon before the weather changes." Darcy sat and held out her arms.

"The sooner the better as far as I'm concerned." Andrea moved into Darcy's lap. "Let's keep it small, okay?" She kissed Darcy, then put her head on Darcy's shoulder. "Whenever I've thought about marriage I pictured myself in a tuxedo."

Darcy held Andrea away so she could see her face. "You'd look wonderfully sexy."

"It wouldn't freak you out?"

"Andrea, my love, are you trying to tell me you're a butch?"

She blushed. "Maybe."

* * *

They were putting the finishing touches on dinner prep when Elle and Tori, Francine and Jennifer, and Julie and Karin arrived. As they greeted everyone, Francine raised her eyebrows at Andrea. Andrea blushed and nodded.

During wine and hors d'oeuvres on the deck Andrea was tense waiting for Tori to sniff out the fact that they'd finally had sex, mind-blowing sex, not just the usual eye sex. By the time they sat at the table for the fig and prosciutto appetizer, she couldn't resist sneaking a peek at Tori.

Tori was watching them with the sweetest smile on her face. Damn, she knew. And, Andrea could see that Tori was happy for them, no teasing about it tonight. Andrea smiled and lifted her glass in Tori's direction, silently toasting her. Tori threw her a kiss and stood to make a toast. "To friends, friendship and love. Thank you, Darcy and Andrea, for sharing your lives and your love with us." Everyone raised their glass and drank to them.

When they had eaten, Darcy stood. "Since I know everyone is wondering and for some reason, Tori, nobody in this usually intrusive crowd has mentioned it, I'm happy to report that Andrea and I have finally done…it. Made love." She grinned. "Many times." The group laughed and shouted congratulations. Darcy waited for everyone to calm down before proceeding. "And, we wanted you all to be the first to know we're getting married in three weeks."

With that the group was on its feet hugging and kissing the blushing brides.

CHAPTER FORTY-FOUR

Almost four weeks later, on a gorgeous Indian summer day in early October, they stood at the rear of a platform built on the beach, Andrea in a tuxedo and Darcy in a gorgeous blue suit.

When they sat down to plan, a small wedding turned out to be impossible and they gave in to the inevitable. After all they would only get married once. And now the more than two hundred guests, family and friends, who had been invited to witness and celebrate their marriage stood on both sides of the red carpet.

The chamber group that had played all afternoon as the guests assembled broke into the "Wedding March" to accompany them down the aisle. First, Andrea and her parents, followed by Julie and Karin, walked down the red carpet to where Tori waited, grinning. Darcy with Maria and Carlo, followed by Elle and Francine, came next.

When they were all standing before her, Tori, a newly certified Universal Life Minister, smiled at Darcy and Andrea, then spoke to the guests. "Please be seated. Since I'm in charge today, I'm going to take a few minutes to make some comments before I join these two ravishing women in matrimony."

"Oh, oh," Darcy whispered.

"I was in love with Darcy first." She stopped and smiled at Andrea. "Then I met Andrea and I have to tell you if I was unencumbered—"

"Unencumbered?" Elle snorted.

The crowd laughed.

Tori smirked. "I meant to say, if I wasn't already married to a marvelous woman, I would have pursued the gorgeous, kind, loving Andrea myself. But what I would have done really doesn't matter because these two, Darcy Silver and Andrea Trapani, from the start, only had eyes for each other. In the last six months, Darcy and Andrea have experienced more in sickness and in health stuff than any couple should in a lifetime together. Yet they've come through it strongly committed to each other and with a love so bright and true it's blinding, yet restorative to those of us lucky enough to spend time with them. Darcy and Andrea hold a special place in my heart, as I'm sure they do for many of you here today to honor them, and, it is my pleasure to be the one to join them together in matrimony. Darcy and Andrea please face each other." They turned and gazed into each other's eyes.

Tori leaned in and whispered. "No eye sex during the ceremony."

Andrea stepped forward onto Tori's foot. "Behave yourself." She spoke softly.

Tori smiled. "Darcy, take Andrea's hand and repeat after me: I, Darcy Maria Silver, take you, Andrea Claudia Trapani, to be my lawfully wedded wife, my constant friend and my faithful partner from this day forward."

Darcy repeated the words in her strong, husky voice, then continued with her own words. "Andrea, you are the love of my life, the reason I chose to live, the reason I will always choose to live. I promise to love you always, to trust you always, to confide in you always, to be with you always as long as I shall live." She looked at Tori who prompted her to repeat the rest of her vows.

"In the presence of our family and friends, I offer you my solemn vow to be your faithful partner in sickness and in health, in good times and in bad and in joy as well as in sorrow. I promise to love you unconditionally, to support you in your goals, to honor and respect you, to laugh with you and cry with you, and to cherish you for as long as we both shall live."

"You may put the ring on Andrea's finger."

Elle handed Darcy the gold band and she slipped it onto Andrea's finger. "Andrea, my soul mate, love of my life, I give you this ring as a symbol of my love and commitment. As it encircles your finger, may it remind you always that you are surrounded by my unending love."

Tori turned to Andrea. Repeat after me: "I, Andrea Claudia Trapani, take you, Darcy Maria Silver, to be my lawfully wedded wife, my constant friend and my faithful partner from this day forward." Andrea repeated the words, then spoke her own.

"Darcy, love of my life. I'm grateful you chose to live for me so now we can live for each other. I promise to love you always, to trust you always, to confide in you always, to be with you always as long as I shall live." She went on to repeat the rest of her vows, then turned to Julie for the ring. She placed the ring on Darcy's finger. "Darcy, with this ring I give my heart and soul to you. It is a symbol of my love and commitment and as it encircles your finger, may it remind you always that you are surrounded by my unending love."

"By the power vested in me by the State of New York," a sob escaped from Tori. They each extended a hand to touch her. She grinned. "It is my pleasure to pronounce you wife and wife. You may kiss the bride."

Darcy wrapped her arms around Andrea. "Kiss me, wife," she whispered.

"Yes, my love." Andrea lowered her head and met Darcy's lips, then deepened the kiss. As they separated, Andrea realized the crowd was clapping and cheering. She blushed.

After the cocktail hour, the DJ announced their first dance as a married couple would be to "At Last" sung by Etta James. At the first notes, they embraced and began to slow dance to the song that said it all for them. Andrea overflowed with love and gratitude and happiness. She straightened so their eyes met and the current between them that hadn't diminished one iota after a mind-boggling amount of sex in the last four weeks, shot through her.

Darcy sang softly. "You are mine."

"And you are mine." Andrea lowered her head and kissed Darcy. She blushed at the cheers and whistles but for once she didn't care.

As night fell the party moved into the heated tent for a formal dinner followed by dancing. In between, Andrea and Darcy posed for photographs and talked to their guests. The party broke up late, but Darcy had arranged for drinks, food and music until the last guest left, and ferries until the caterer was finished for the night.

CHAPTER FORTY-FIVE

The eight of them sat around the table eating the breakfast feast the wedding party had prepared for the brides: cottage cheese pancakes, vegetable frittata, home fries, fresh fruit salad, champagne, orange juice and coffee. Tori, Elle, Julie, Karin, Francine and Jennifer would be leaving this evening but Andrea and Darcy would remain at the beach house for a couple of days then head back to spend two days with Maria and Carlo and Andrea's parents in the city before the four of them flew to Sicily. That night, Francine and Jennifer would move into the basement apartment to house sit and Andrea and Darcy would fly to Greece the next evening.

After a few toasts, they settled down to eating and rehashing the wedding.

Elle turned to Darcy. "I was surprised to see Gerri there. I figured after the fiasco with Candace, she'd never speak to you again."

"That and the fact that I treated her like shit when we were together, you mean?"

Elle laughed. "That too."

"Andrea and I decided I should try to make peace with her. After all, she was responsible for bringing us together. And aside from that, she made sure I was taken care of before she left."

"And Candace?" Tori asked.

Darcy glanced at Karin. "We're talking. I'm working on it in therapy. And when we get back, Candace and I are going to see a family therapist together. I hope we'll be all right."

Tori reached for another pancake. "Julie, did you notice your surgical team drooling while these two lovebirds were dancing?"

"Well, in their defense, they did hear some intimate things during the surgery," she smiled at Andrea who was in full blush, "and they feel a certain amount of ownership of the relationship. I believe many of them are in love with the fair Andrea."

Darcy kissed Andrea. "My blushing bride. Between orgasms and embarrassment, she's always rosy-cheeked."

Andrea tucked her head into Darcy's shoulder. "You all are going to kill me."

Francine grinned. "On a lighter note, have you finalized your honeymoon plans yet?"

Andrea put her fork down. "We've left it loose on purpose, but we'll spend about a month in Greece and Turkey, a lot of the time on the beach relaxing but also doing some sightseeing. Carlo and Maria are spending the month in Trapani with my parents so they can check out whether they want to settle there. After Greece, we'll go to Trapani and spend a couple of weeks with Maria and Carlo and my parents. I'm hoping Maria and Carlo will decide to live in Trapani so our families will be close, but we'll help them settle wherever they want. And then after New Year's week in Paris with all of you and the rest of the inner circle, we'll fly home to start our life together."

Darcy kissed Andrea's temple and fingered her hair. "Speaking of our life together, should I tell them my news, sweetie?"

Andrea looked up. "Yes."

Darcy grinned. "My father-in-law is writing a book about the Italian resistance and when he heard from Carlo that I had a half-completed manuscript on the subject, he insisted on reading it. He loved it and suggested we combine our efforts to jointly write the book. With him as co-author it's almost guaranteed to be published."

"And that's not all." Andrea grinned. "Tell them the rest, Darcy."

"When I studied with Gaetano at Columbia, he encouraged me to get a PhD in history. Now, thanks to him, I've been hired to teach two courses during the spring semester."

Tori's eyes filled. "Oh, Darcy, you always wanted to teach at the college level. It's wonderful that the woman of your dreams comes with the job of your dreams. Oops, did I say come, Andrea? Why does it always come down to sex with you two?"

Andrea reddened and threw a leftover pancake at Tori. "You are an evil woman."

Tori snorted. "And what about you, Andrea my love? Does the marriage come" —Tori wiggled her eyebrows— "with anything besides the gorgeous, intelligent, sexy Darcy for you?"

"In fact, it does, smartass. I get to share her impertinent friends. And, Darcy and my mom are going to fund and I'm going to run a low-cost clinic for women and children in the Bronx."

"I'm really excited." She kissed Darcy.

Tori laughed. "I won't comment on that, Andrea, but you are the perfect straight woman, even if you are a lesbian."

"Be nice to my sweet doctor, Tori." Darcy hugged Andrea. "Come on, let's clean up breakfast and take a walk on the beach."

With good conversation, good food and lots of laughter, the rest of the day flew by. After dinner they walked their friends to the dock and waved as the ferry carried them back to the city. Darcy took Andrea's hand as they strolled to the house, really alone for the first time in several weeks.

"Happy?" Darcy asked, when they entered the house.

Andrea squeezed her hand. "I'm finally alone with my wife, why wouldn't I be happy?"

"It's cool tonight. How about I build a fire in the suite? I'd love to see you naked in the firelight."

Picturing them both naked in front of the fireplace, Andrea's internal fire sparked immediately. She pulled Darcy close, cupped her buttocks and nibbled her earlobe. "You'll be naked too?"

"Of course, my lovely sexy doctor wife. You know we always do tit for tat."

Bella Books, Inc.

Women. Books. Even Better Together.

P.O. Box 10543
Tallahassee, FL 32302

Phone: 800-729-4992
www.bellabooks.com